TALES OF MR KEUNER

THE GERMAN LIST

This publication was supported by a grant
from the Goethe-Institut, India

Seagull Books, 2018

The graphic novel *Geschichten vom Herrn Keuner* by Bertolt Brecht and Ulf K. was
first published in 2014 by Suhrkamp Verlag, Berlin.

ISBN 978 0 8574 2 471 6

British Library Cataloguing-in-Publication Data
A catalogue record for this book is available from the British Library

Typeset by Seagull Books, Calcutta, India
Printed and bound by Hyam Enterprises, Calcutta, India

CONTENTS

TALES OF MR
KEUNER

FROM BERTOLT BRECHT AND ULF K.

TRANSLATED BY
JAMES REIDEL

LONDON NEW YORK CALCUTTA

TALES OF MR
KEUNER

THE HARDSHIP OF THE BEST

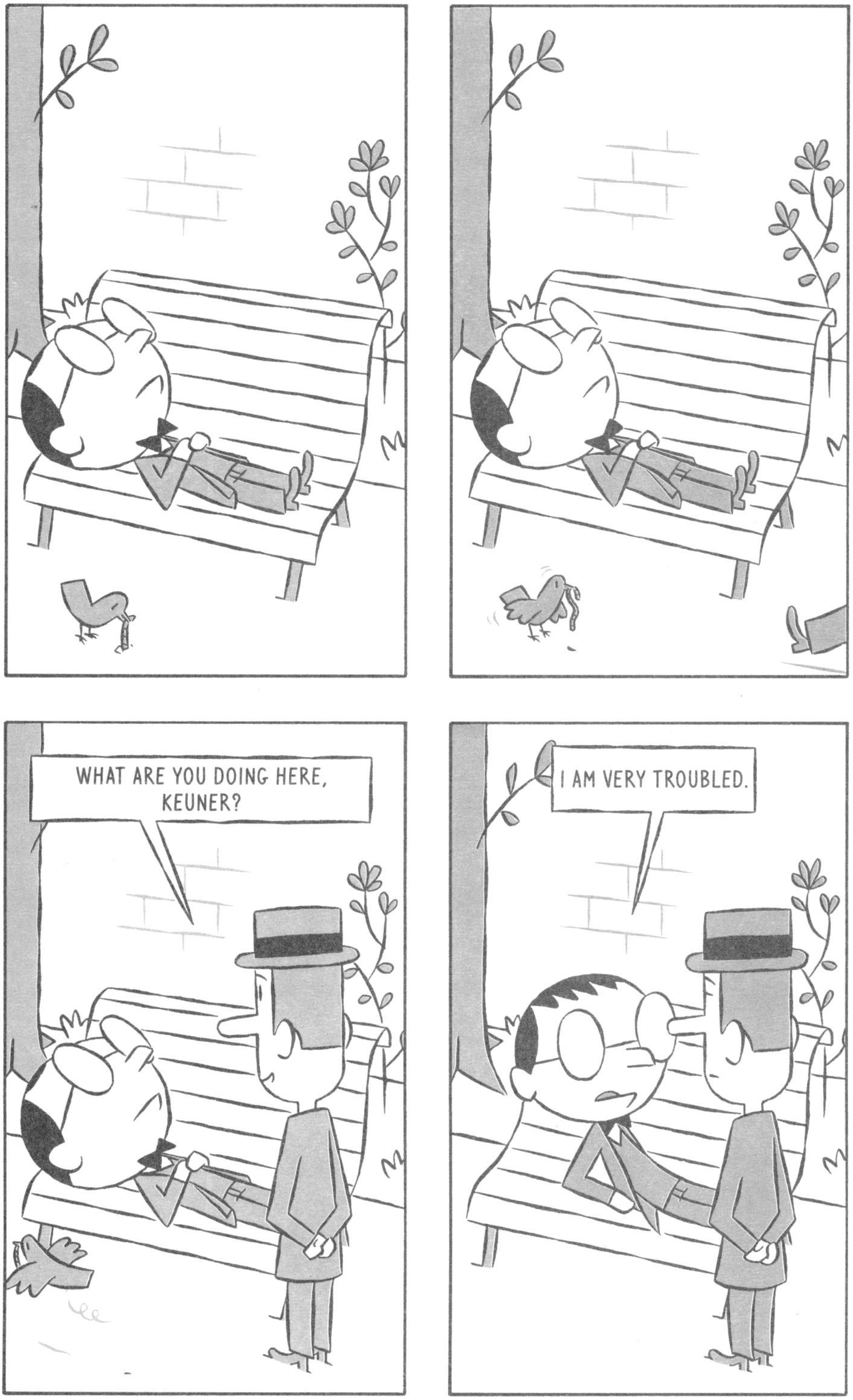
WHAT ARE YOU DOING HERE, KEUNER?
I AM VERY TROUBLED.

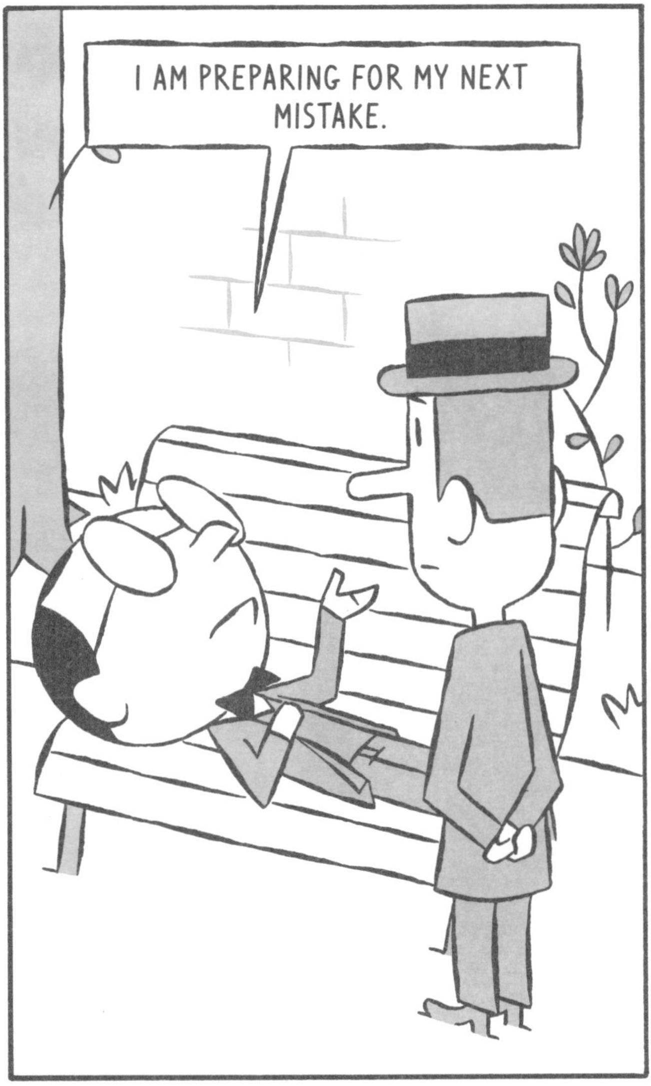
I AM PREPARING FOR MY NEXT MISTAKE.

MR KEUNER AND GERMAN POLITICS

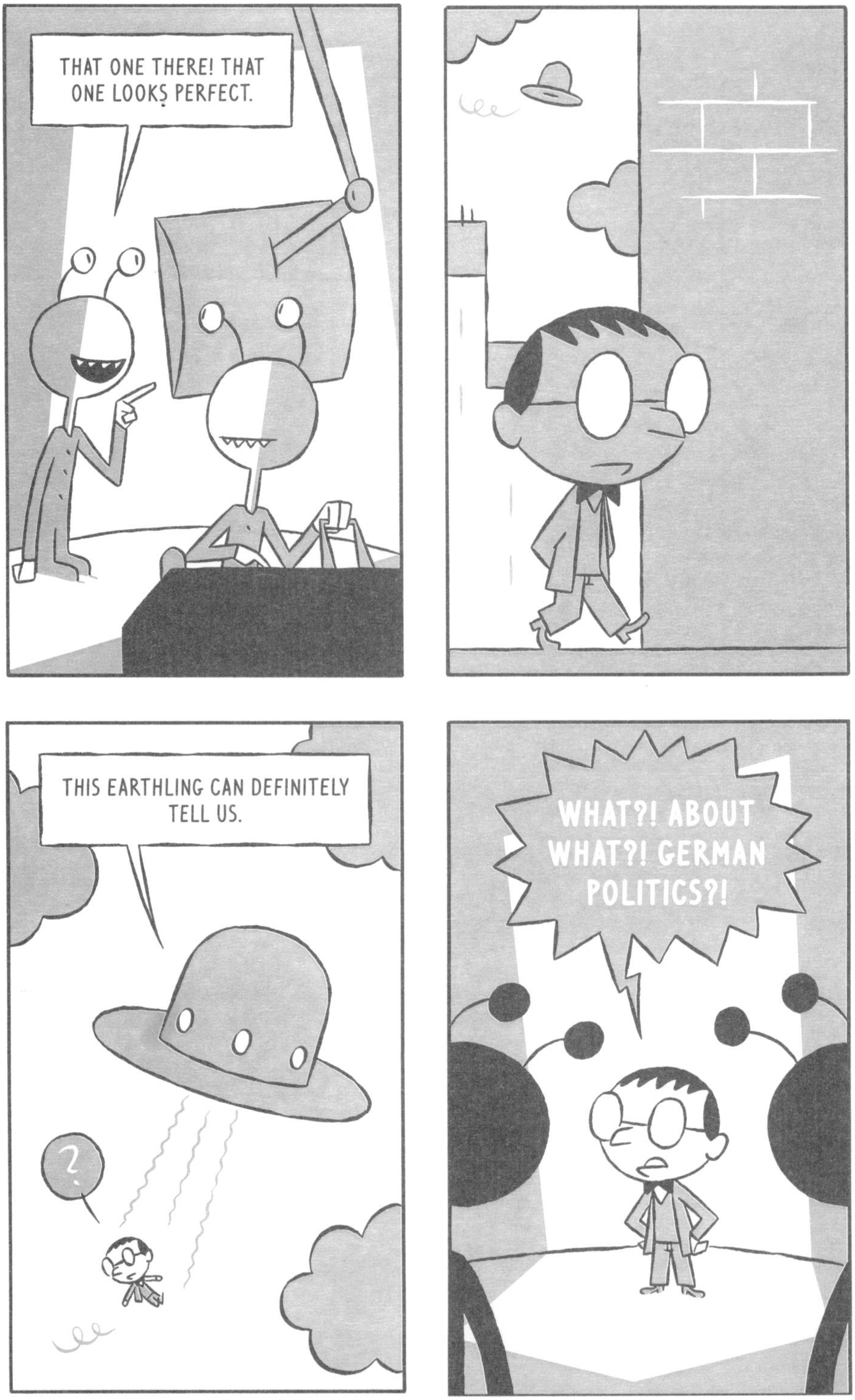
THAT ONE THERE! THAT ONE LOOKS PERFECT.
THIS EARTHLING CAN DEFINITELY TELL US.
?
WHAT?! ABOUT WHAT?! GERMAN POLITICS?!

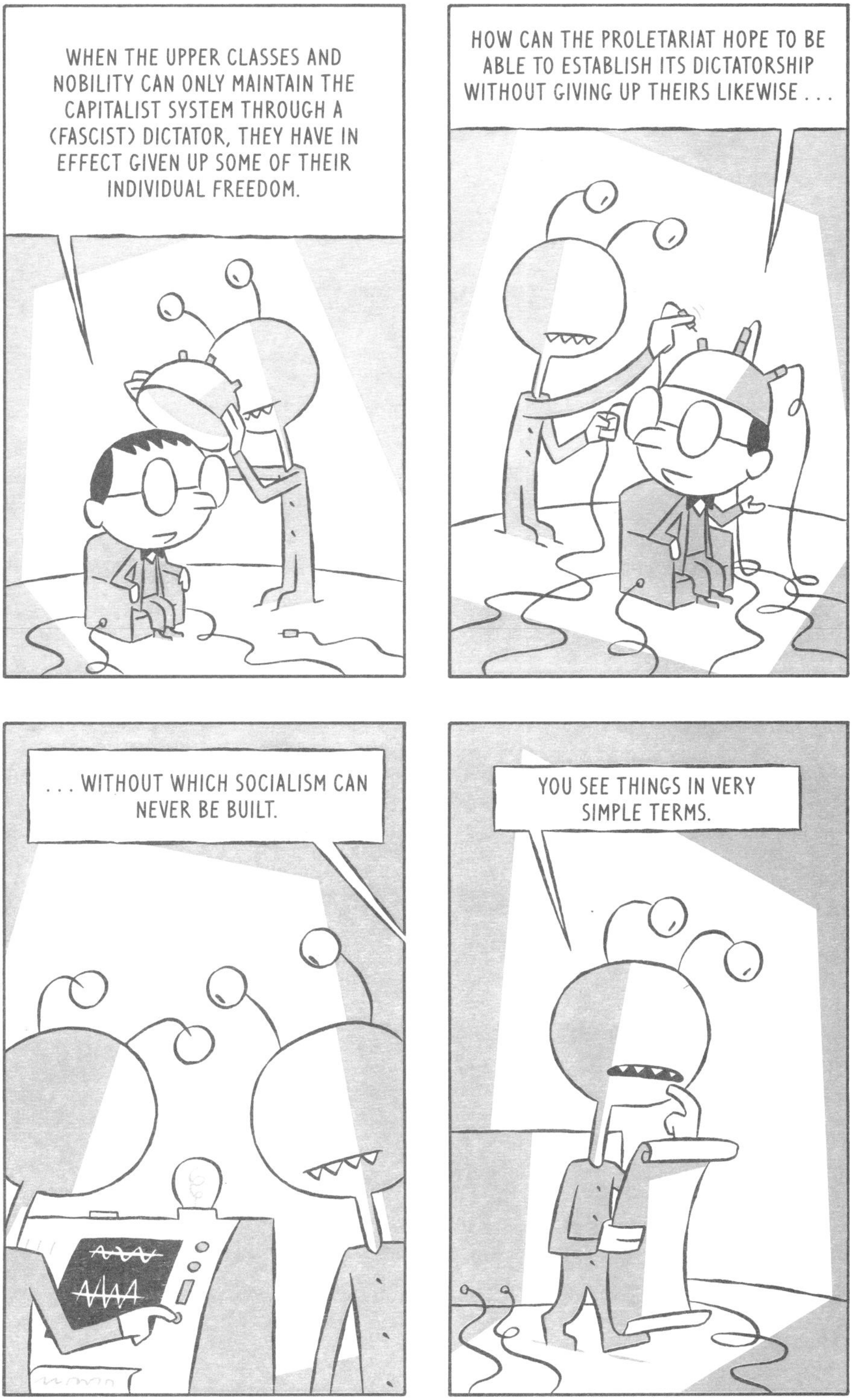
WHEN THE UPPER CLASSES AND NOBILITY CAN ONLY MAINTAIN THE CAPITALIST SYSTEM THROUGH A (FASCIST) DICTATOR, THEY HAVE IN EFFECT GIVEN UP SOME OF THEIR INDIVIDUAL FREEDOM.
HOW CAN THE PROLETARIAT HOPE TO BE ABLE TO ESTABLISH ITS DICTATORSHIP WITHOUT GIVING UP THEIRS LIKEWISE . . .
. . . WITHOUT WHICH SOCIALISM CAN NEVER BE BUILT.
YOU SEE THINGS IN VERY SIMPLE TERMS.

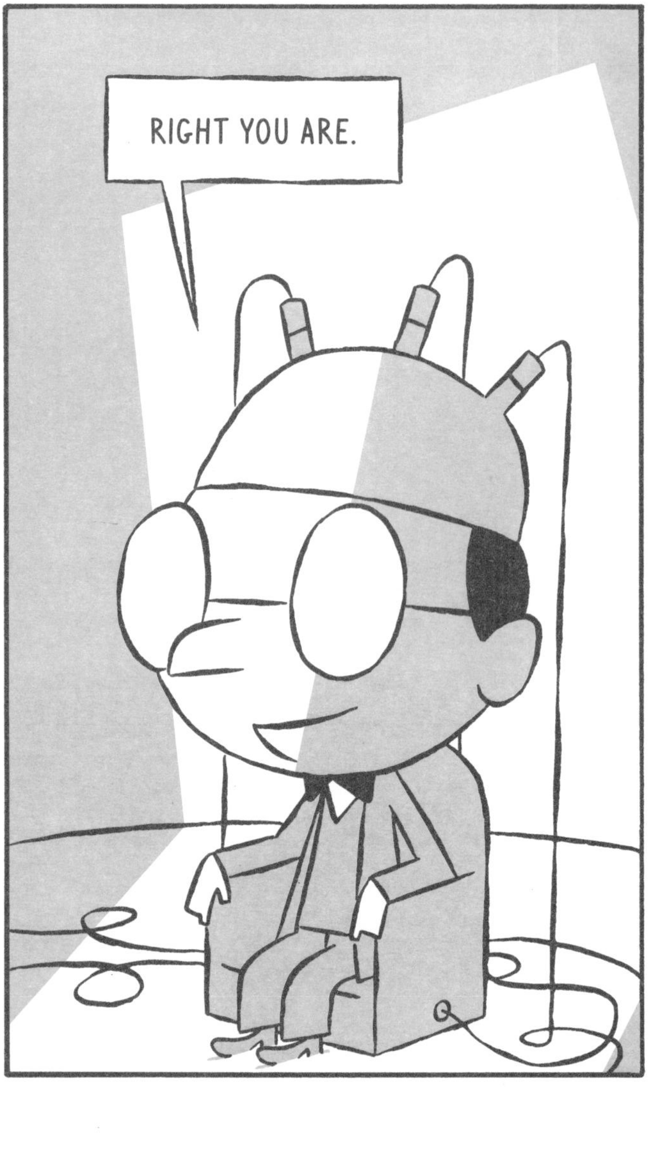
RIGHT YOU ARE.

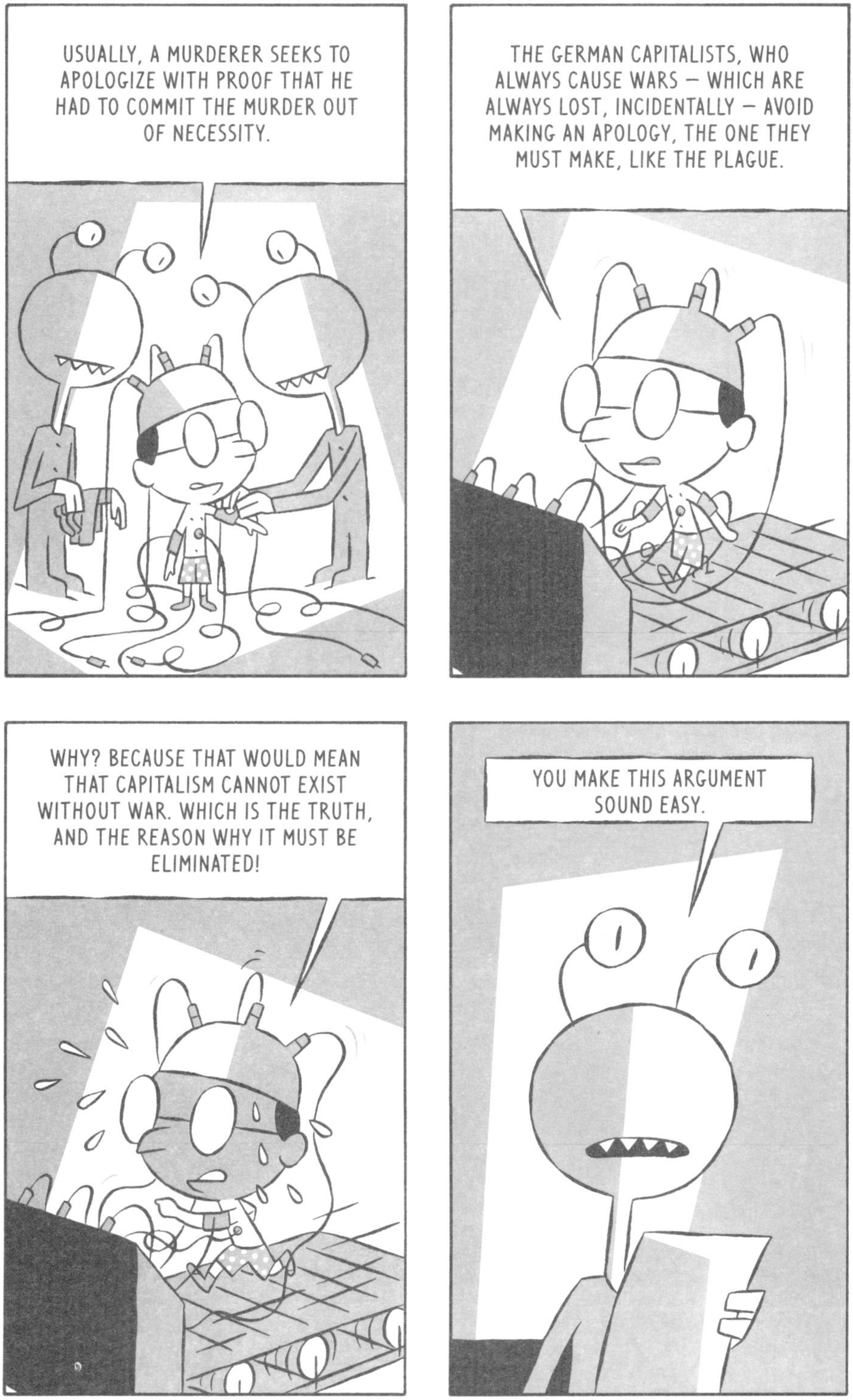
USUALLY, A MURDERER SEEKS TO APOLOGIZE WITH PROOF THAT HE HAD TO COMMIT THE MURDER OUT OF NECESSITY.
THE GERMAN CAPITALISTS, WHO ALWAYS CAUSE WARS — WHICH ARE ALWAYS LOST, INCIDENTALLY — AVOID MAKING AN APOLOGY, THE ONE THEY MUST MAKE, LIKE THE PLAGUE.
WHY? BECAUSE THAT WOULD MEAN THAT CAPITALISM CANNOT EXIST WITHOUT WAR. WHICH IS THE TRUTH, AND THE REASON WHY IT MUST BE ELIMINATED!
YOU MAKE THIS ARGUMENT SOUND EASY.

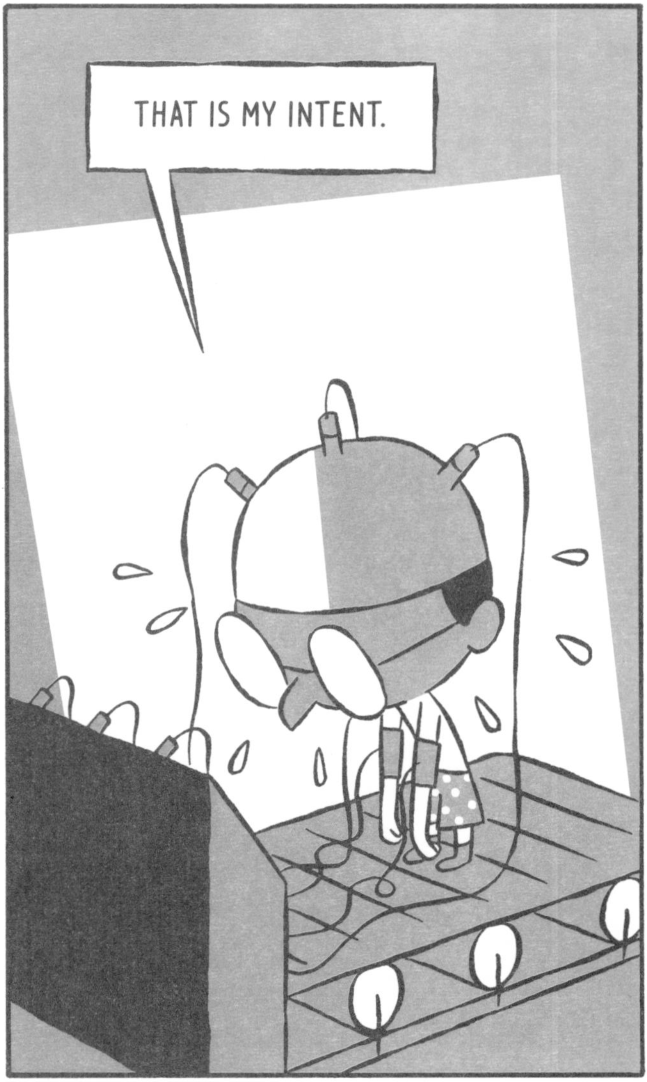
THAT IS MY INTENT.

I AM FOR THE POLICE STATE!
WHAT?! YOU HAD A POLICE STATE FOR TWELVE LONG YEARS!
FOR TWELVE LONG YEARS CRIMINALS HAD SERVED AS POLICE AGAINST DECENT PEOPLE. THEY ARE DEPOSED, BUT THEY HAVEN'T DISAPPEARED.
IF DECENT PEOPLE NOW REFUSE TO SERVE AS POLICE AGAINST THESE CRIMINALS, WHAT WILL THOSE PEOPLE DO NEXT?
BUT WHAT ABOUT FREEDOM?

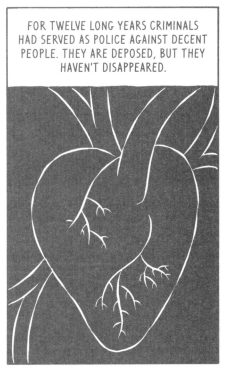

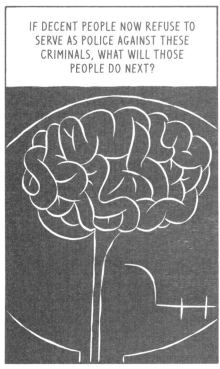

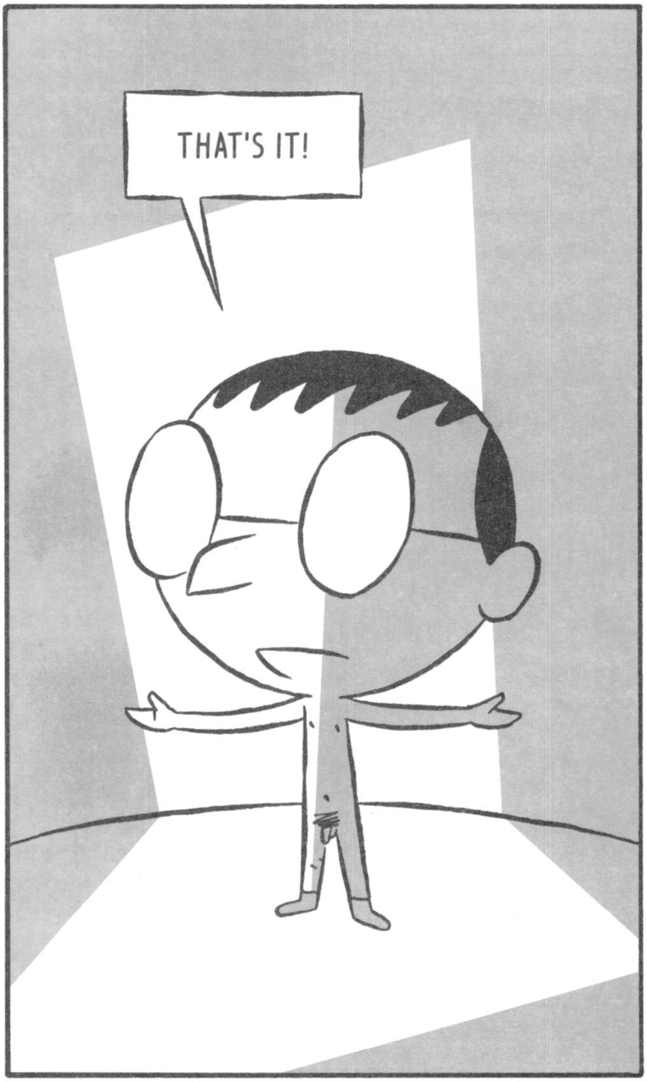
THAT'S IT!

IF SHARKS WERE HUMAN

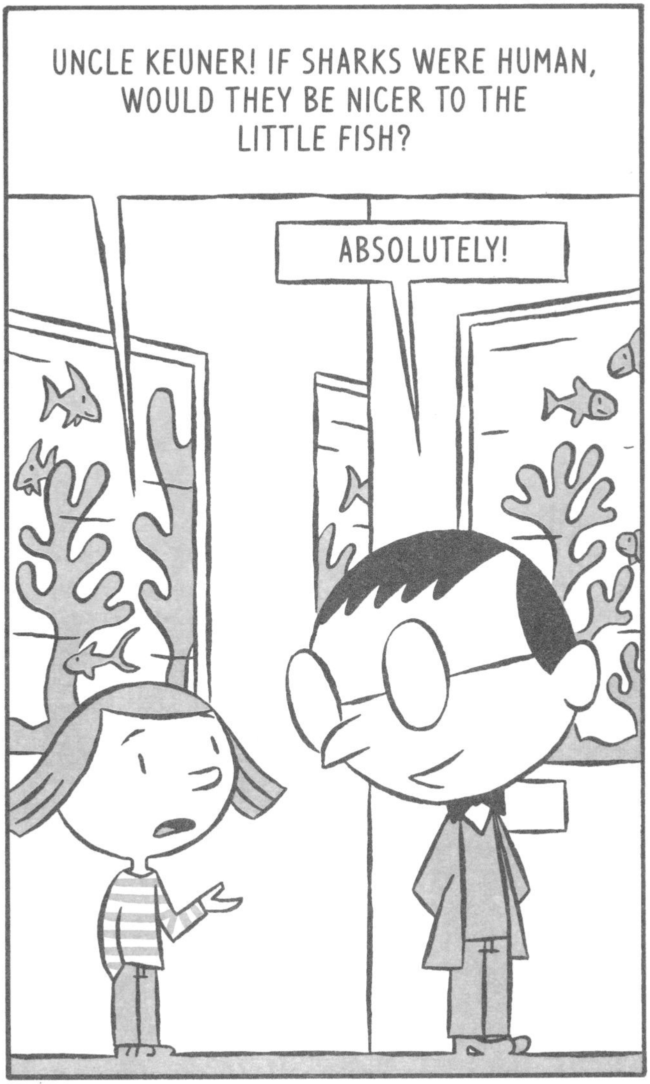
UNCLE KEUNER! IF SHARKS WERE HUMAN, WOULD THEY BE NICER TO THE LITTLE FISH?
ABSOLUTELY!

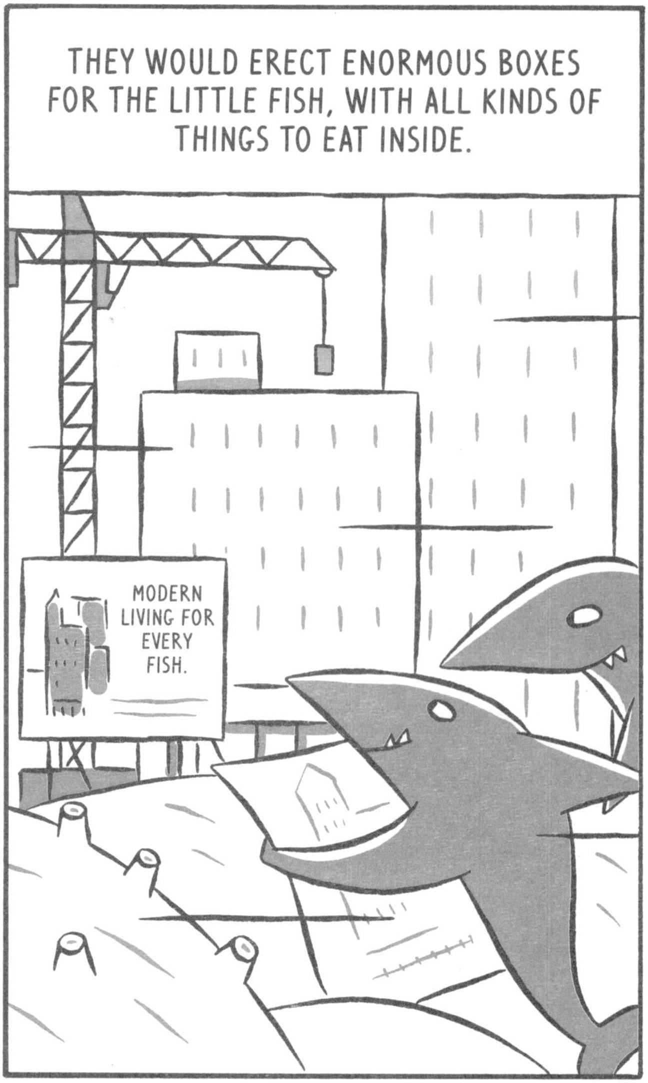
THEY WOULD ERECT ENORMOUS BOXES FOR THE LITTLE FISH, WITH ALL KINDS OF THINGS TO EAT INSIDE.
MODERN LIVING FOR EVERY FISH.

THEN THEY WOULD PROVIDE SCHOOLS FOR THE LITTLE FISH, WHERE THEY WOULD TEACH THEM HOW TO SWIM INTO THE JAWS OF THE SHARKS.

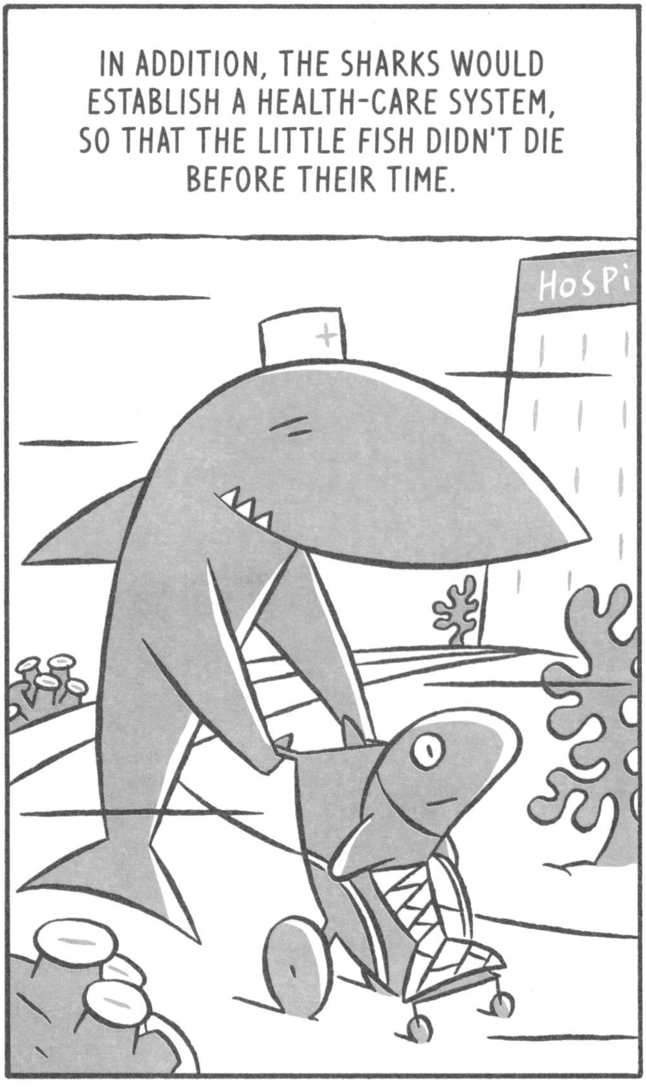
IN ADDITION, THE SHARKS WOULD ESTABLISH A HEALTH-CARE SYSTEM, SO THAT THE LITTLE FISH DIDN'T DIE BEFORE THEIR TIME.
HOSPI

AND BECAUSE HAPPY FISHLINGS TASTE BETTER THAN SAD ONES, BIG CELEBRATIONS WOULD ALWAYS BE PROVIDED.

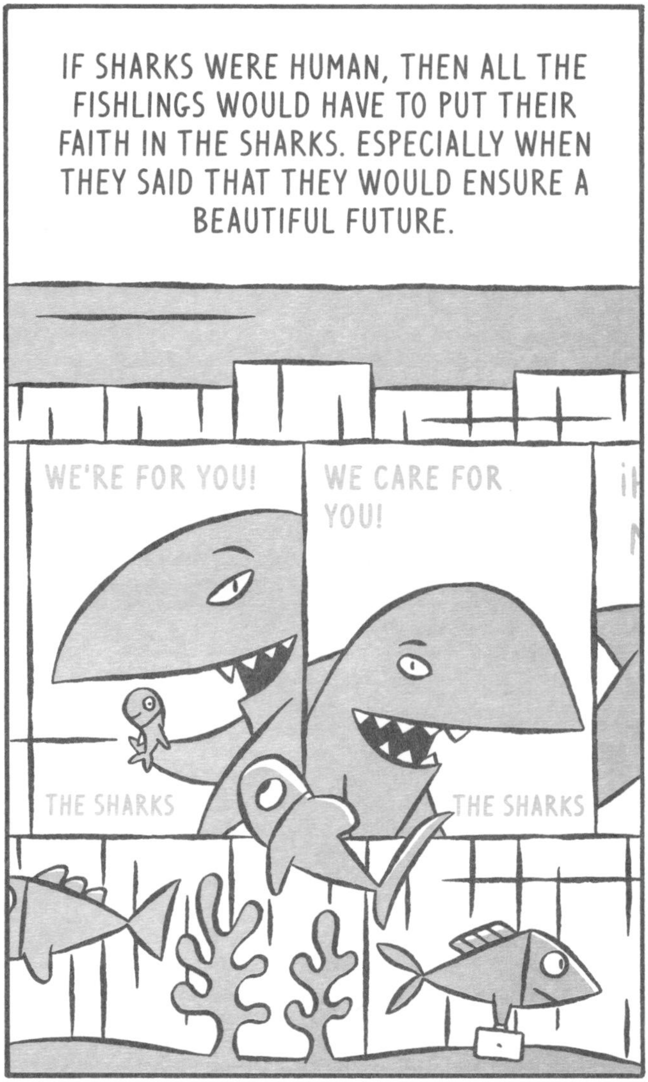
IF SHARKS WERE HUMAN, THEN ALL THE FISHLINGS WOULD HAVE TO PUT THEIR FAITH IN THE SHARKS. ESPECIALLY WHEN THEY SAID THAT THEY WOULD ENSURE A BEAUTIFUL FUTURE.
WE'RE FOR YOU!
THE SHARKS
WE CARE FOR YOU!
THE SHARKS

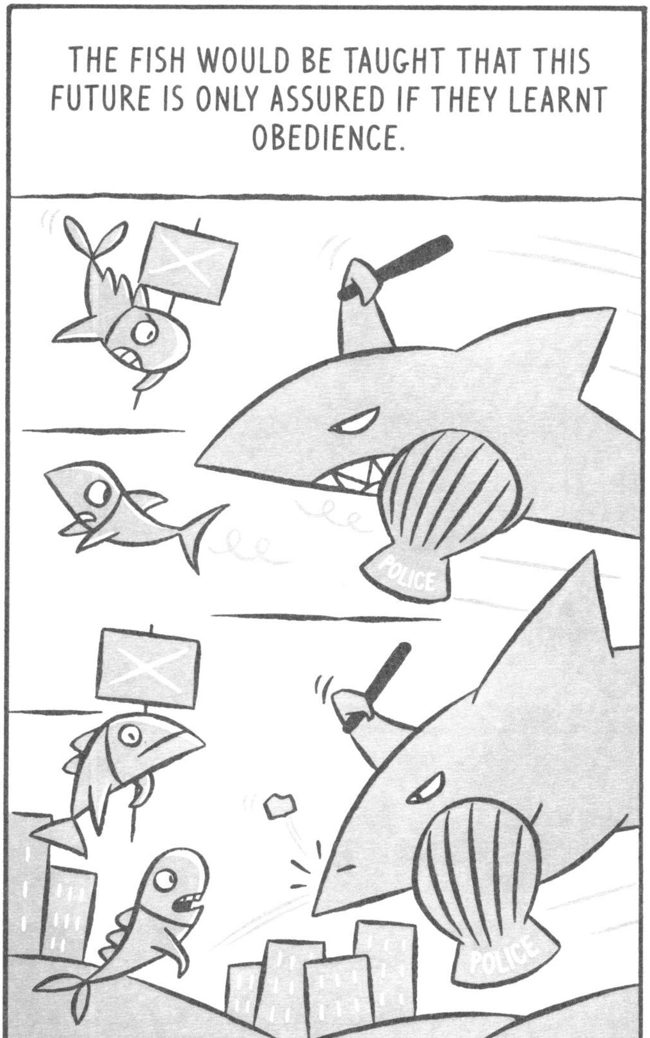
THE FISH WOULD BE TAUGHT THAT THIS FUTURE IS ONLY ASSURED IF THEY LEARNT OBEDIENCE.
POLICE
POLICE

THE SHARKS WOULD TEACH THE FISHLINGS
THAT THE FISHLINGS OF OTHER SHARKS
WERE DIFFERENT.

THEN THEY WOULD LEAD THEIR OWN FISH INTO WAR TO CONQUER THE ENEMY FISH BOXES.

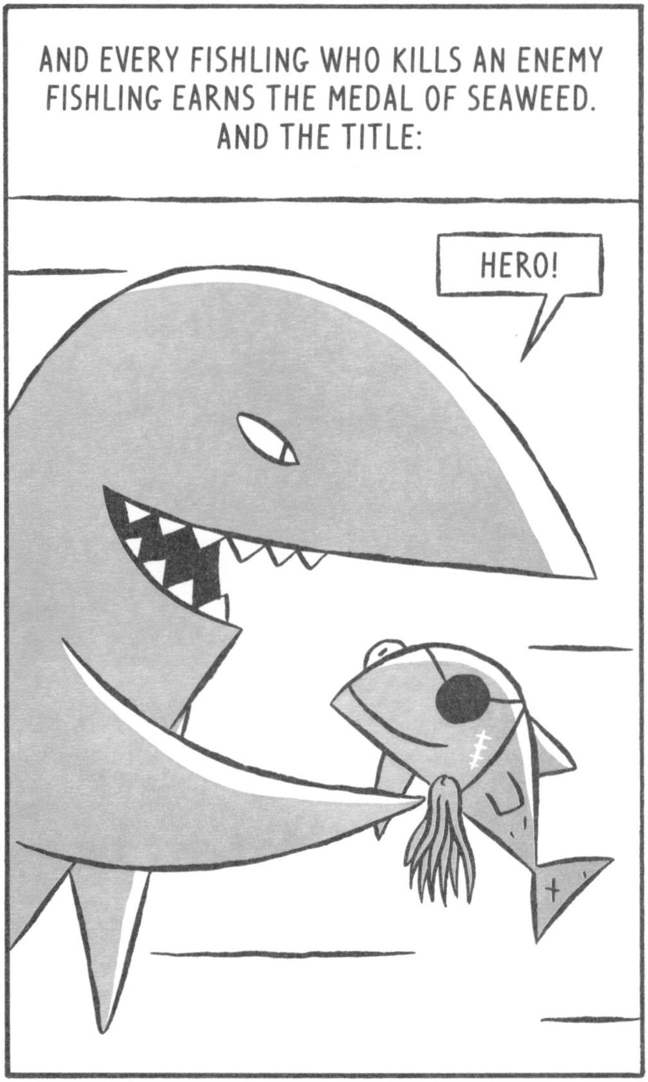
AND EVERY FISHLING WHO KILLS AN ENEMY FISHLING EARNS THE MEDAL OF SEAWEED. AND THE TITLE:
HERO!

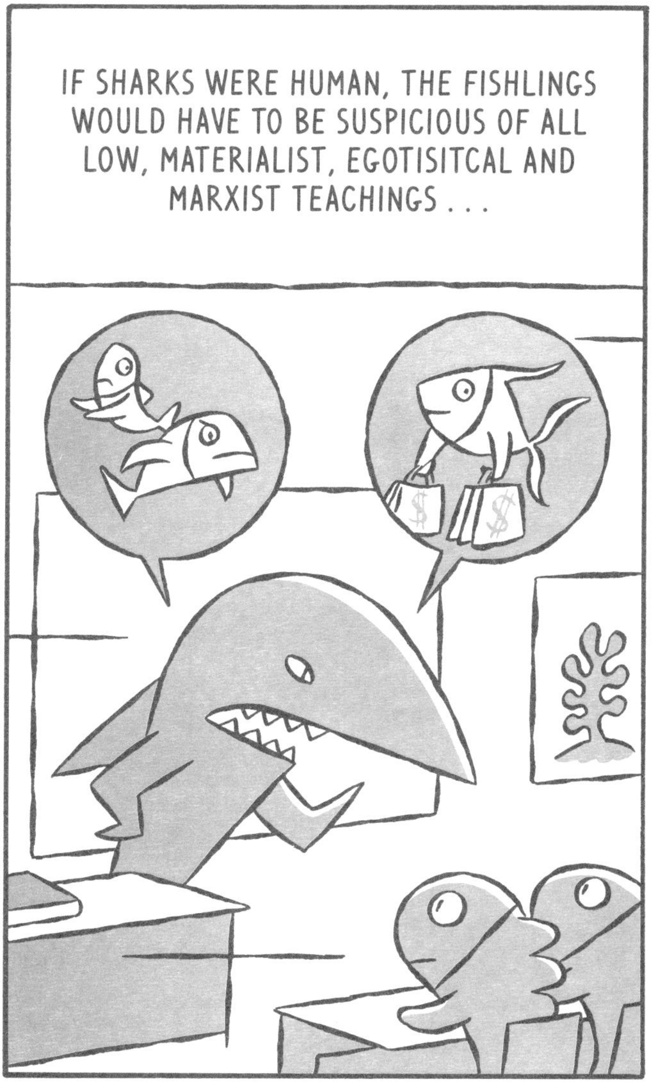
IF SHARKS WERE HUMAN, THE FISHLINGS WOULD HAVE TO BE SUSPICIOUS OF ALL LOW, MATERIALIST, EGOTISITCAL AND MARXIST TEACHINGS . . .

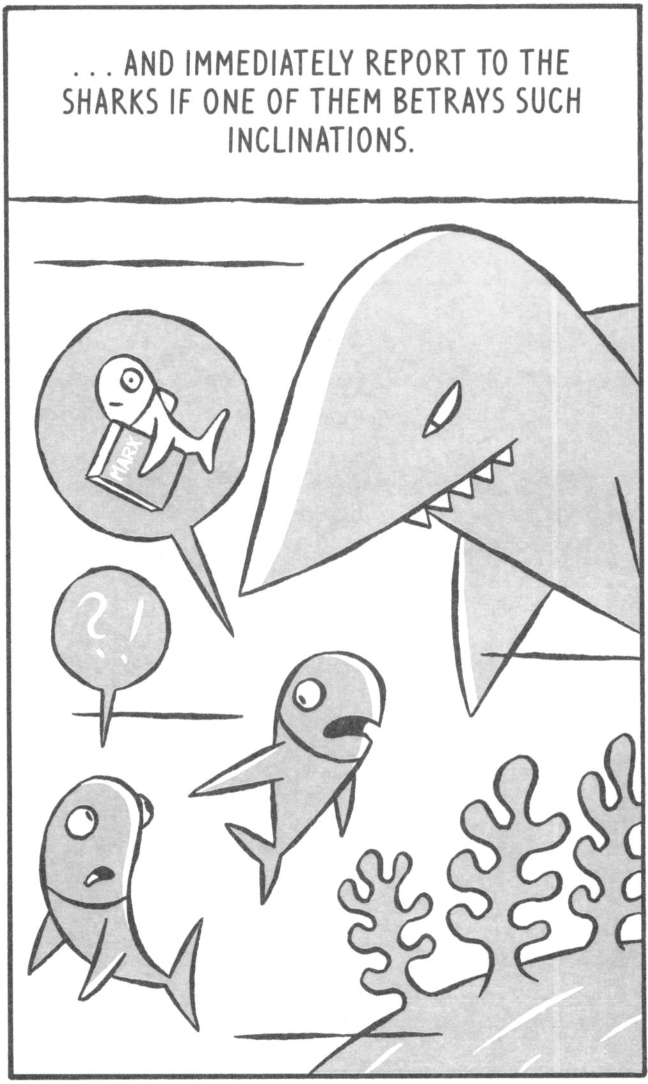
. . . AND IMMEDIATELY REPORT TO THE SHARKS IF ONE OF THEM BETRAYS SUCH INCLINATIONS.
MARX
?!

NATURALLY, THERE WOULD BE ART BY
THE SHARKS. THE IMAGES WOULD HAVE
GORGEOUS COLOUR . . .

THE GOLDEN
JAWS.

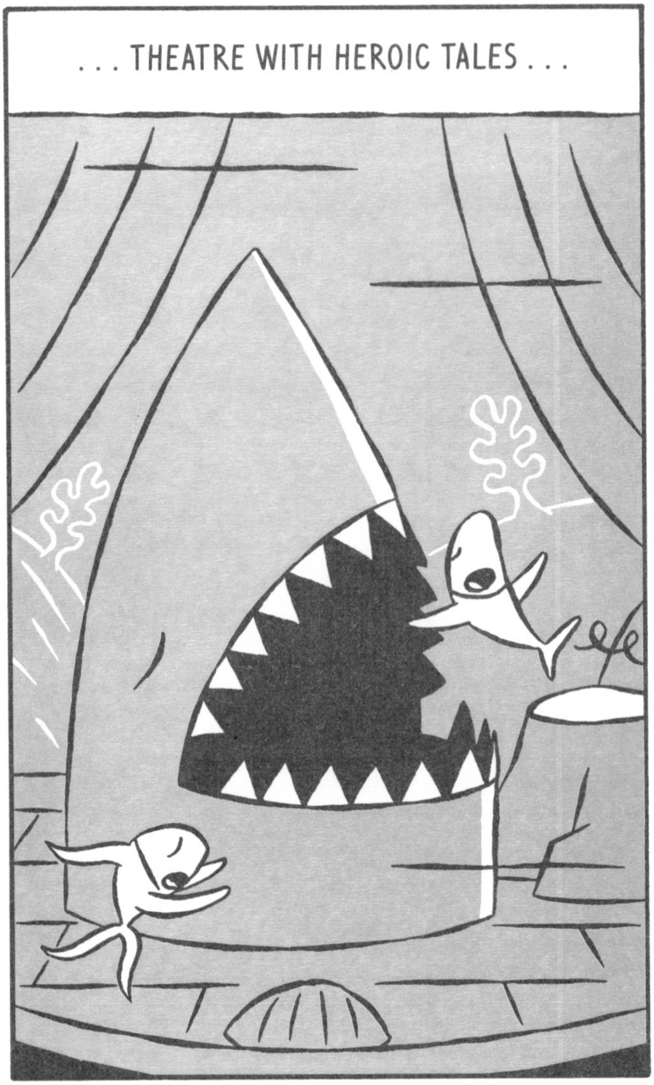
. . . THEATRE WITH HEROIC TALES . . .

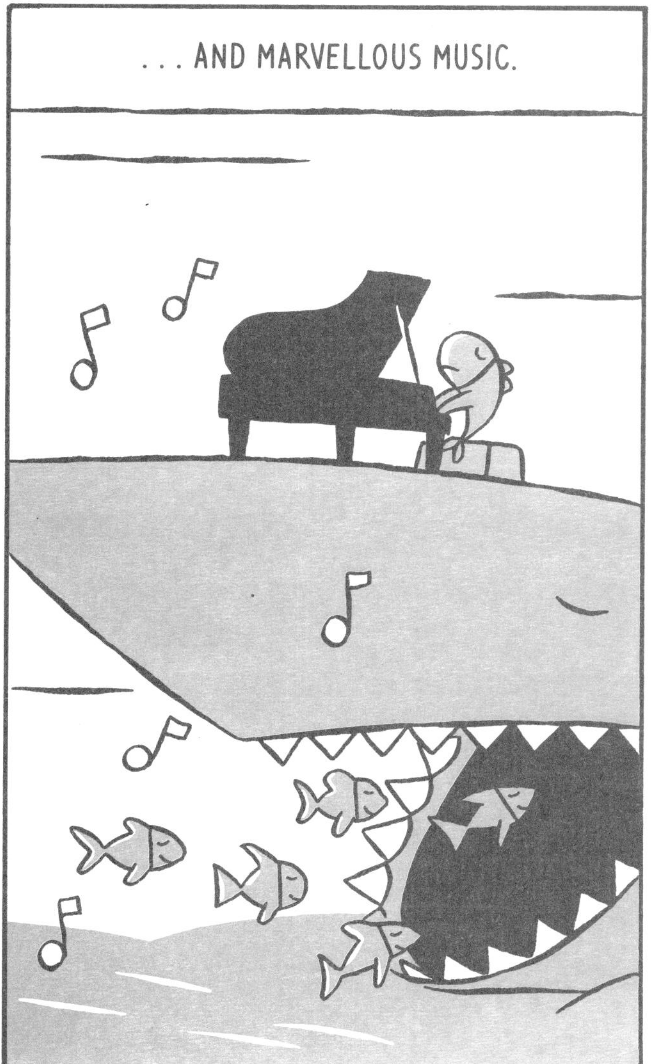
. . . AND MARVELLOUS MUSIC.

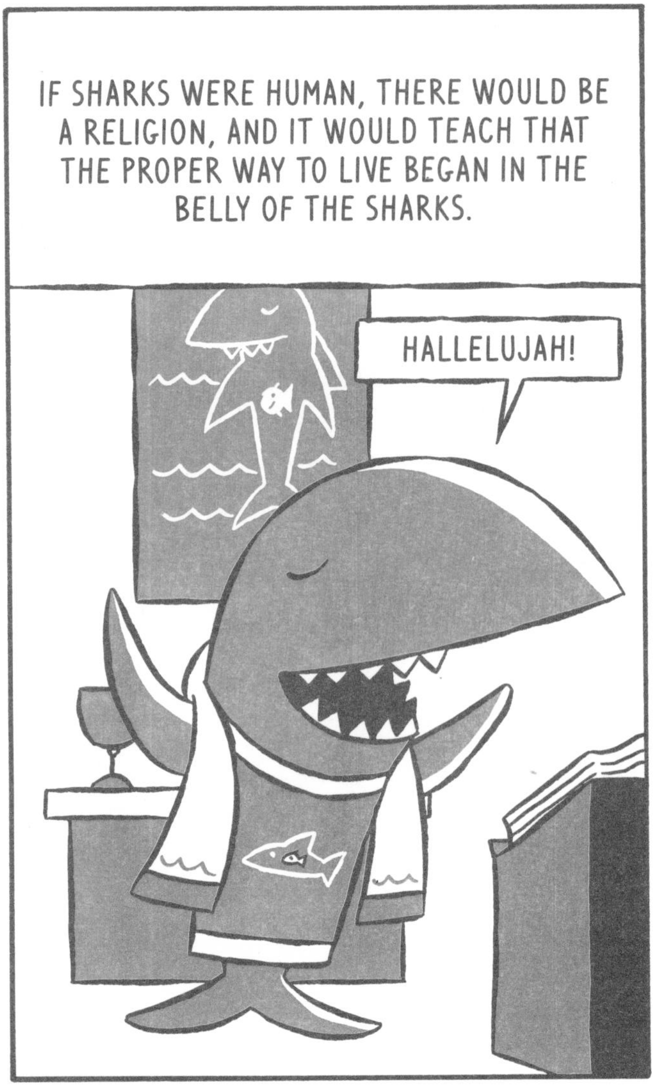
IF SHARKS WERE HUMAN, THERE WOULD BE A RELIGION, AND IT WOULD TEACH THAT THE PROPER WAY TO LIVE BEGAN IN THE BELLY OF THE SHARKS.
HALLELUJAH!

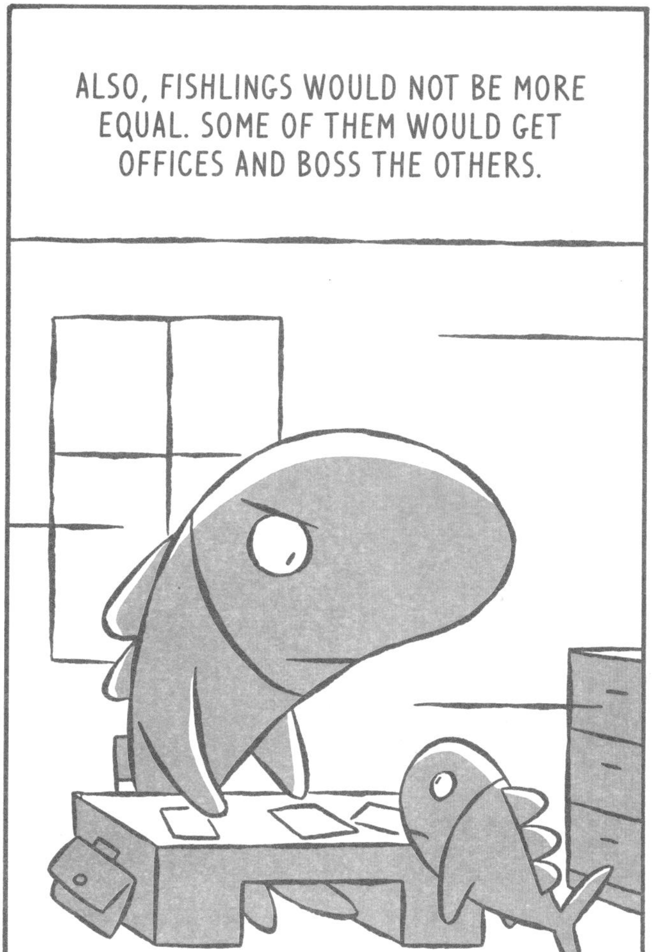
ALSO, FISHLINGS WOULD NOT BE MORE EQUAL. SOME OF THEM WOULD GET OFFICES AND BOSS THE OTHERS.

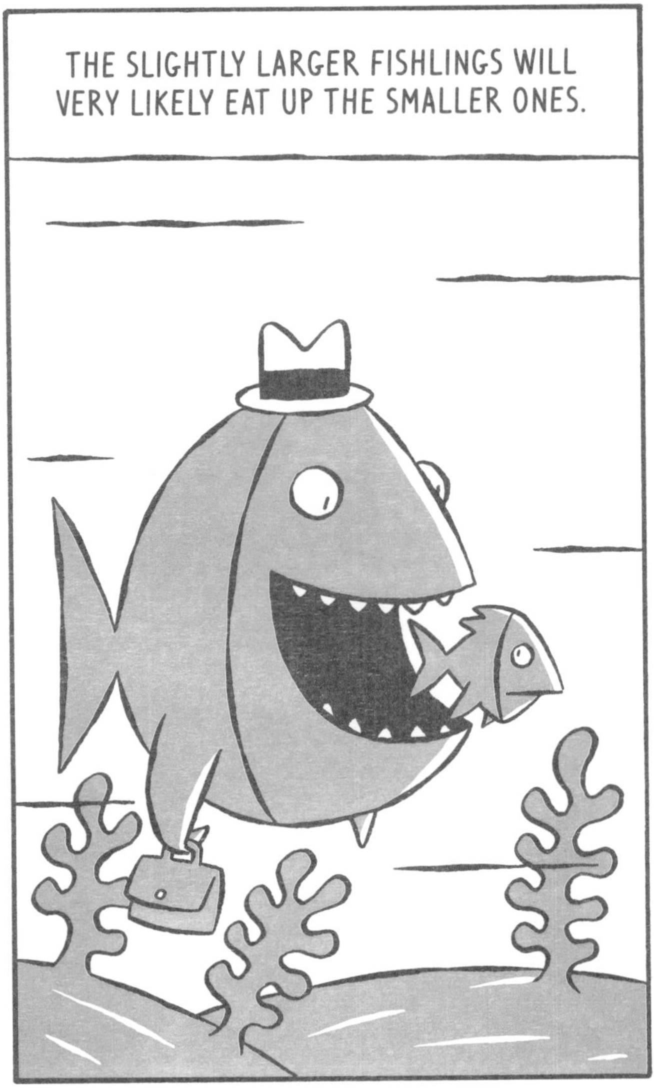
THE SLIGHTLY LARGER FISHLINGS WILL VERY LIKELY EAT UP THE SMALLER ONES.

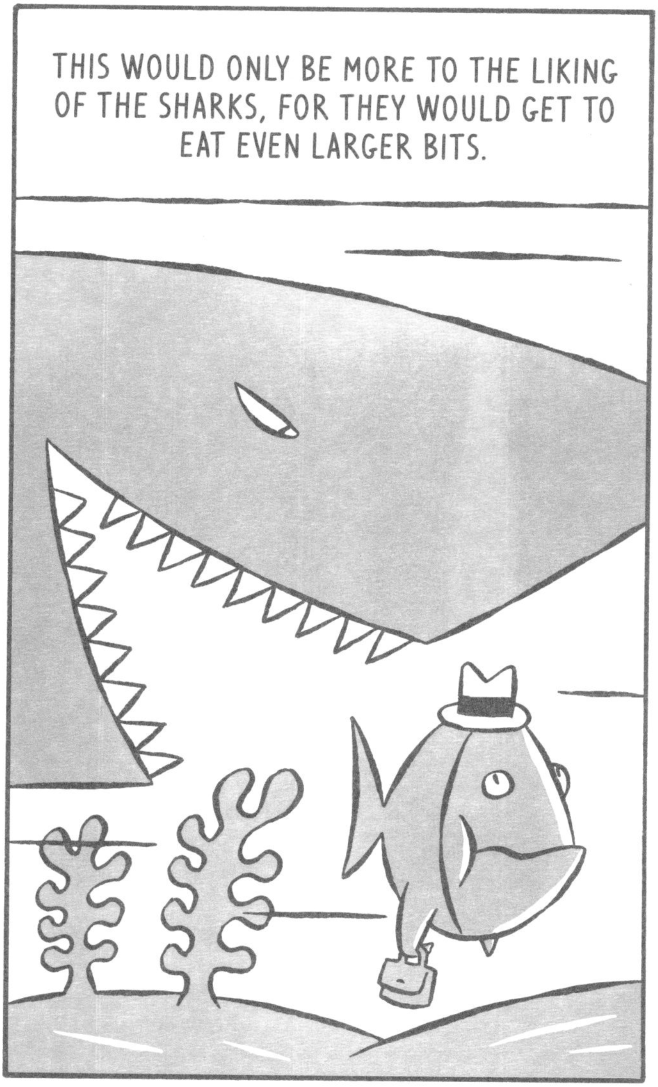
THIS WOULD ONLY BE MORE TO THE LIKING OF THE SHARKS, FOR THEY WOULD GET TO EAT EVEN LARGER BITS.

SOON CIVILIZATION WOULD ONLY EXIST IN THE OCEANS IF SHARKS WERE HUMAN . . . AND NOW LET'S GO EAT FISH . . . NO, ICE CREAM.

FORM AND SUBSTANCE

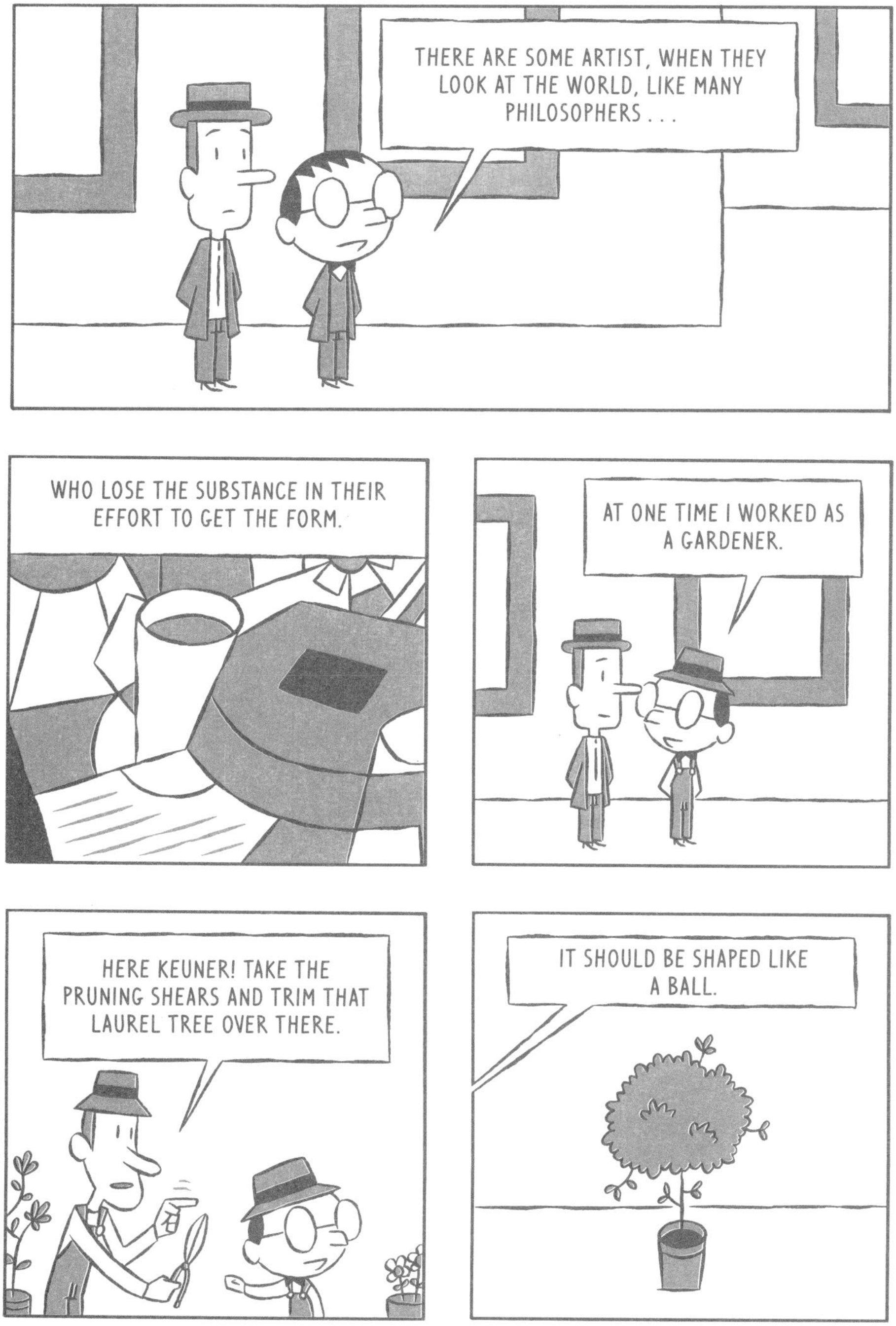
THERE ARE SOME ARTIST, WHEN THEY LOOK AT THE WORLD, LIKE MANY PHILOSOPHERS . . .
WHO LOSE THE SUBSTANCE IN THEIR EFFORT TO GET THE FORM.
AT ONE TIME I WORKED AS A GARDENER.
HERE KEUNER! TAKE THE PRUNING SHEARS AND TRIM THAT LAUREL TREE OVER THERE.
IT SHOULD BE SHAPED LIKE A BALL.

GOOD, THAT IS THE BALL, BUT WHERE IS THE LAUREL?

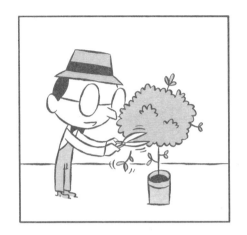

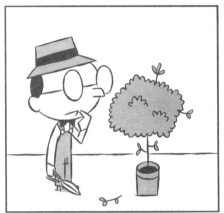

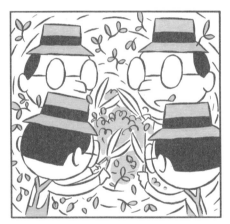

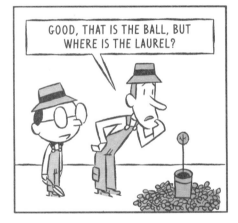

ANCIENT WORLD

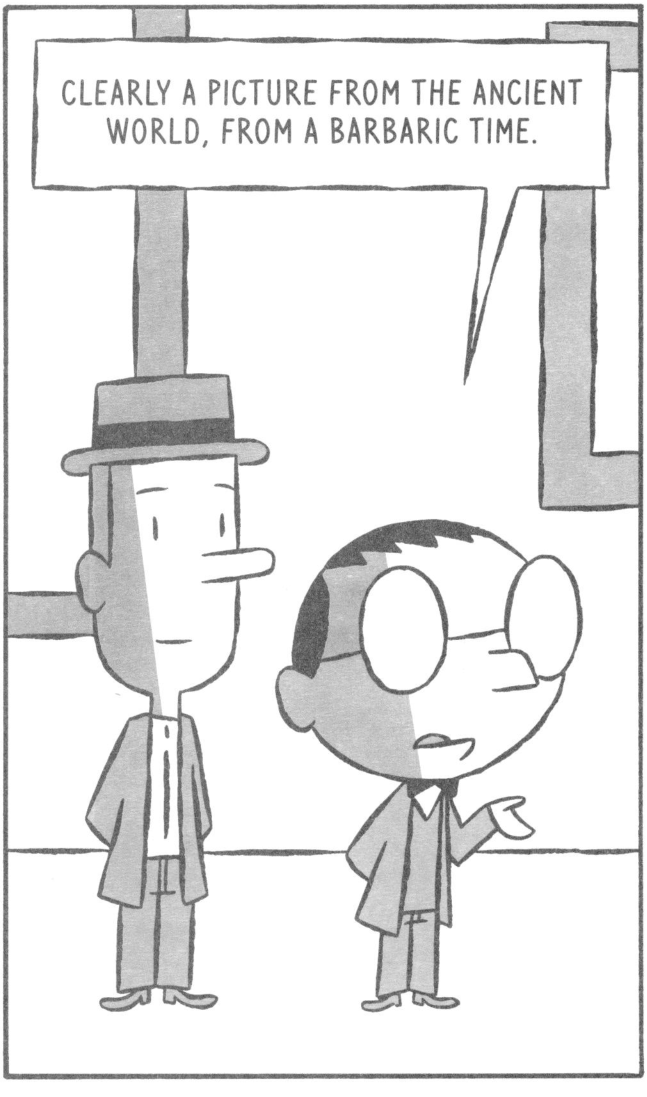
CLEARLY A PICTURE FROM THE ANCIENT WORLD, FROM A BARBARIC TIME.

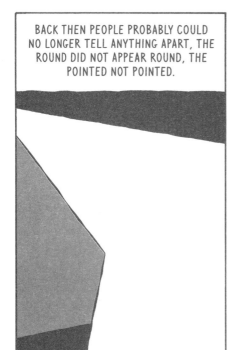

BACK THEN PEOPLE PROBABLY COULD
NO LONGER TELL ANYTHING APART, THE
ROUND DID NOT APPEAR ROUND, THE
POINTED NOT POINTED.

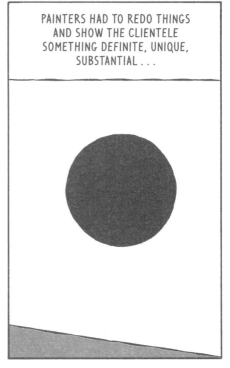

PAINTERS HAD TO REDO THINGS
AND SHOW THE CLIENTELE
SOMETHING DEFINITE, UNIQUE,
SUBSTANTIAL . . .

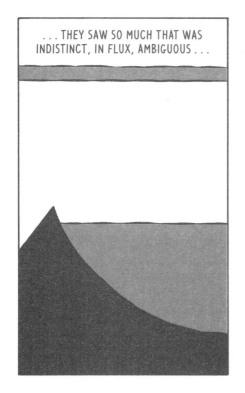

. . . THEY SAW SO MUCH THAT WAS
INDISTINCT, IN FLUX, AMBIGUOUS . . .

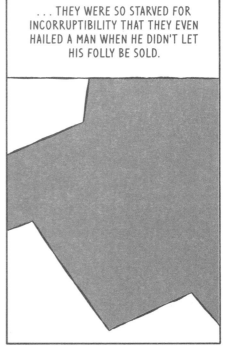

. . . THEY WERE SO STARVED FOR
INCORRUPTIBILITY THAT THEY EVEN
HAILED A MAN WHEN HE DIDN'T LET
HIS FOLLY BE SOLD.

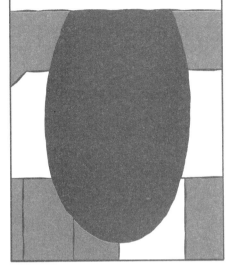

YOU CAN SEE IN THIS PAINTING FROM THE ANCIENT WORLD THAT LABOUR WAS DIVIDED UP AMONG THE MANY. THOSE WHO DETERMINED THE FORM DIDN'T CARE ABOUT THE PURPOSE OF THE OBJECT . . .

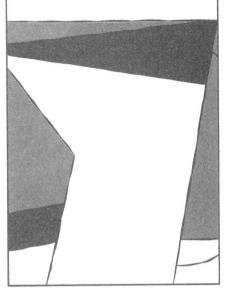

. . . YOU CANNOT POUR WATER FROM THIS PITCHER. MANY PEOPLE BACK THEN MUST HAVE BEEN REGARDED AS SIMPLY UTILITARIAN OBJECTS.

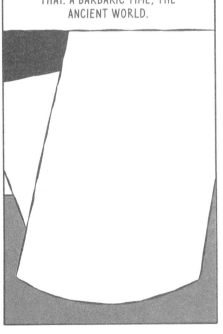

AND THE ARTISTS HAD TO RESIST THAT. A BARBARIC TIME, THE ANCIENT WORLD.

I HATE CORRECTING YOU, KEUNER, BUT THIS IS A MODERN PAINTING.

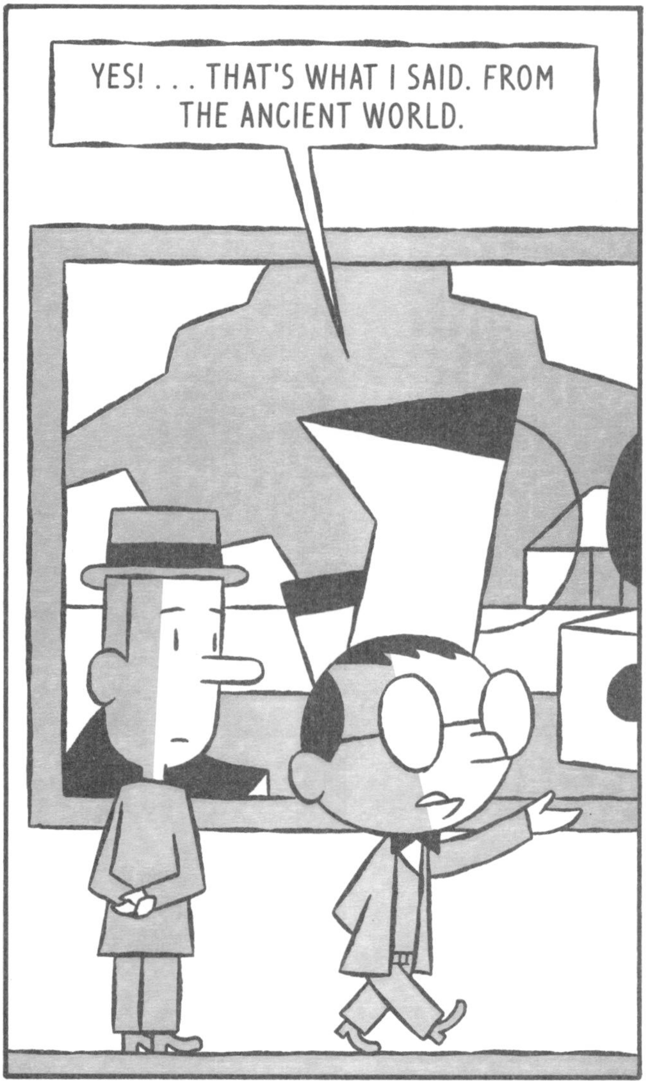
YES! . . . THAT'S WHAT I SAID. FROM THE ANCIENT WORLD.

MEASURES AGAINST AUTHORITY

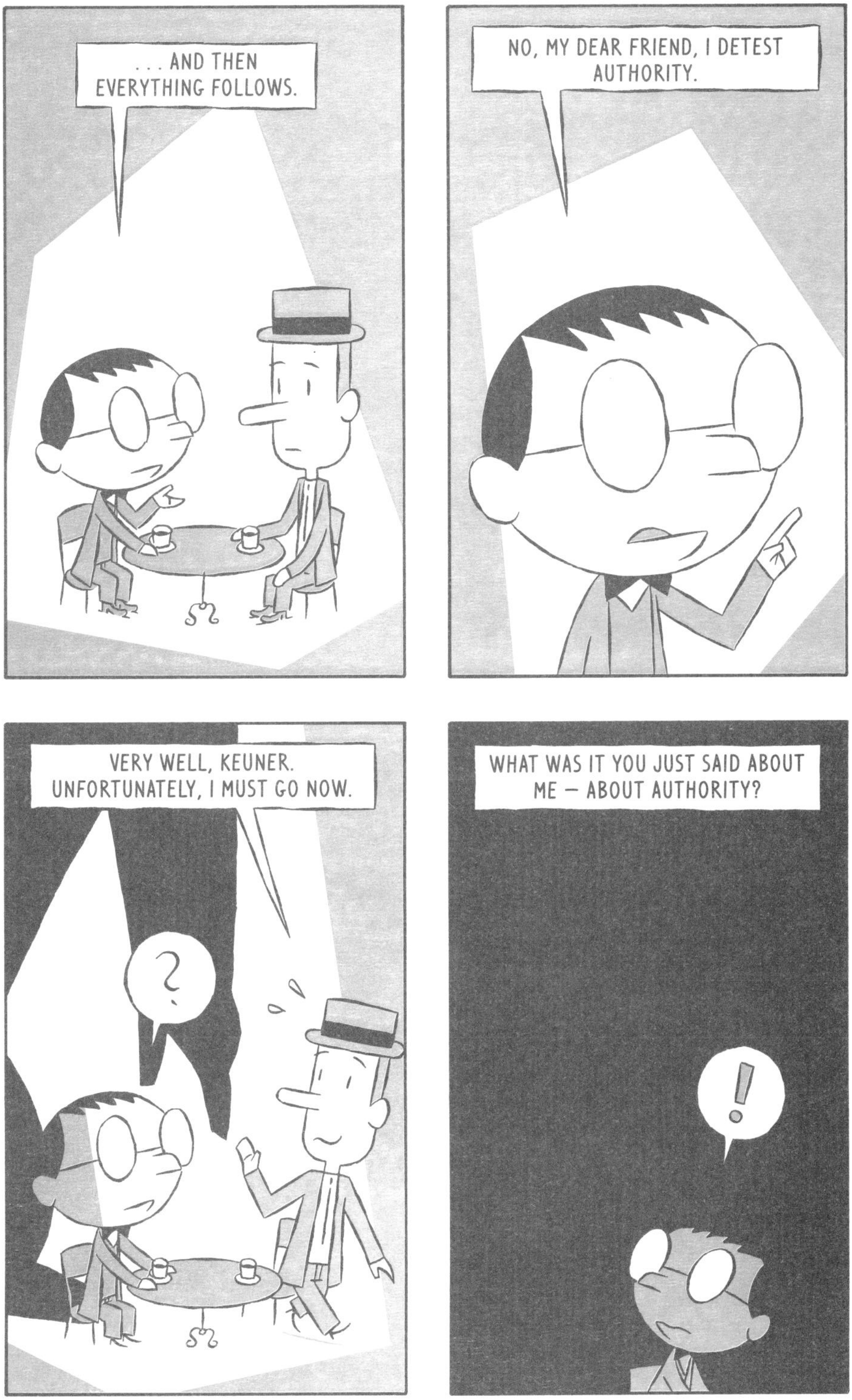
. . . AND THEN EVERYTHING FOLLOWS.
NO, MY DEAR FRIEND, I DETEST AUTHORITY.
VERY WELL, KEUNER. UNFORTUNATELY, I MUST GO NOW.
?
WHAT WAS IT YOU JUST SAID ABOUT ME — ABOUT AUTHORITY?
!

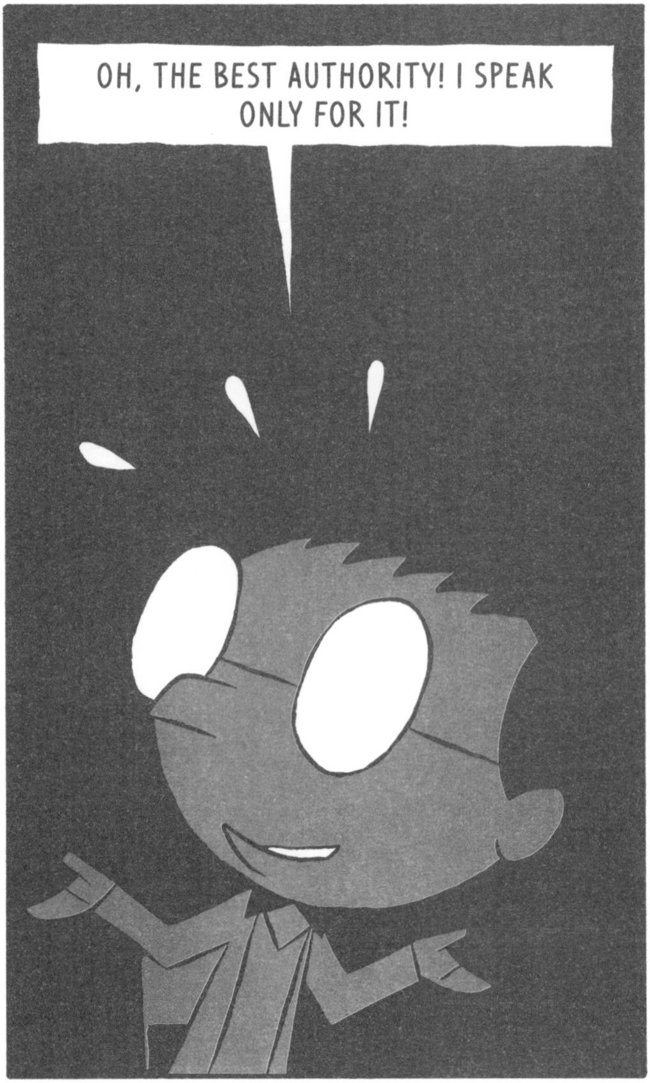
OH, THE BEST AUTHORITY! I SPEAK ONLY FOR IT!

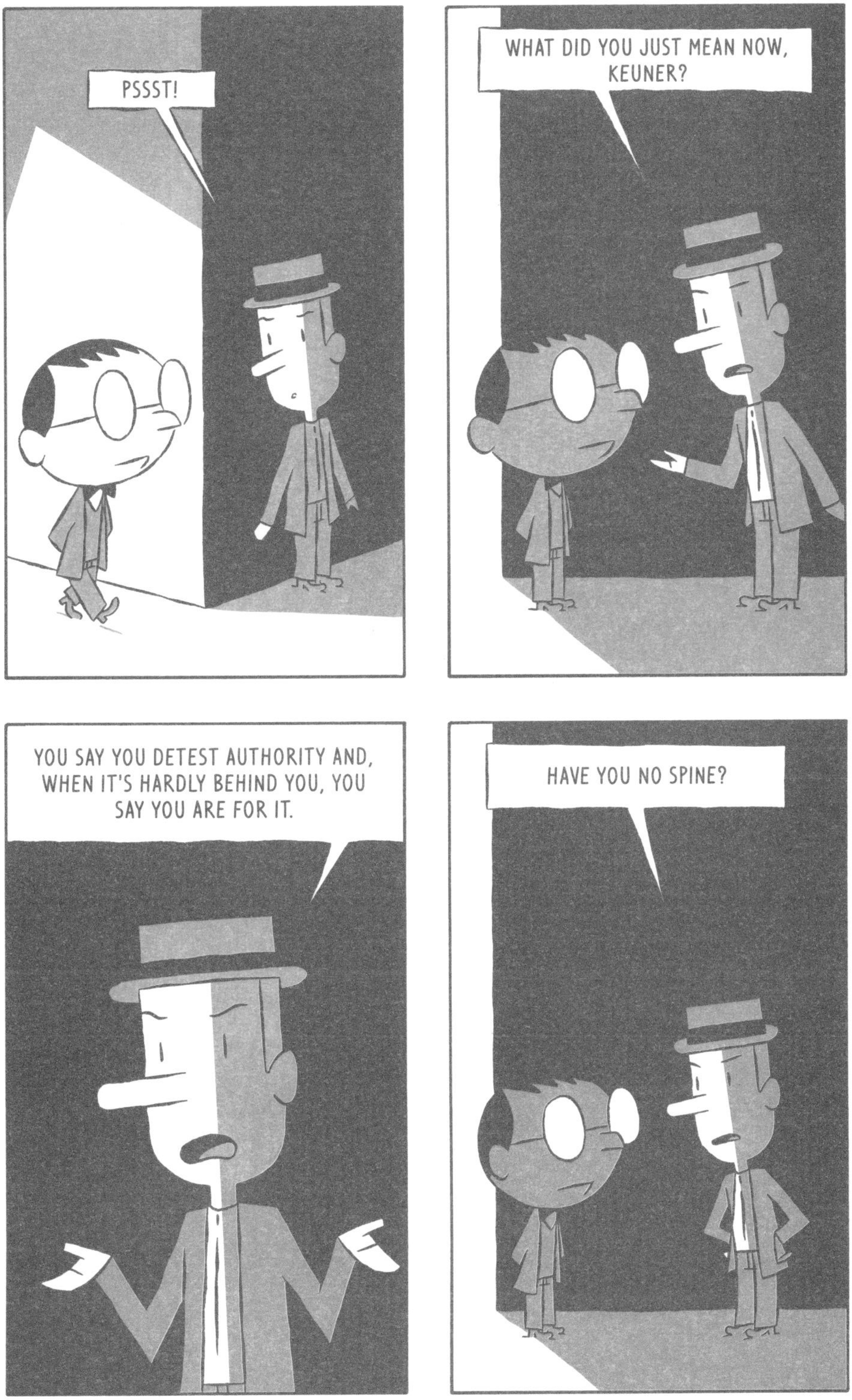
PSSST!
WHAT DID YOU JUST MEAN NOW, KEUNER?
YOU SAY YOU DETEST AUTHORITY AND, WHEN IT'S HARDLY BEHIND YOU, YOU SAY YOU ARE FOR IT.
HAVE YOU NO SPINE?

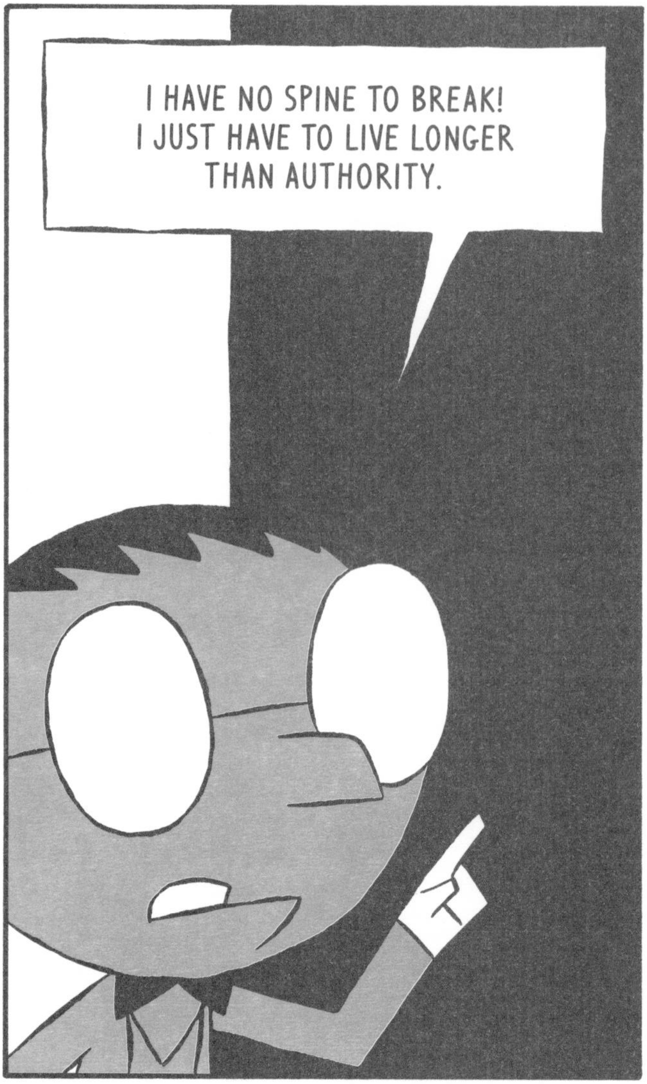
I HAVE NO SPINE TO BREAK!
I JUST HAVE TO LIVE LONGER
THAN AUTHORITY.

MY DEAR FRIEND, I WILL TELL YOU A STORY, THEN YOU WILL UNDERSTAND WHY I HAVE NO SPINE TO BREAK.

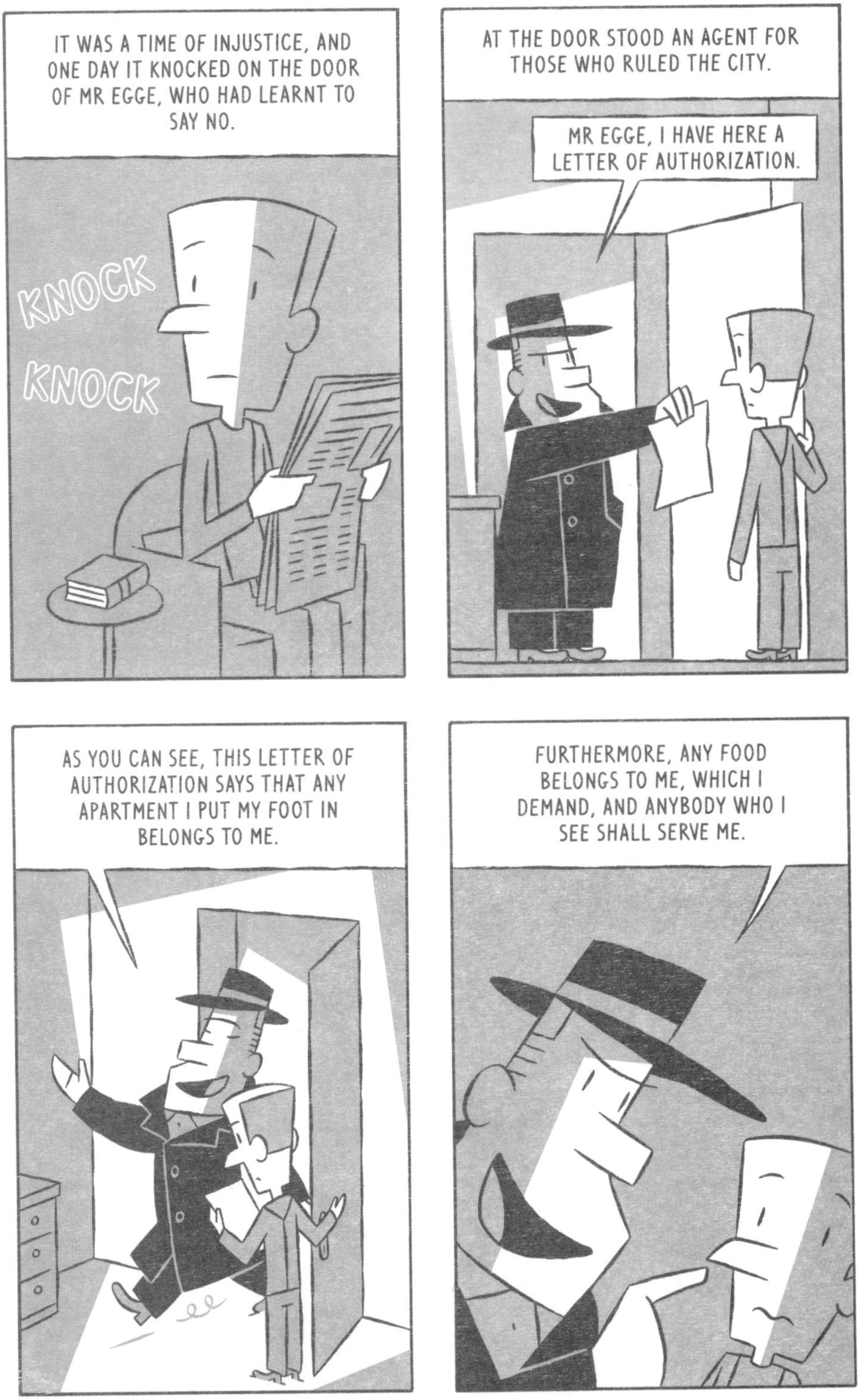
IT WAS A TIME OF INJUSTICE, AND ONE DAY IT KNOCKED ON THE DOOR OF MR EGGE, WHO HAD LEARNT TO SAY NO.
KNOCK
KNOCK
AT THE DOOR STOOD AN AGENT FOR THOSE WHO RULED THE CITY.
MR EGGE, I HAVE HERE A LETTER OF AUTHORIZATION.
AS YOU CAN SEE, THIS LETTER OF AUTHORIZATION SAYS THAT ANY APARTMENT I PUT MY FOOT IN BELONGS TO ME.
FURTHERMORE, ANY FOOD BELONGS TO ME, WHICH I DEMAND, AND ANYBODY WHO I SEE SHALL SERVE ME.

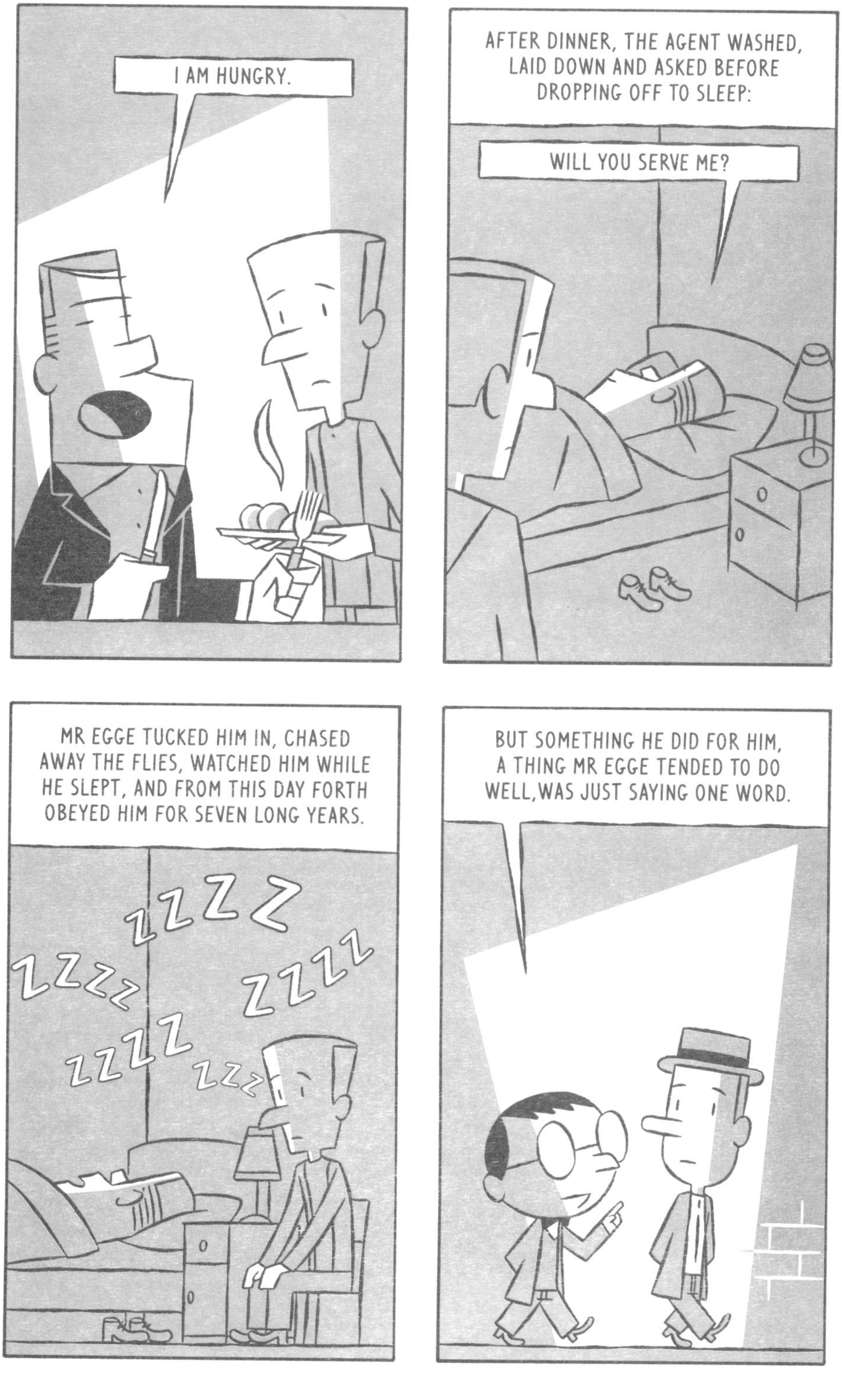
I AM HUNGRY.
AFTER DINNER, THE AGENT WASHED, LAID DOWN AND ASKED BEFORE DROPPING OFF TO SLEEP:
WILL YOU SERVE ME?
MR EGGE TUCKED HIM IN, CHASED AWAY THE FLIES, WATCHED HIM WHILE HE SLEPT, AND FROM THIS DAY FORTH OBEYED HIM FOR SEVEN LONG YEARS.
ZZZZ
ZZZZ
ZZZZ
ZZZZ
ZZZ
BUT SOMETHING HE DID FOR HIM, A THING MR EGGE TENDED TO DO WELL,WAS JUST SAYING ONE WORD.

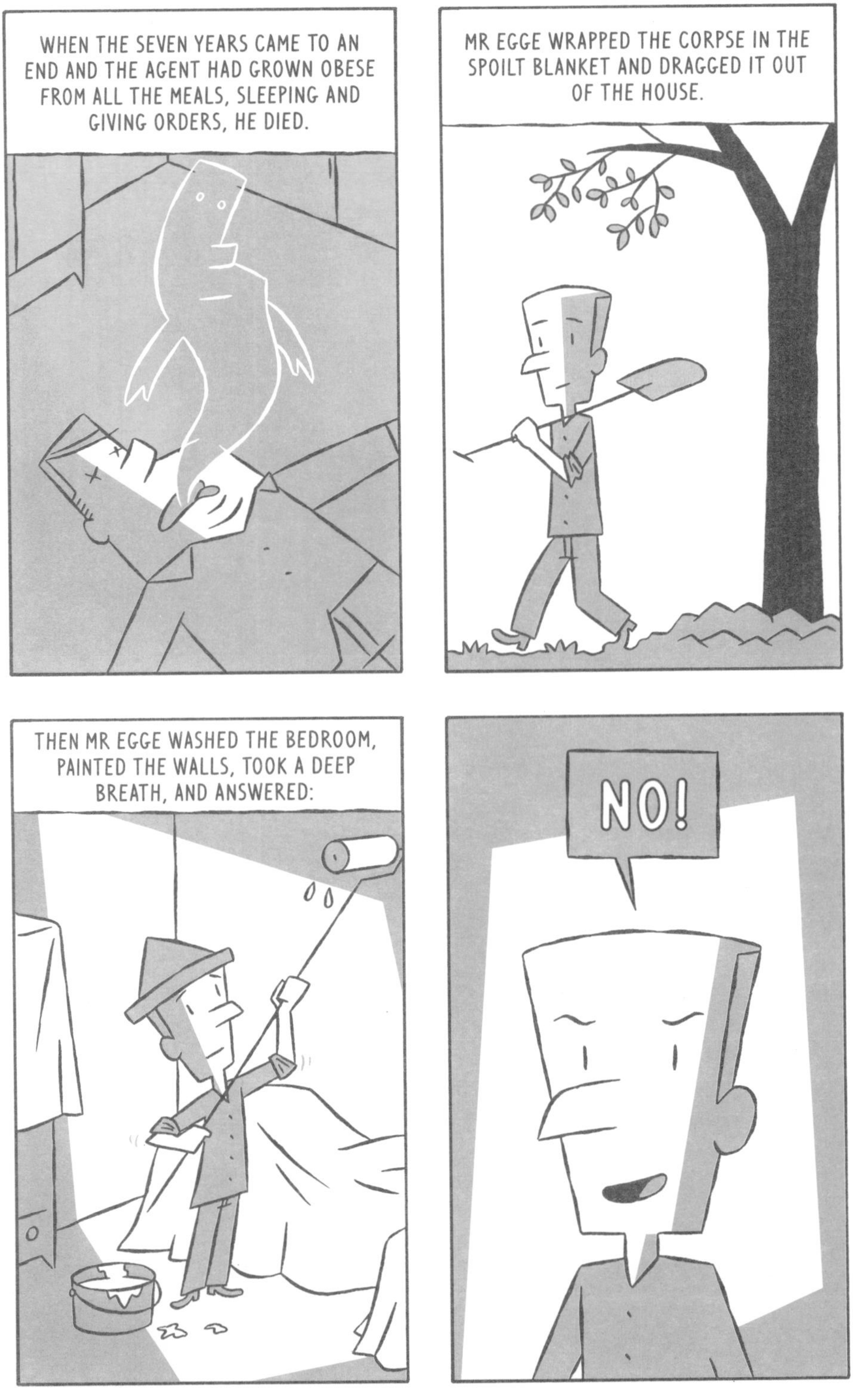
WHEN THE SEVEN YEARS CAME TO AN END AND THE AGENT HAD GROWN OBESE FROM ALL THE MEALS, SLEEPING AND GIVING ORDERS, HE DIED.
MR EGGE WRAPPED THE CORPSE IN THE SPOILT BLANKET AND DRAGGED IT OUT OF THE HOUSE.
THEN MR EGGE WASHED THE BEDROOM, PAINTED THE WALLS, TOOK A DEEP BREATH, AND ANSWERED:
NO!

MR KEUNER AND ORIGINALITY

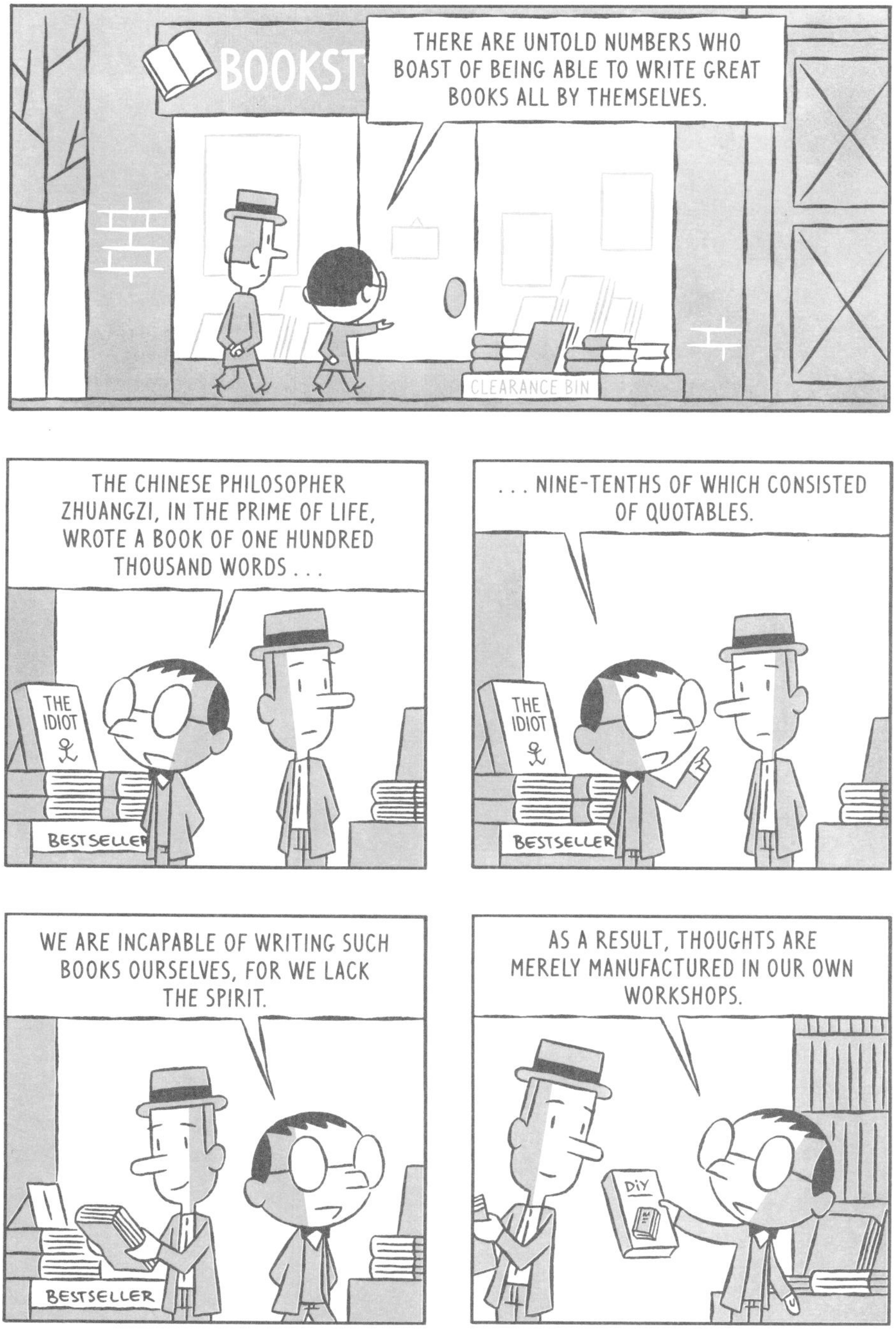
BOOKST
THERE ARE UNTOLD NUMBERS WHO BOAST OF BEING ABLE TO WRITE GREAT BOOKS ALL BY THEMSELVES.
CLEARANCE BIN
THE CHINESE PHILOSOPHER ZHUANGZI, IN THE PRIME OF LIFE, WROTE A BOOK OF ONE HUNDRED THOUSAND WORDS . . .
THE IDIOT
BESTSELLER
. . . NINE-TENTHS OF WHICH CONSISTED OF QUOTABLES.
THE IDIOT
BESTSELLER
WE ARE INCAPABLE OF WRITING SUCH BOOKS OURSELVES, FOR WE LACK THE SPIRIT.
BESTSELLER
AS A RESULT, THOUGHTS ARE MERELY MANUFACTURED IN OUR OWN WORKSHOPS.
DiY

THERE IS NEITHER ANY THOUGHT ONE CAN BORROW, NOR THE FORMULATION OF ANY THOUGHT ONE COULD QUOTE.

THESE WRITERS REQUIRE VERY LITTLE IN THEIR OCCUPATION.

WITHOUT ANY ASSISTANCE, ONLY WITH THE MOST MISERABLE MATERIAL — THAT WHICH AN INDIVIDUAL CAN CARRY IN HIS ARMS — THEY BUILD THEIR HUTS.

LARGER STRUCTURES THEY KNOW NOTHING ABOUT, ONLY THOSE ONE MAN IS CAPABLE OF BUILDING.

MR KEUNER AND CALISTHENICS

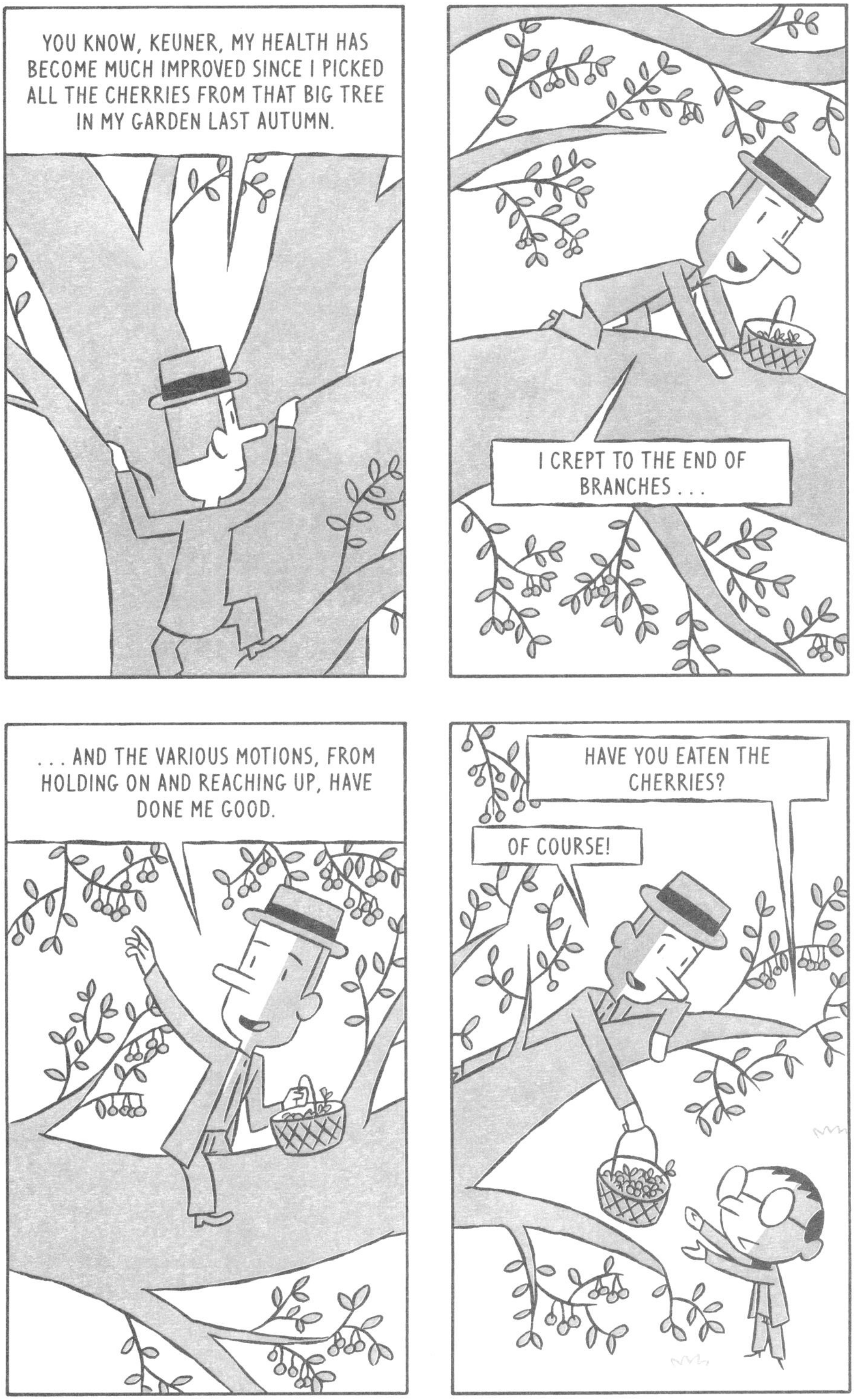
YOU KNOW, KEUNER, MY HEALTH HAS BECOME MUCH IMPROVED SINCE I PICKED ALL THE CHERRIES FROM THAT BIG TREE IN MY GARDEN LAST AUTUMN.
I CREPT TO THE END OF BRANCHES . . .
. . . AND THE VARIOUS MOTIONS, FROM HOLDING ON AND REACHING UP, HAVE DONE ME GOOD.
HAVE YOU EATEN THE CHERRIES?
OF COURSE!

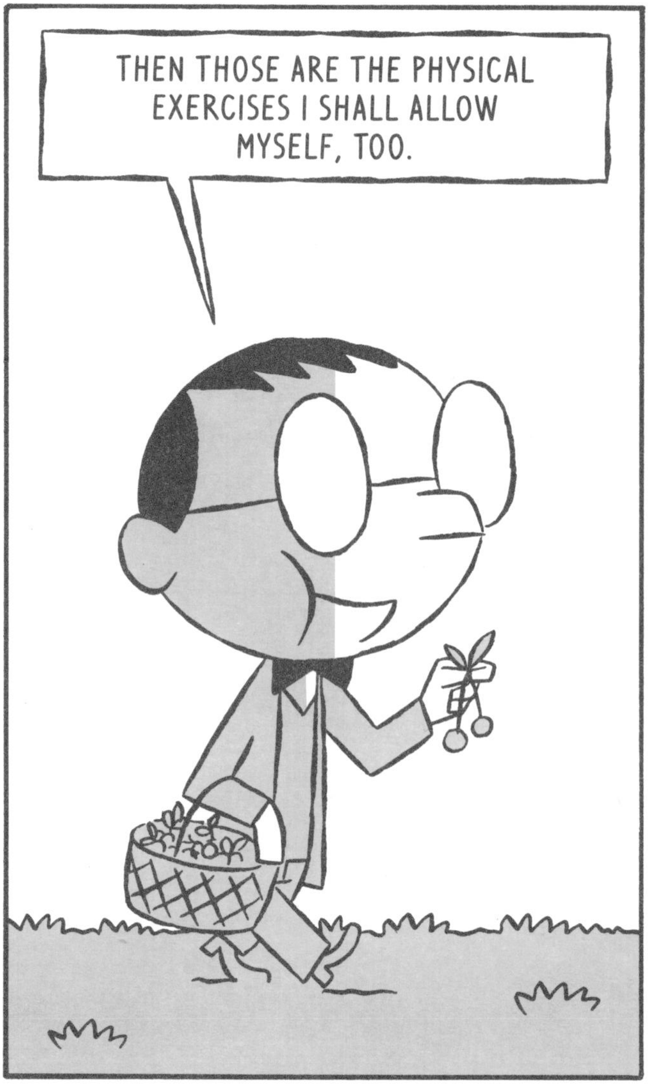
THEN THOSE ARE THE PHYSICAL EXERCISES I SHALL ALLOW MYSELF, TOO.

KEUNER

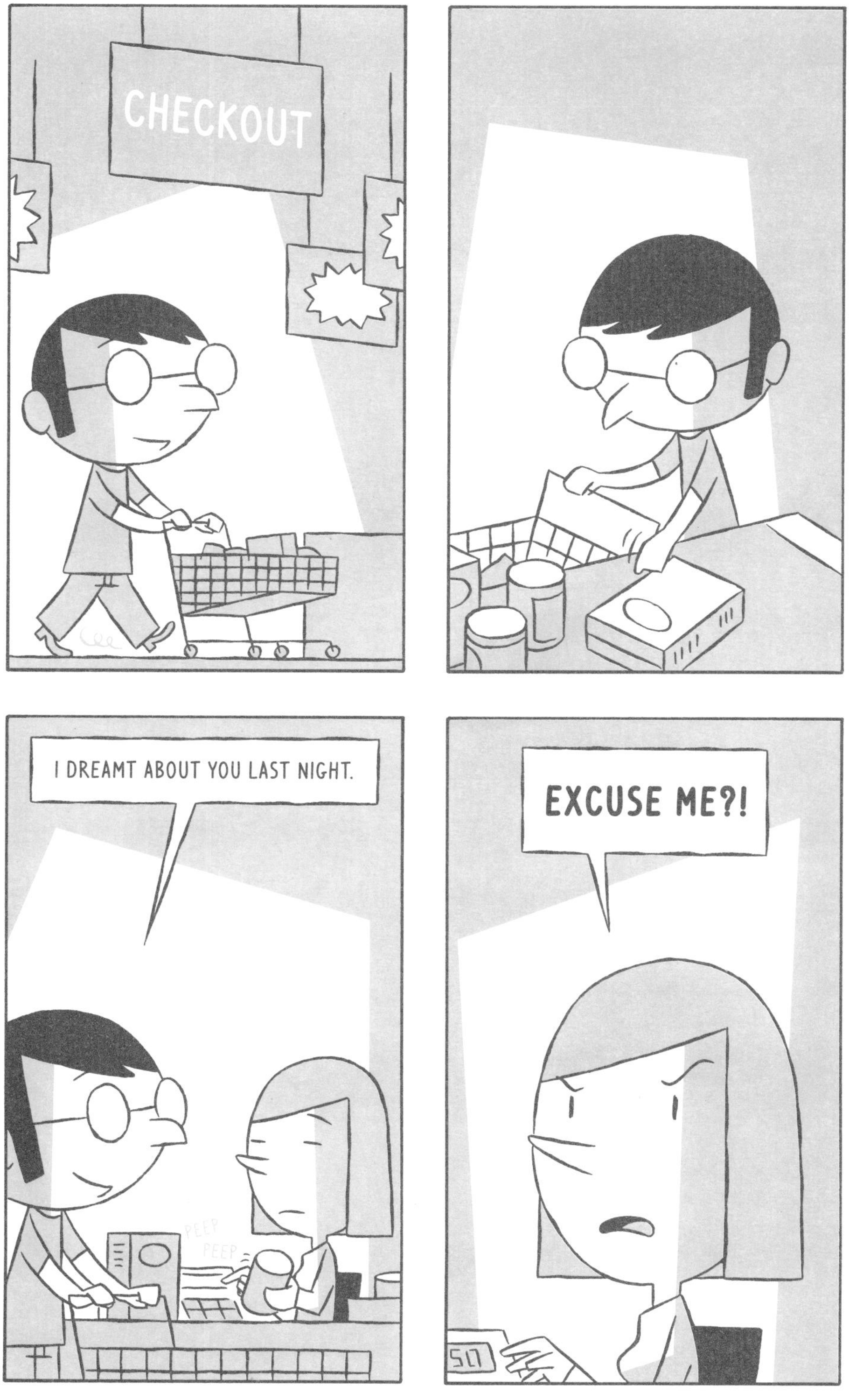
CHECKOUT
I DREAMT ABOUT YOU LAST NIGHT.
PEEP PEEP
EXCUSE ME?!

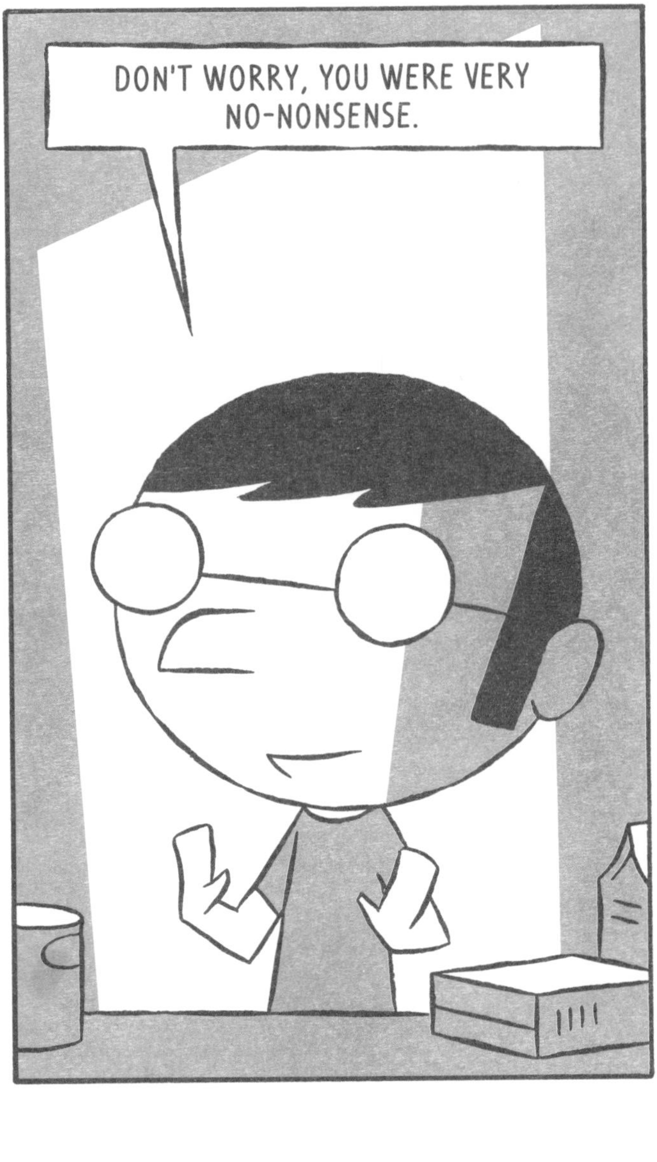
DON'T WORRY, YOU WERE VERY NO-NONSENSE.

IF KEUNER LOVED SOMEONE

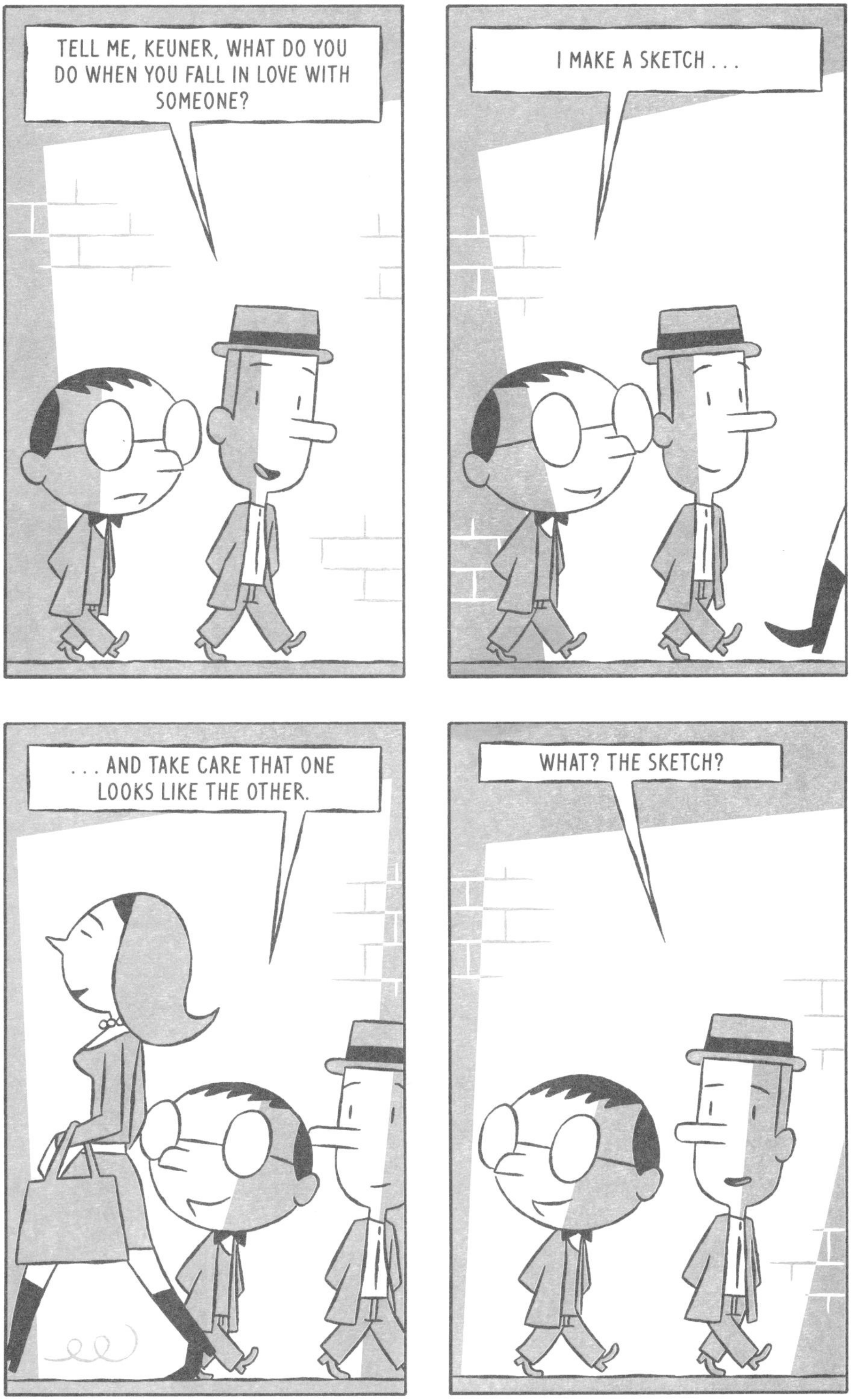
TELL ME, KEUNER, WHAT DO YOU DO WHEN YOU FALL IN LOVE WITH SOMEONE?
I MAKE A SKETCH . . .
. . . AND TAKE CARE THAT ONE LOOKS LIKE THE OTHER.
WHAT? THE SKETCH?

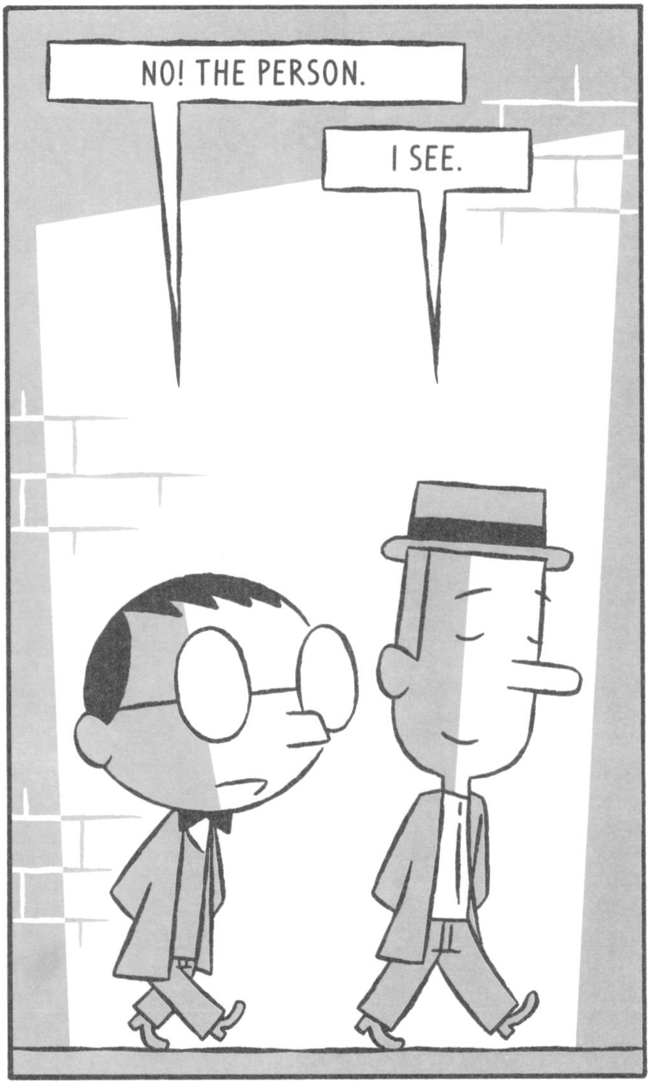
NO! THE PERSON.
I SEE.

SUCCESS

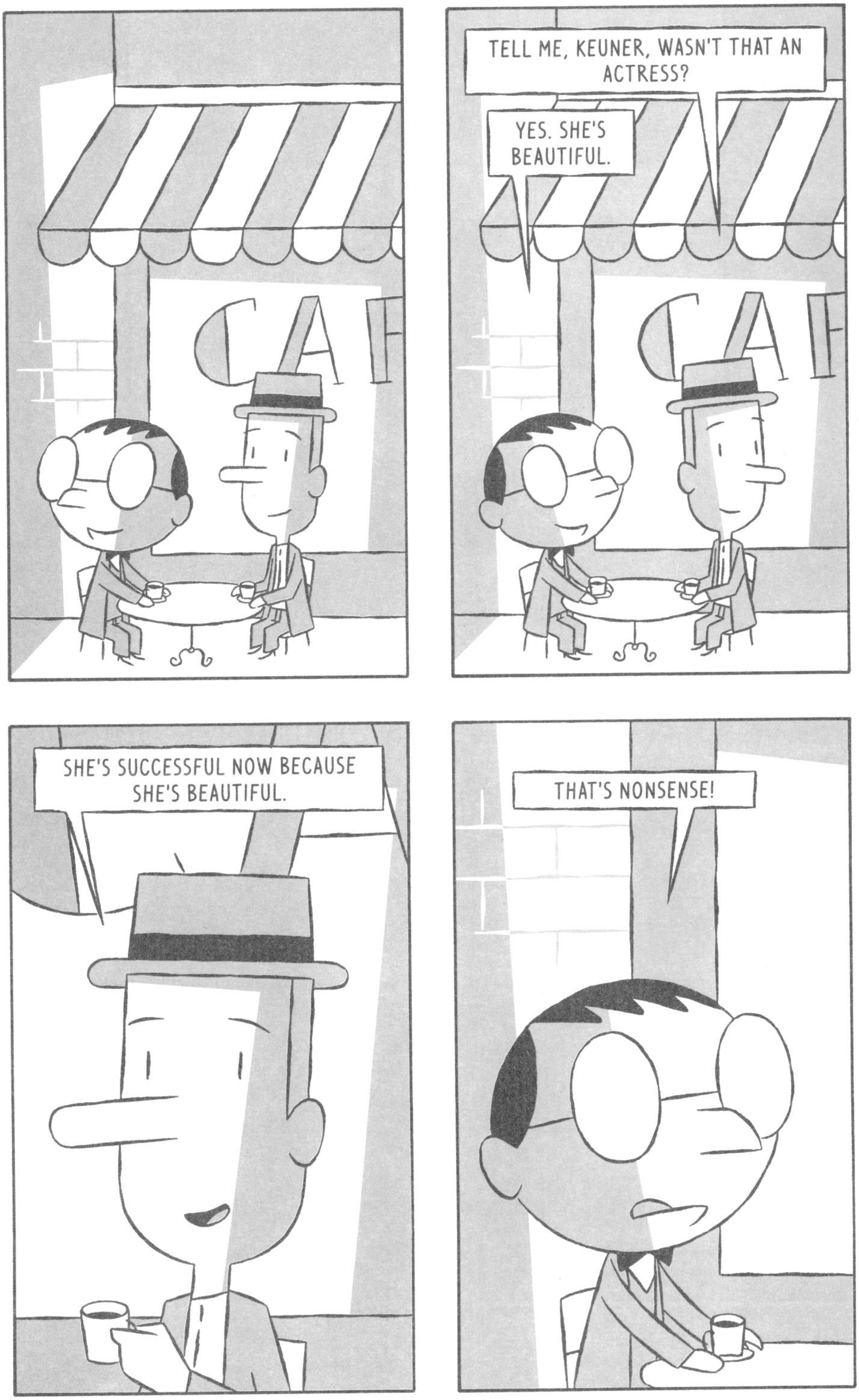
TELL ME, KEUNER, WASN'T THAT AN ACTRESS?
YES. SHE'S BEAUTIFUL.
SHE'S SUCCESSFUL NOW BECAUSE SHE'S BEAUTIFUL.
THAT'S NONSENSE!

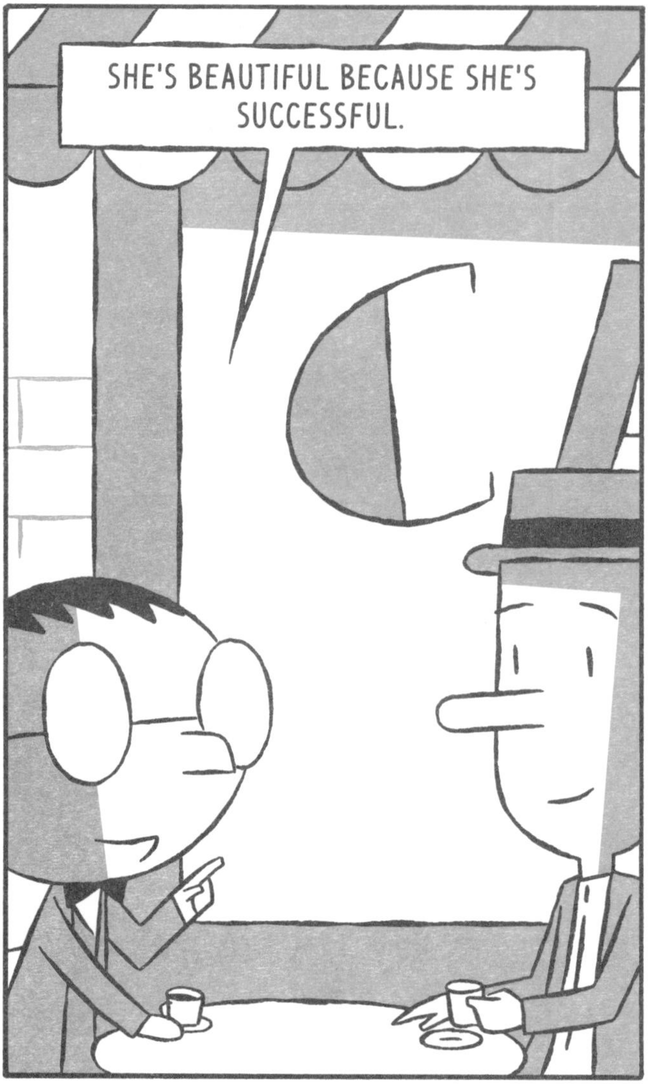
SHE'S BEAUTIFUL BECAUSE SHE'S SUCCESSFUL.

MR KEUNER AND THE ACTRESS

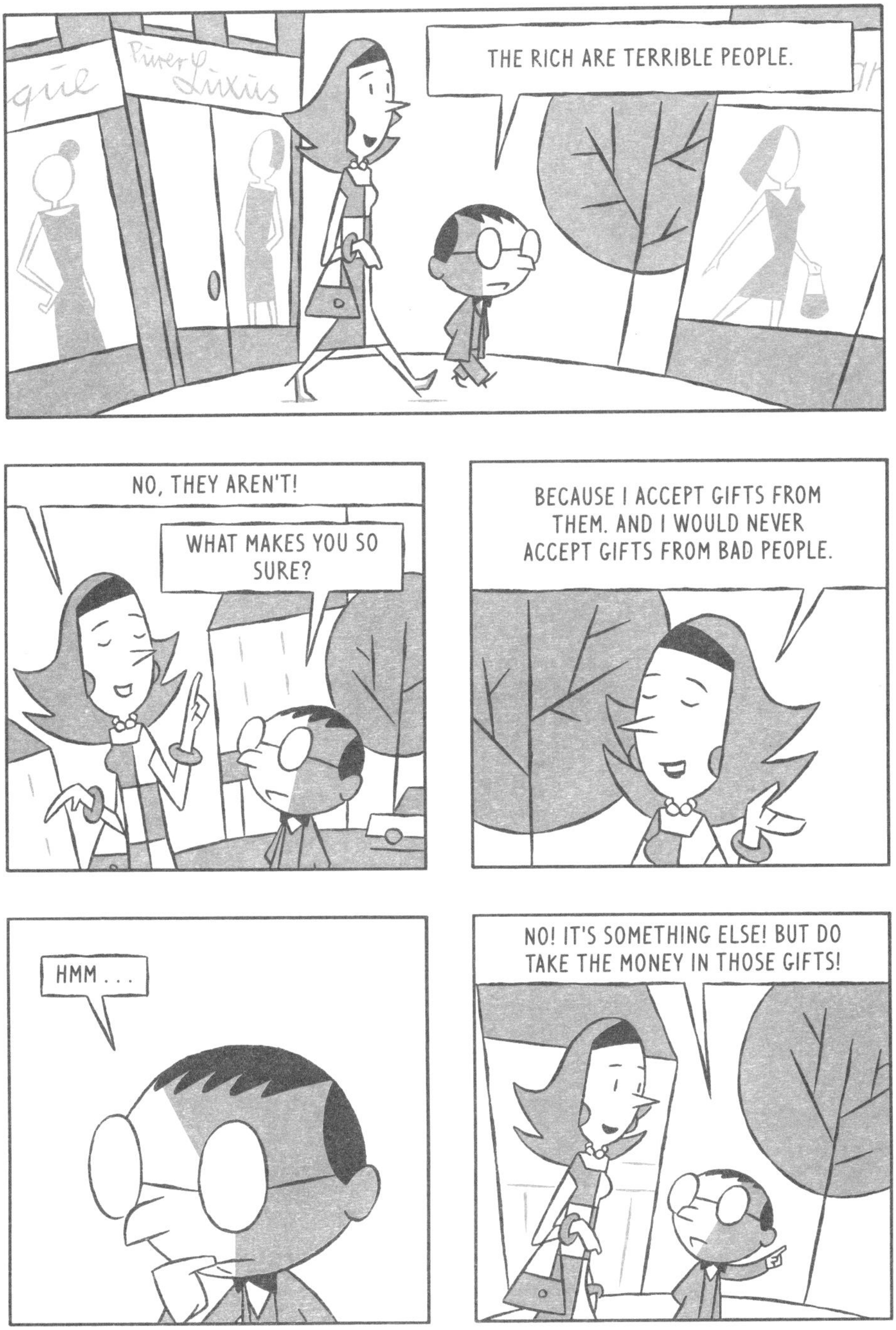

THE RICH ARE TERRIBLE PEOPLE.
NO, THEY AREN'T!
WHAT MAKES YOU SO SURE?
BECAUSE I ACCEPT GIFTS FROM THEM. AND I WOULD NEVER ACCEPT GIFTS FROM BAD PEOPLE.
HMM . . .
NO! IT'S SOMETHING ELSE! BUT DO TAKE THE MONEY IN THOSE GIFTS!

THEY DIDN'T PAY FOR THOSE GIFTS, THEY STOLE THEM INSTEAD!

TAKE THE STOLEN GOODS FROM THESE TERRIBLE PEOPLE SO THAT YOU CAN BE A GOOD ACTRESS.

CAN'T I BE A GOOD ACTRESS WITHOUT THE MONEY TOO?

NO! NO! NO!

FRIENDLY TURNS

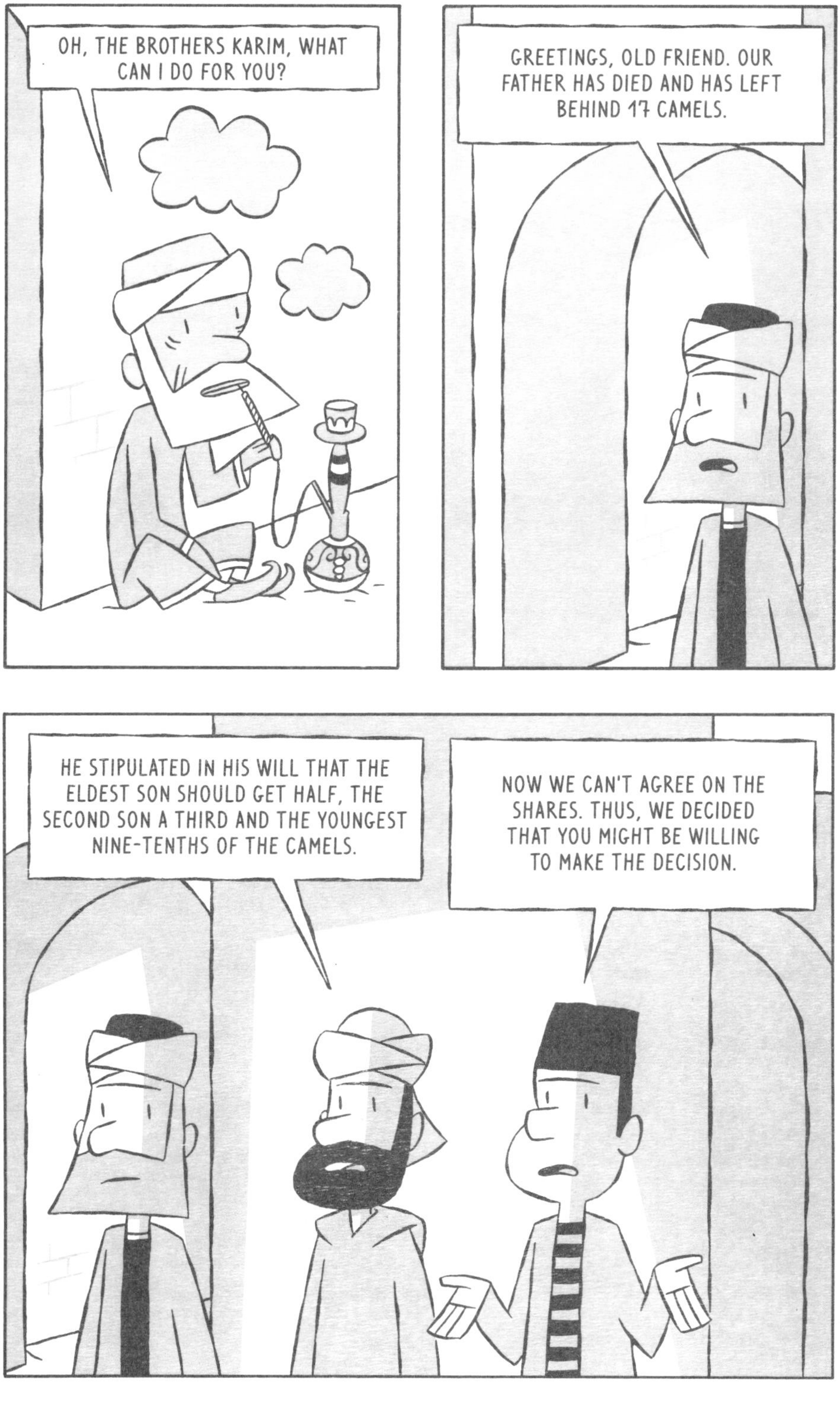
OH, THE BROTHERS KARIM, WHAT CAN I DO FOR YOU?
GREETINGS, OLD FRIEND. OUR FATHER HAS DIED AND HAS LEFT BEHIND 17 CAMELS.
HE STIPULATED IN HIS WILL THAT THE ELDEST SON SHOULD GET HALF, THE SECOND SON A THIRD AND THE YOUNGEST NINE-TENTHS OF THE CAMELS.
NOW WE CAN'T AGREE ON THE SHARES. THUS, WE DECIDED THAT YOU MIGHT BE WILLING TO MAKE THE DECISION.

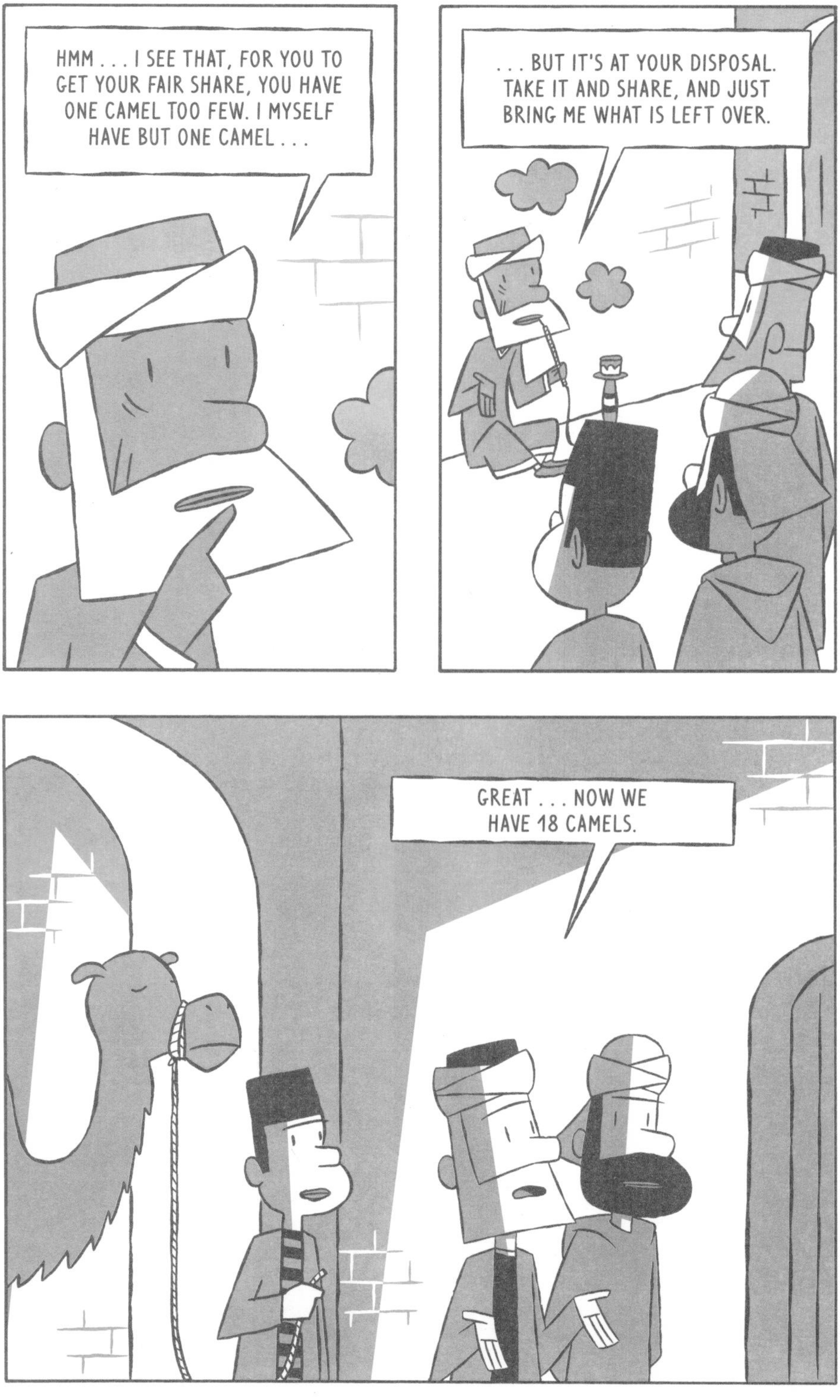
HMM . . . I SEE THAT, FOR YOU TO GET YOUR FAIR SHARE, YOU HAVE ONE CAMEL TOO FEW. I MYSELF HAVE BUT ONE CAMEL . . .
. . . BUT IT'S AT YOUR DISPOSAL. TAKE IT AND SHARE, AND JUST BRING ME WHAT IS LEFT OVER.
GREAT . . . NOW WE HAVE 18 CAMELS.

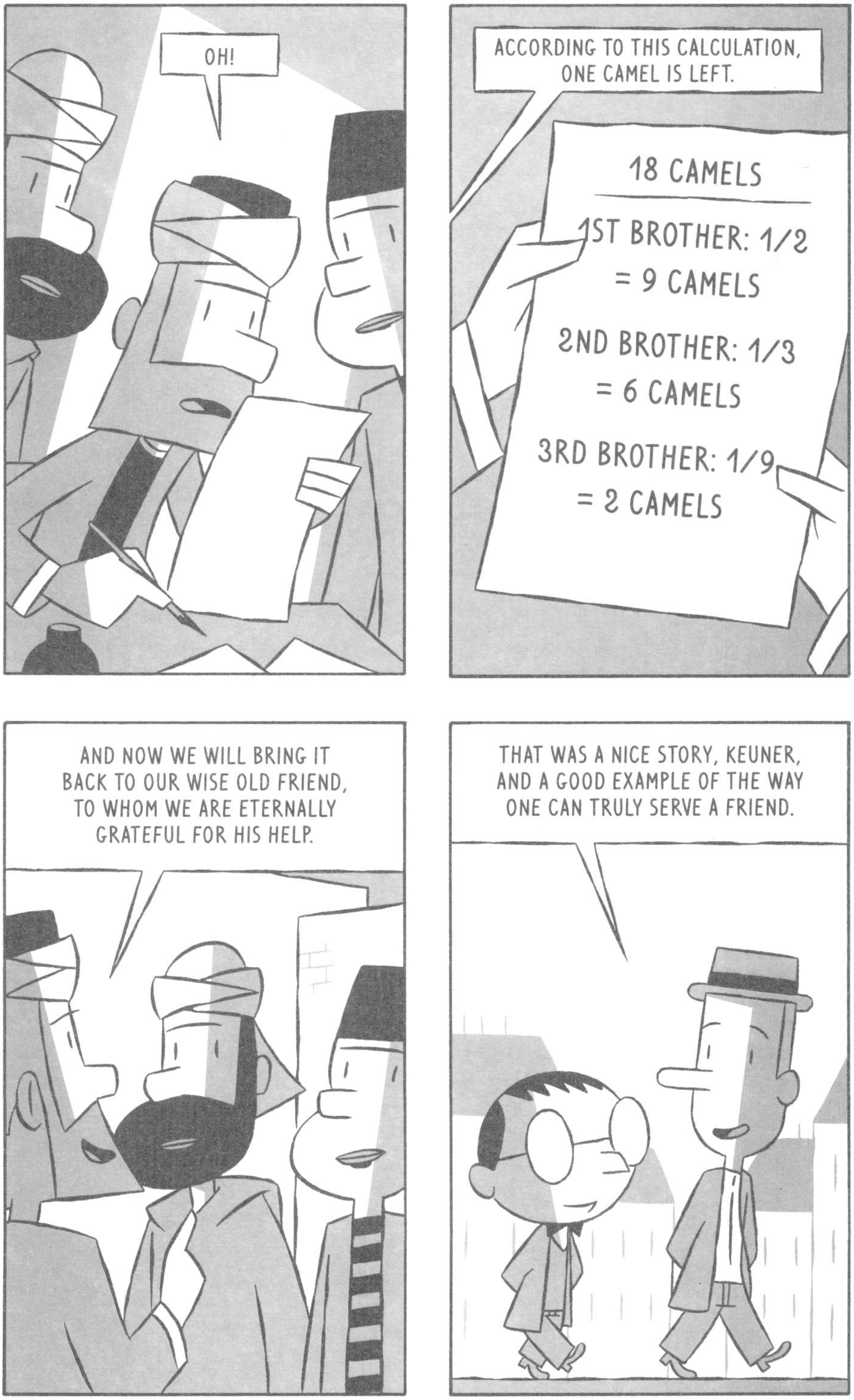
OH!
ACCORDING TO THIS CALCULATION, ONE CAMEL IS LEFT.
18 CAMELS
1ST BROTHER: 1/2 = 9 CAMELS
2ND BROTHER: 1/3 = 6 CAMELS
3RD BROTHER: 1/9 = 2 CAMELS
AND NOW WE WILL BRING IT BACK TO OUR WISE OLD FRIEND, TO WHOM WE ARE ETERNALLY GRATEFUL FOR HIS HELP.
THAT WAS A NICE STORY, KEUNER, AND A GOOD EXAMPLE OF THE WAY ONE CAN TRULY SERVE A FRIEND.

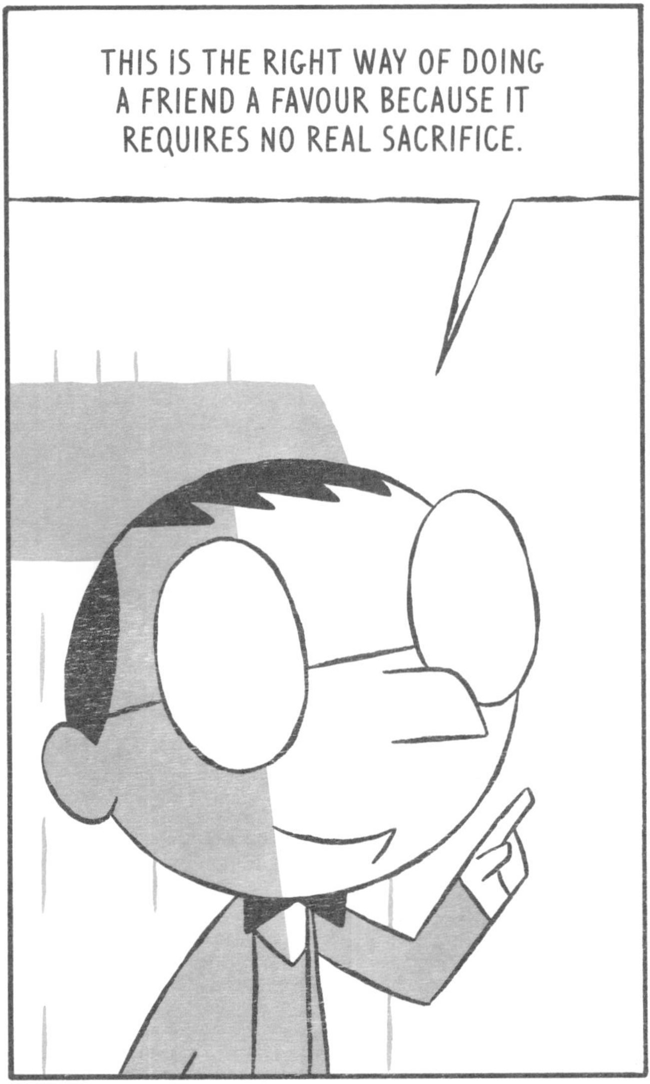
THIS IS THE RIGHT WAY OF DOING A FRIEND A FAVOUR BECAUSE IT REQUIRES NO REAL SACRIFICE.

MR KEUNER AND DEATH

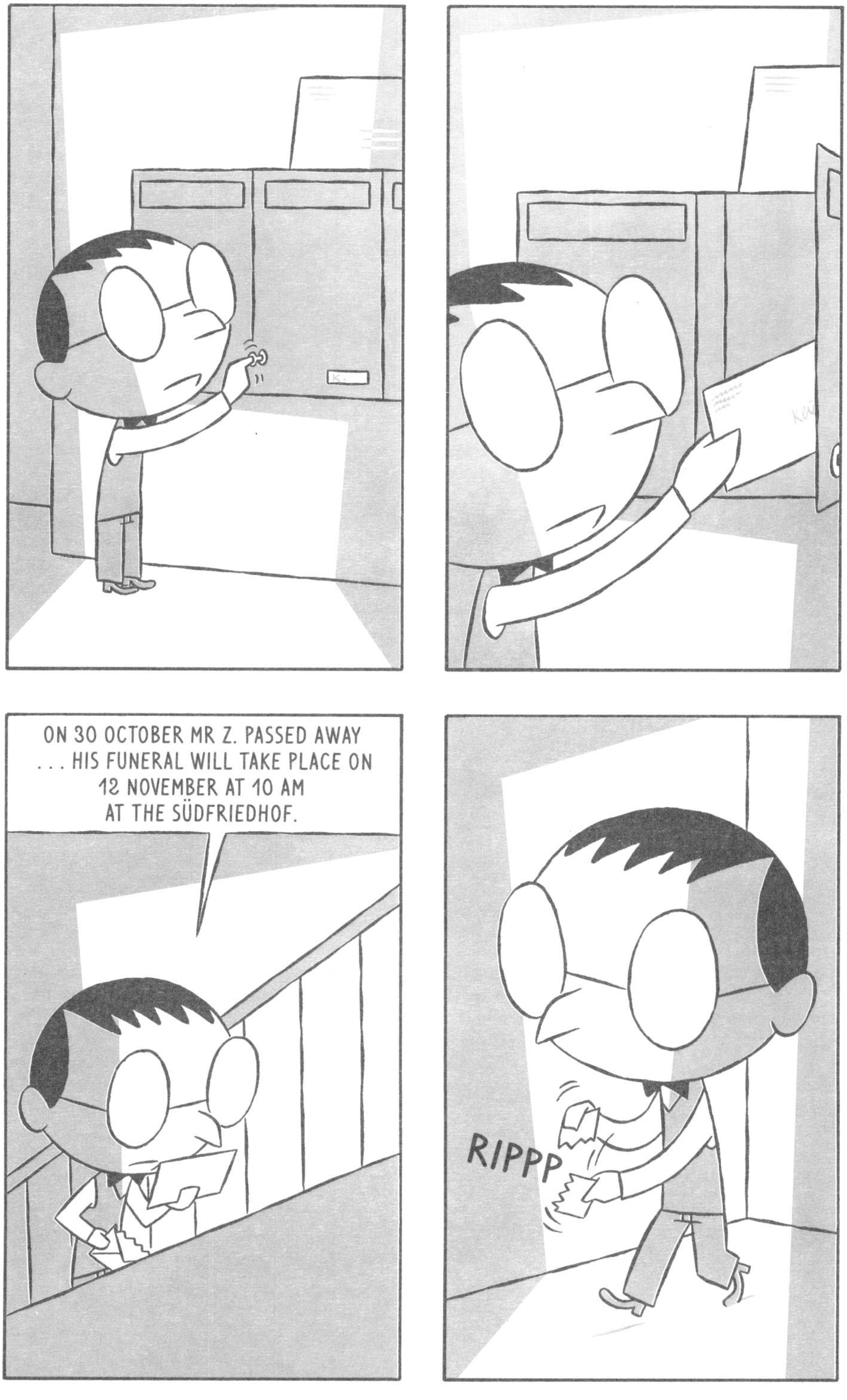
ON 30 OCTOBER MR Z. PASSED AWAY . . . HIS FUNERAL WILL TAKE PLACE ON 12 NOVEMBER AT 10 AM AT THE SÜDFRIEDHOF.
RIPPP

MR KEUNER AVOIDED FUNERALS.

THE REUNION

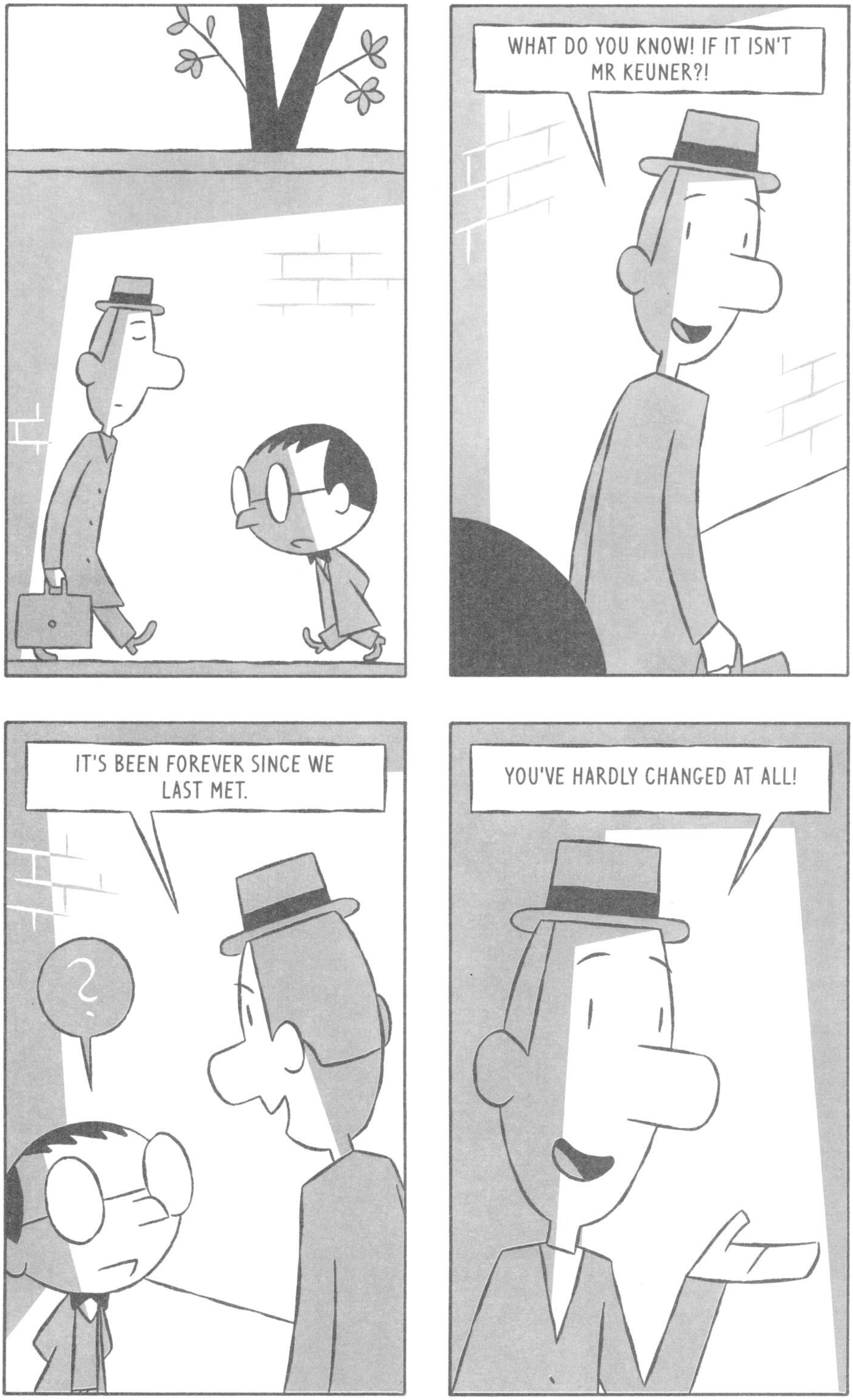
WHAT DO YOU KNOW! IF IT ISN'T MR KEUNER?!
IT'S BEEN FOREVER SINCE WE LAST MET.
?
YOU'VE HARDLY CHANGED AT ALL!

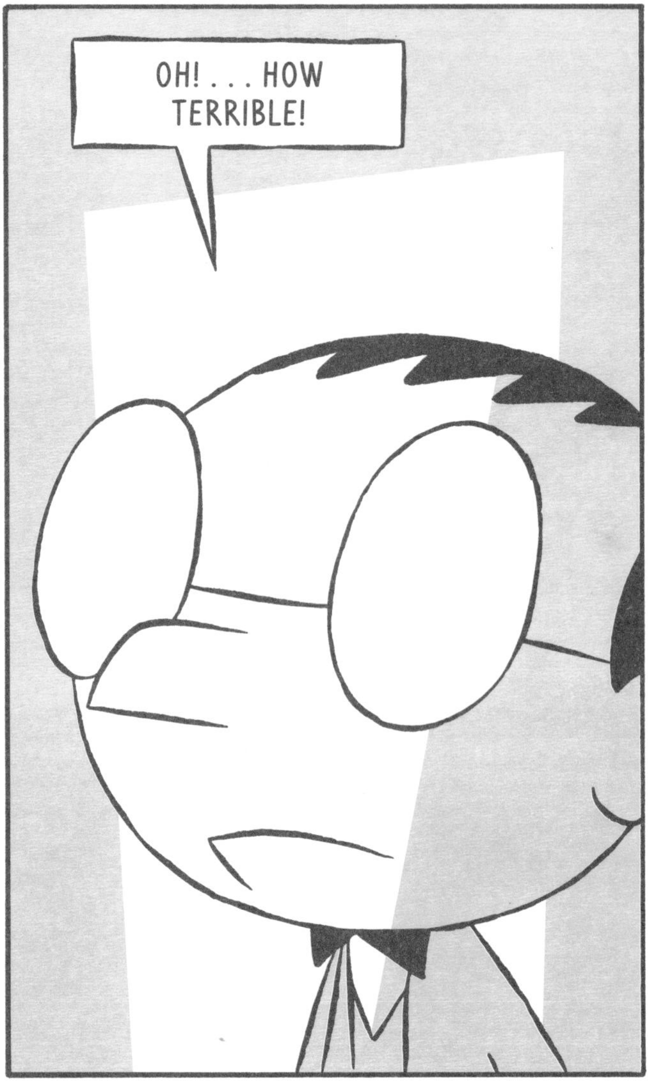
OH! . . . HOW TERRIBLE!

DISPENSING JUSTICE

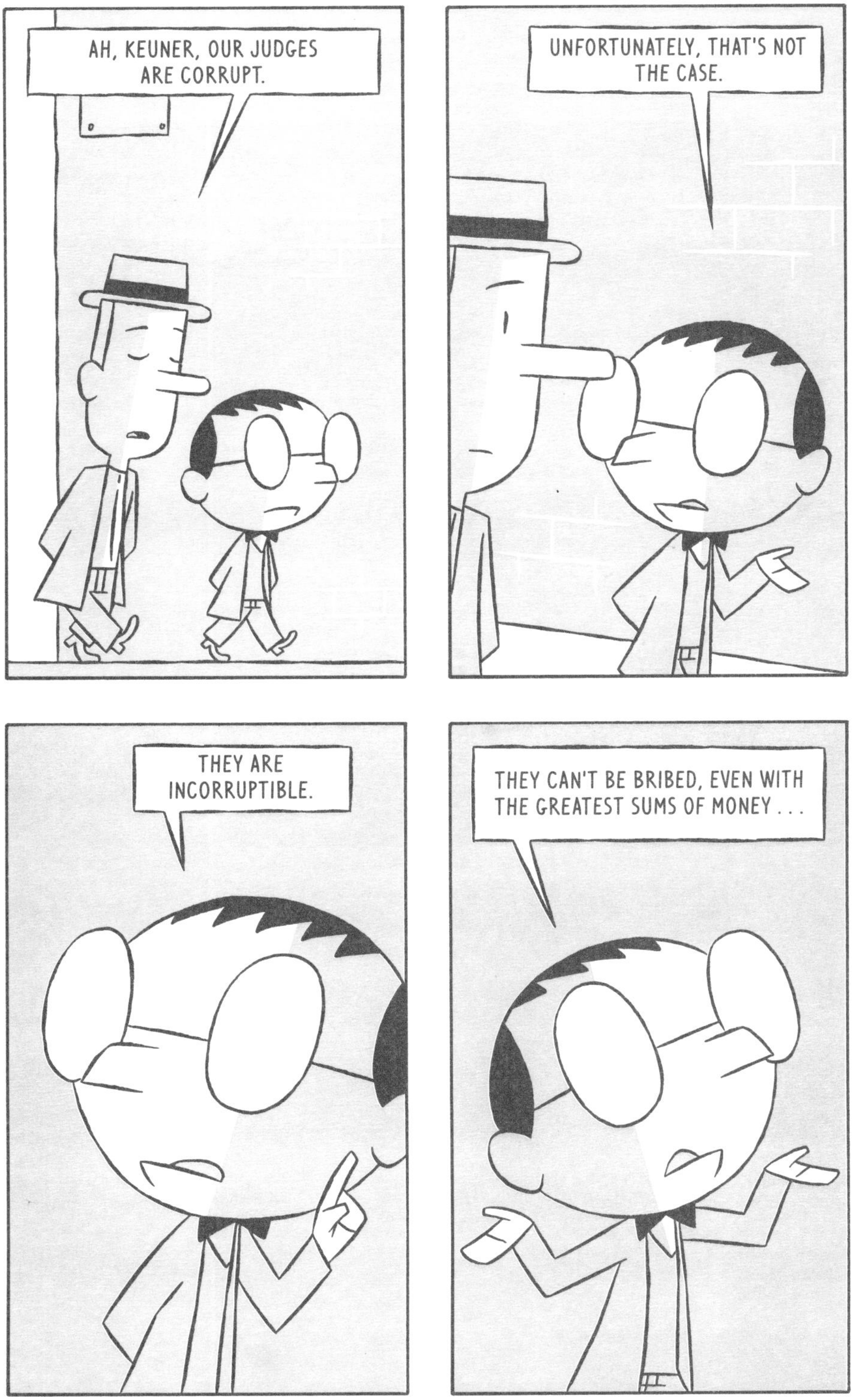
AH, KEUNER, OUR JUDGES ARE CORRUPT.
UNFORTUNATELY, THAT'S NOT THE CASE.
THEY ARE INCORRUPTIBLE.
THEY CAN'T BE BRIBED, EVEN WITH THE GREATEST SUMS OF MONEY . . .

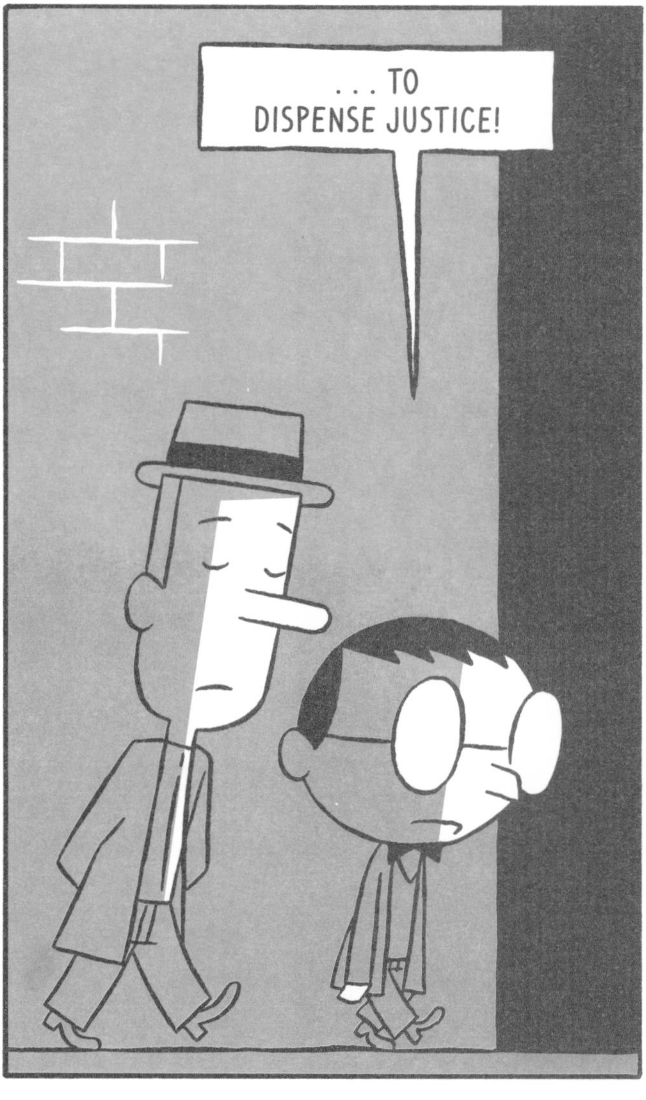
. . . TO
DISPENSE JUSTICE!

A GOOD ANSWER

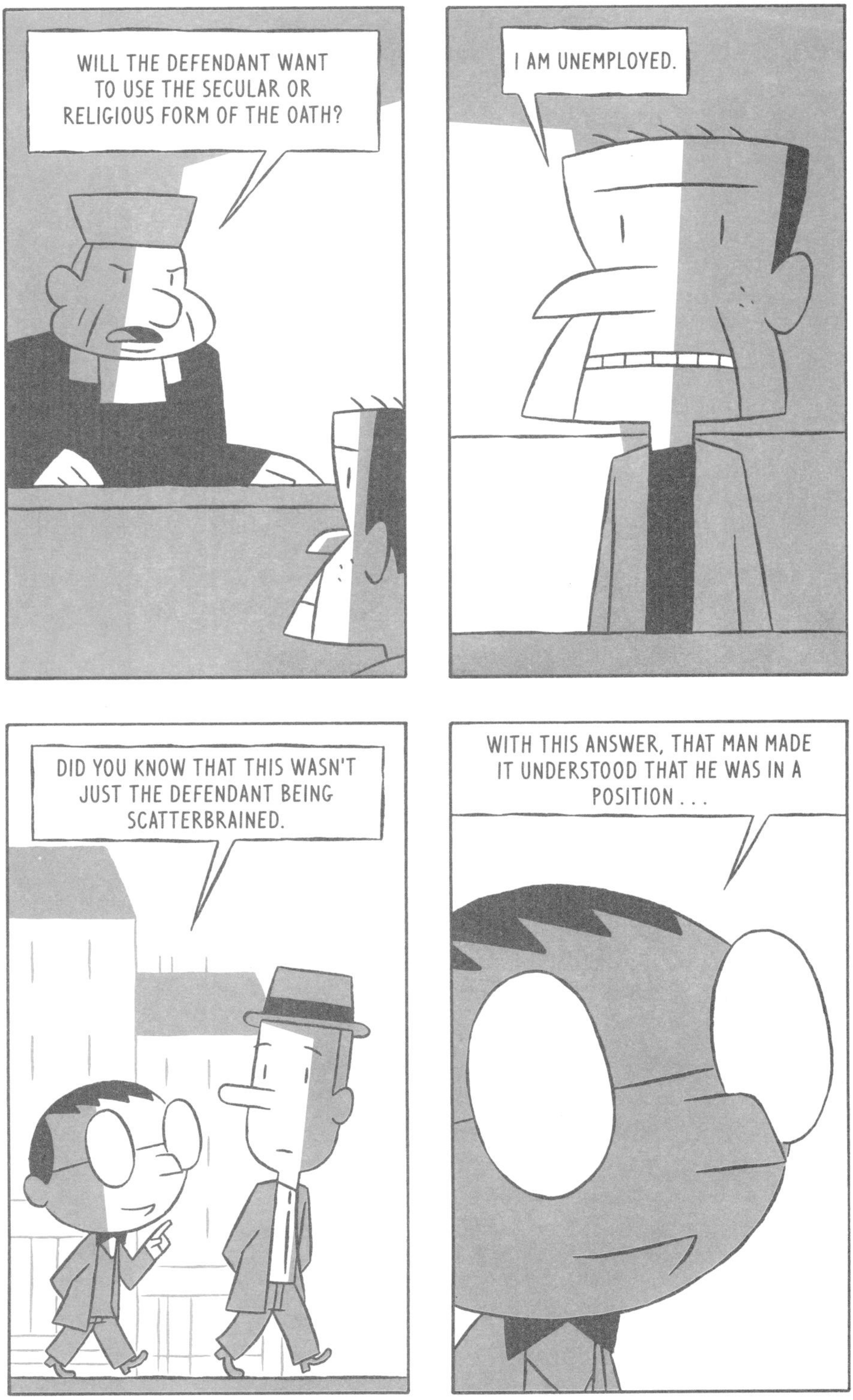
WILL THE DEFENDANT WANT TO USE THE SECULAR OR RELIGIOUS FORM OF THE OATH?
I AM UNEMPLOYED.
DID YOU KNOW THAT THIS WASN'T JUST THE DEFENDANT BEING SCATTERBRAINED.
WITH THIS ANSWER, THAT MAN MADE IT UNDERSTOOD THAT HE WAS IN A POSITION . . .

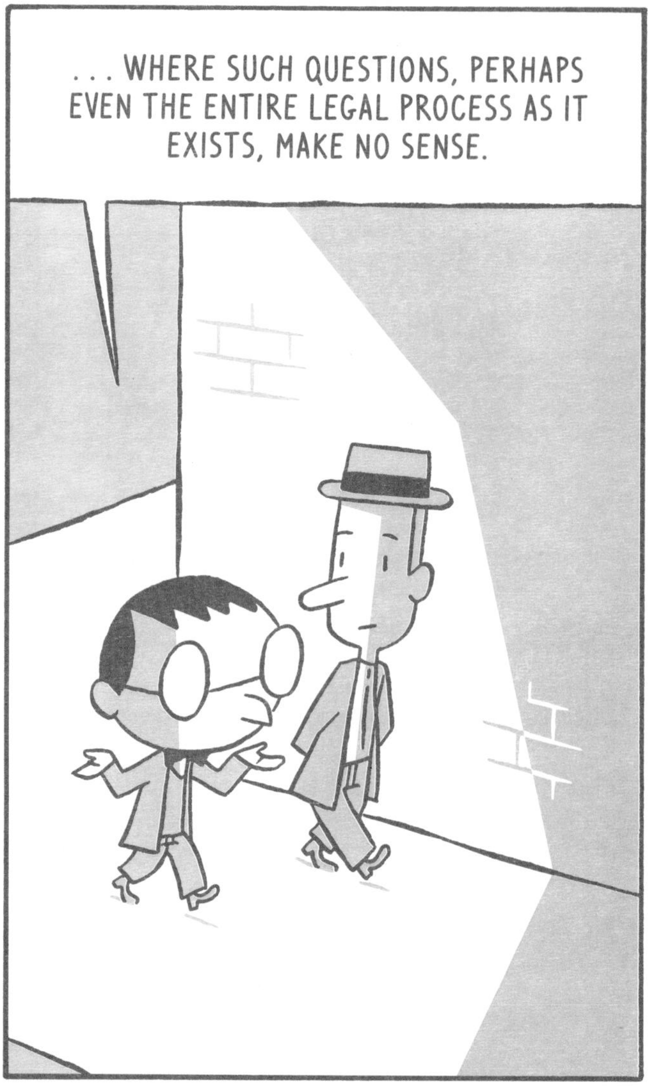
. . . WHERE SUCH QUESTIONS, PERHAPS EVEN THE ENTIRE LEGAL PROCESS AS IT EXISTS, MAKE NO SENSE.

ON THE CULLING OF BEASTS

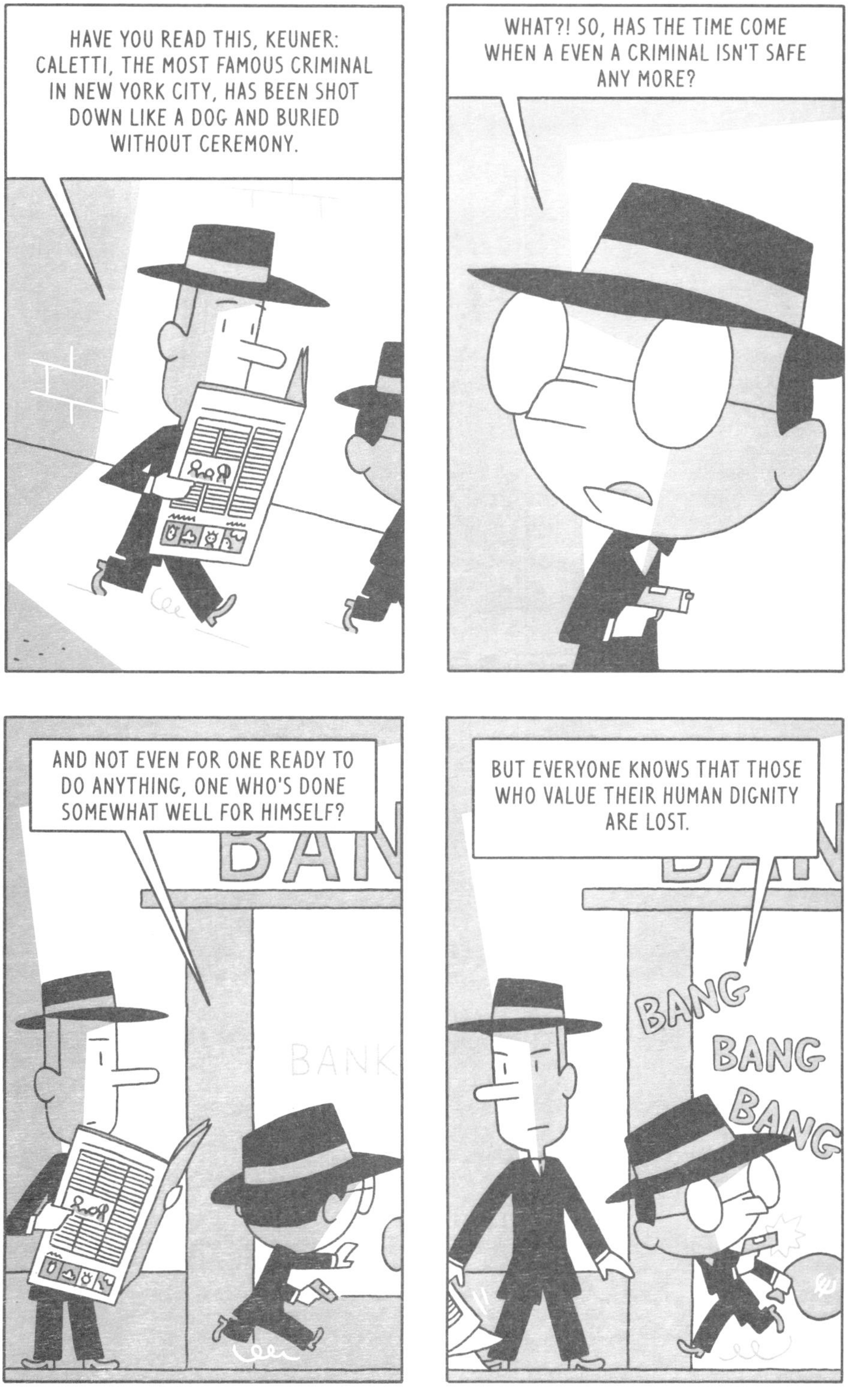
HAVE YOU READ THIS, KEUNER: CALETTI, THE MOST FAMOUS CRIMINAL IN NEW YORK CITY, HAS BEEN SHOT DOWN LIKE A DOG AND BURIED WITHOUT CEREMONY.
WHAT?! SO, HAS THE TIME COME WHEN A EVEN A CRIMINAL ISN'T SAFE ANY MORE?
AND NOT EVEN FOR ONE READY TO DO ANYTHING, ONE WHO'S DONE SOMEWHAT WELL FOR HIMSELF?
BAN
BANK
BUT EVERYONE KNOWS THAT THOSE WHO VALUE THEIR HUMAN DIGNITY ARE LOST.
BANG
BANG
BANG

BUT THOSE WHO GIVE THEIRS UP? SHOULD THE EXPRESSION BE: HE WHO ESCAPES THE DEPTHS FALLS AT THE TOP?

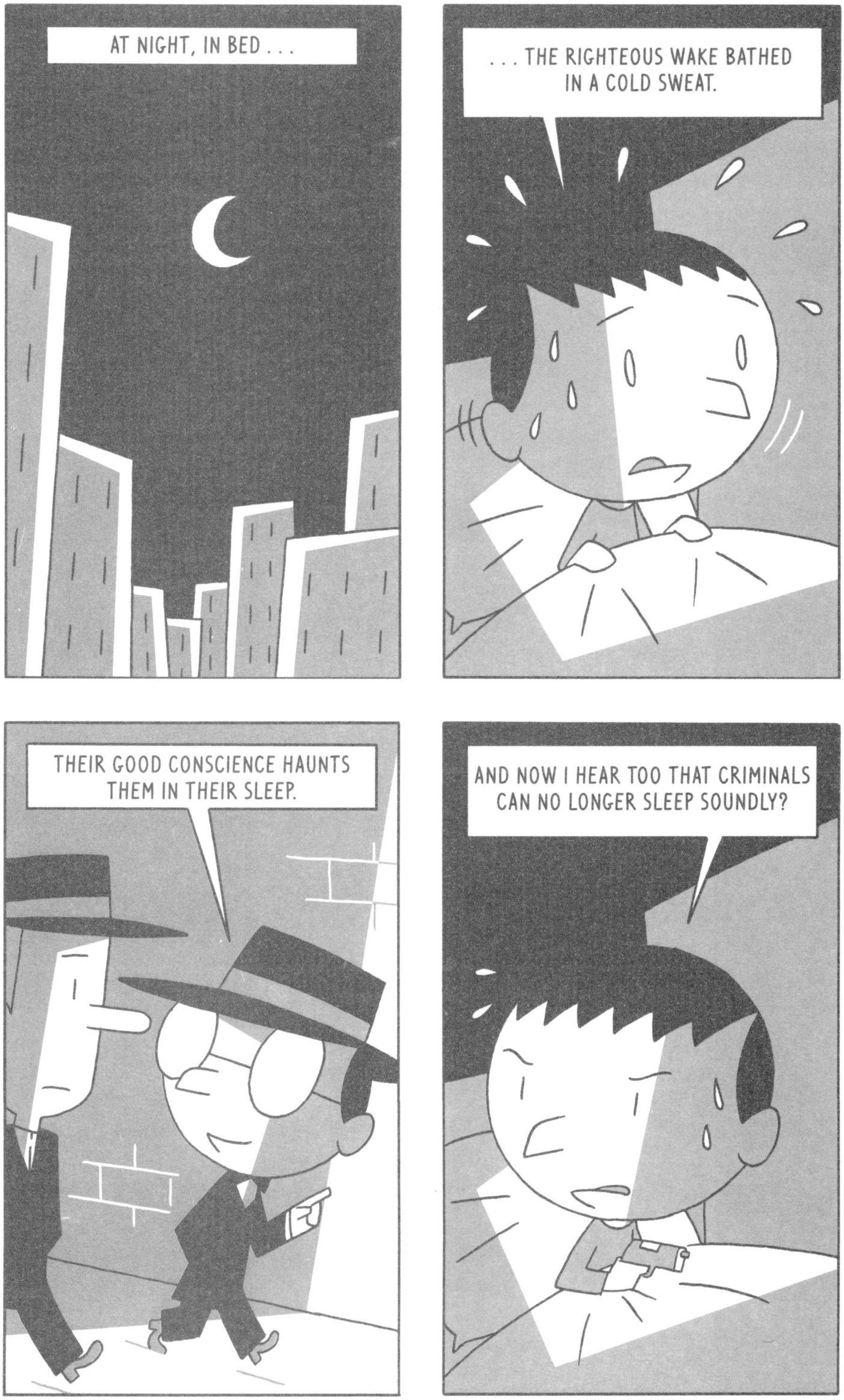
AT NIGHT, IN BED . . .
. . . THE RIGHTEOUS WAKE BATHED IN A COLD SWEAT.
THEIR GOOD CONSCIENCE HAUNTS THEM IN THEIR SLEEP.
AND NOW I HEAR TOO THAT CRIMINALS CAN NO LONGER SLEEP SOUNDLY?

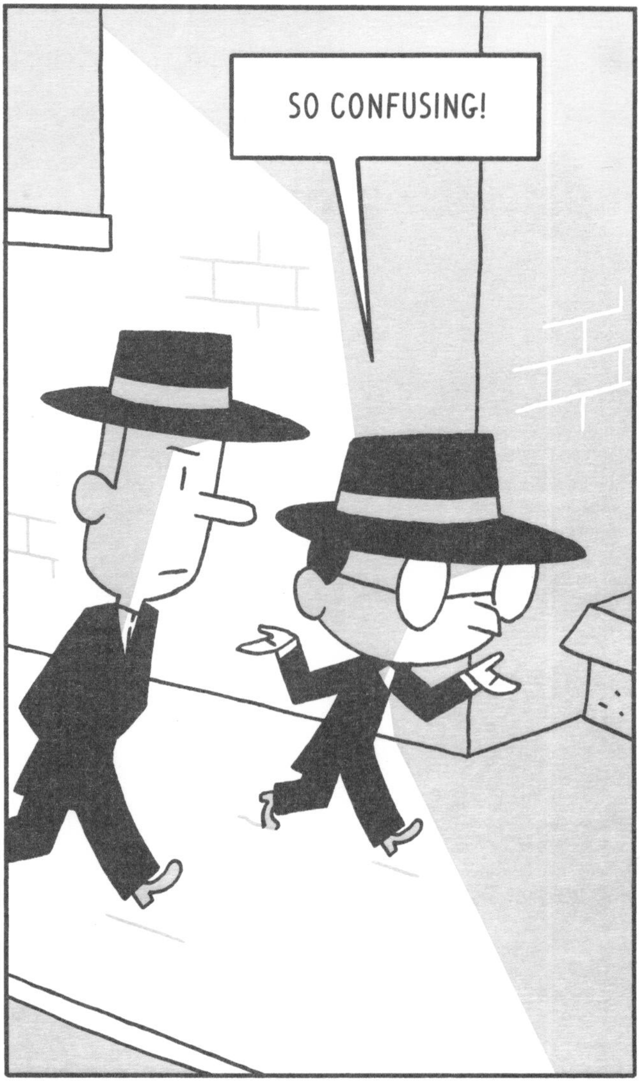
SO CONFUSING!

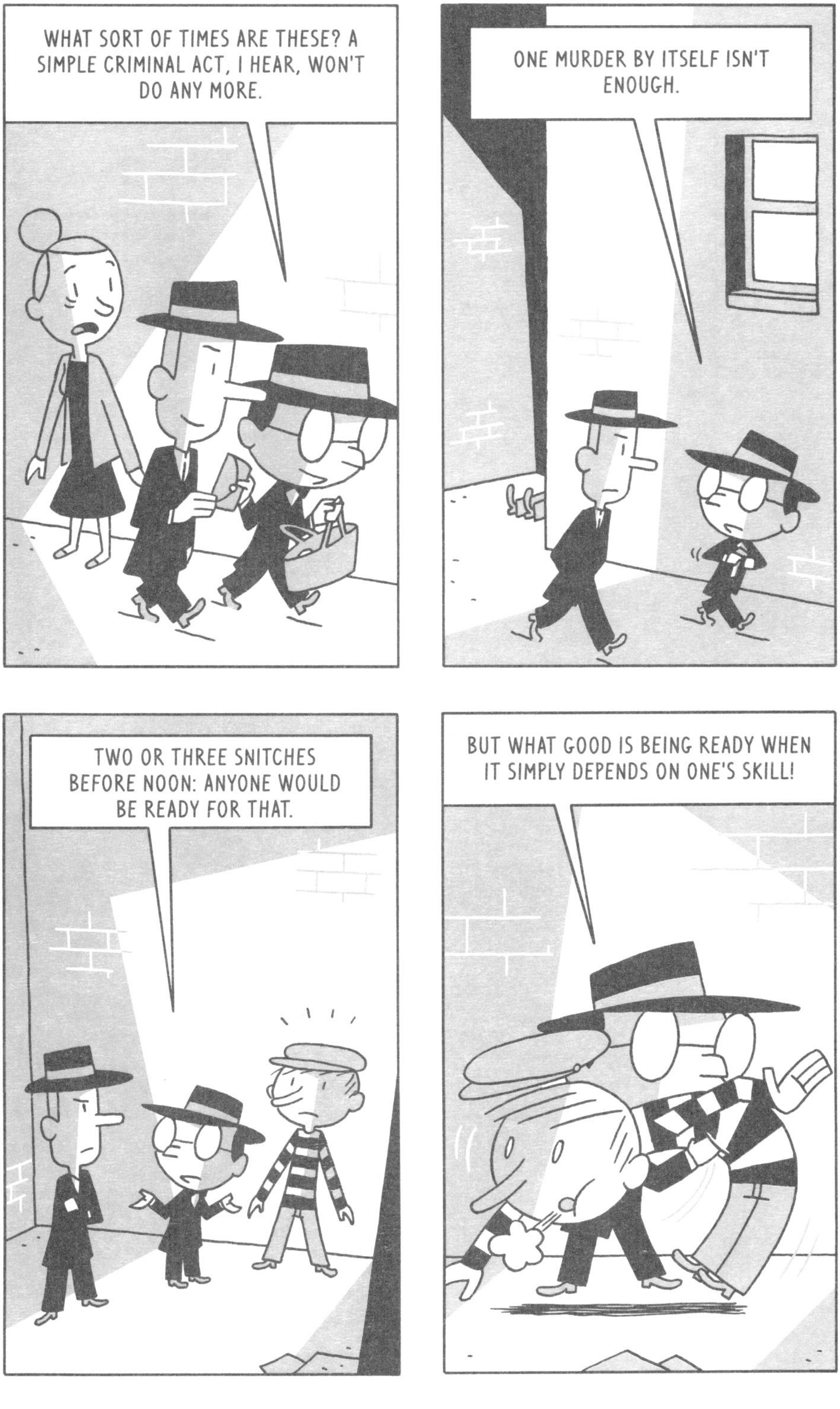
WHAT SORT OF TIMES ARE THESE? A SIMPLE CRIMINAL ACT, I HEAR, WON'T DO ANY MORE.
ONE MURDER BY ITSELF ISN'T ENOUGH.
TWO OR THREE SNITCHES BEFORE NOON: ANYONE WOULD BE READY FOR THAT.
BUT WHAT GOOD IS BEING READY WHEN IT SIMPLY DEPENDS ON ONE'S SKILL!

EVEN A LACK OF PRINCIPLES DOESN'T CUT IT:
EFFORT IS WHAT MAKES THE CUT!!

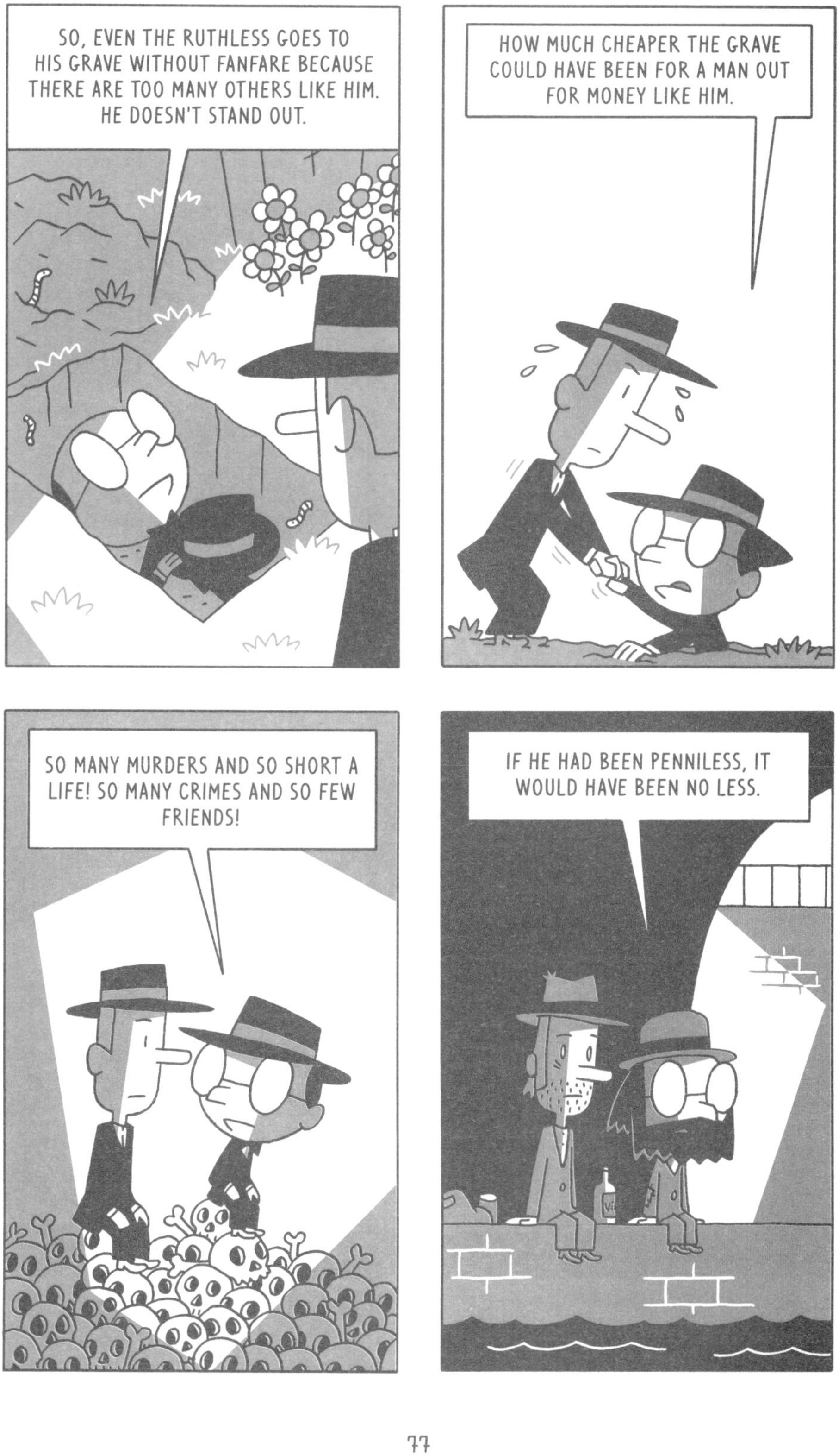
SO, EVEN THE RUTHLESS GOES TO HIS GRAVE WITHOUT FANFARE BECAUSE THERE ARE TOO MANY OTHERS LIKE HIM. HE DOESN'T STAND OUT.
HOW MUCH CHEAPER THE GRAVE COULD HAVE BEEN FOR A MAN OUT FOR MONEY LIKE HIM.
SO MANY MURDERS AND SO SHORT A LIFE! SO MANY CRIMES AND SO FEW FRIENDS!
IF HE HAD BEEN PENNILESS, IT WOULD HAVE BEEN NO LESS.

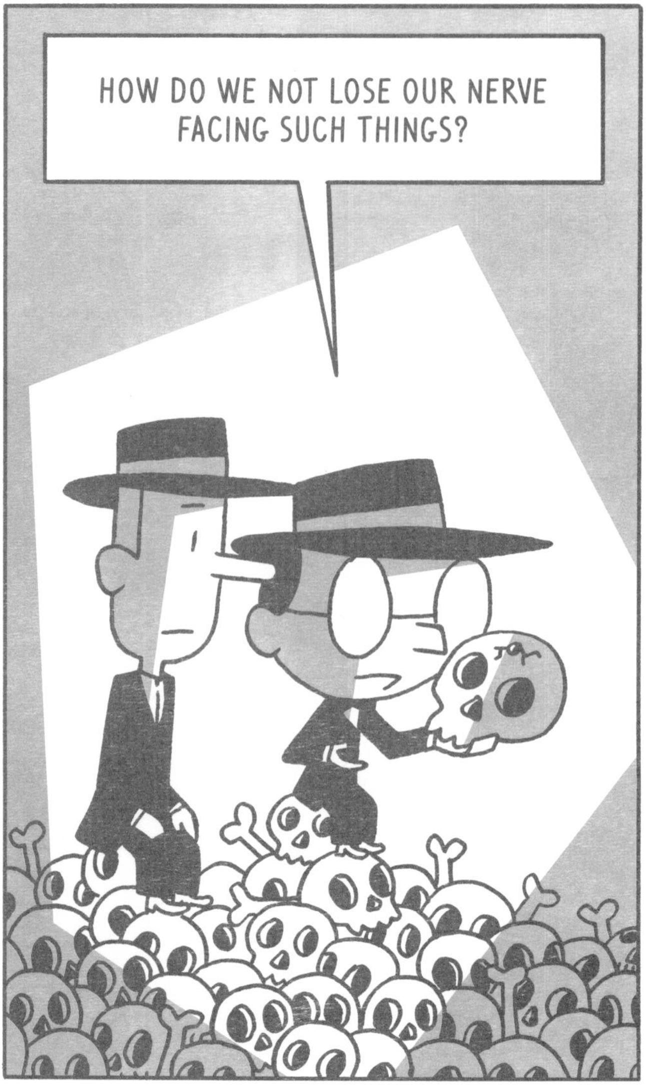
HOW DO WE NOT LOSE OUR NERVE FACING SUCH THINGS?

THE RIGHT TO BE POWERLESS

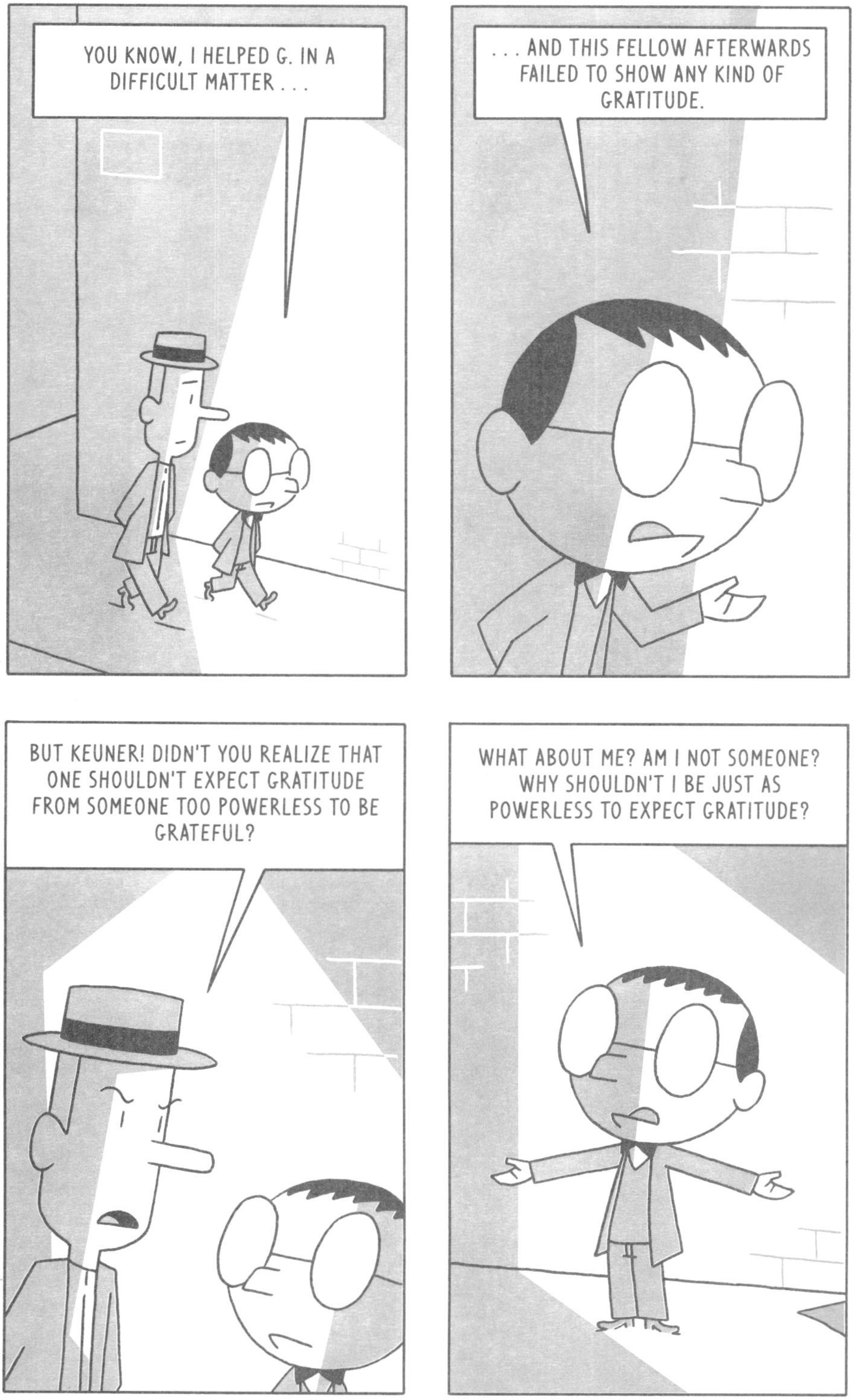

YOU KNOW, I HELPED G. IN A DIFFICULT MATTER . . .
. . . AND THIS FELLOW AFTERWARDS FAILED TO SHOW ANY KIND OF GRATITUDE.
BUT KEUNER! DIDN'T YOU REALIZE THAT ONE SHOULDN'T EXPECT GRATITUDE FROM SOMEONE TOO POWERLESS TO BE GRATEFUL?
WHAT ABOUT ME? AM I NOT SOMEONE? WHY SHOULDN'T I BE JUST AS POWERLESS TO EXPECT GRATITUDE?

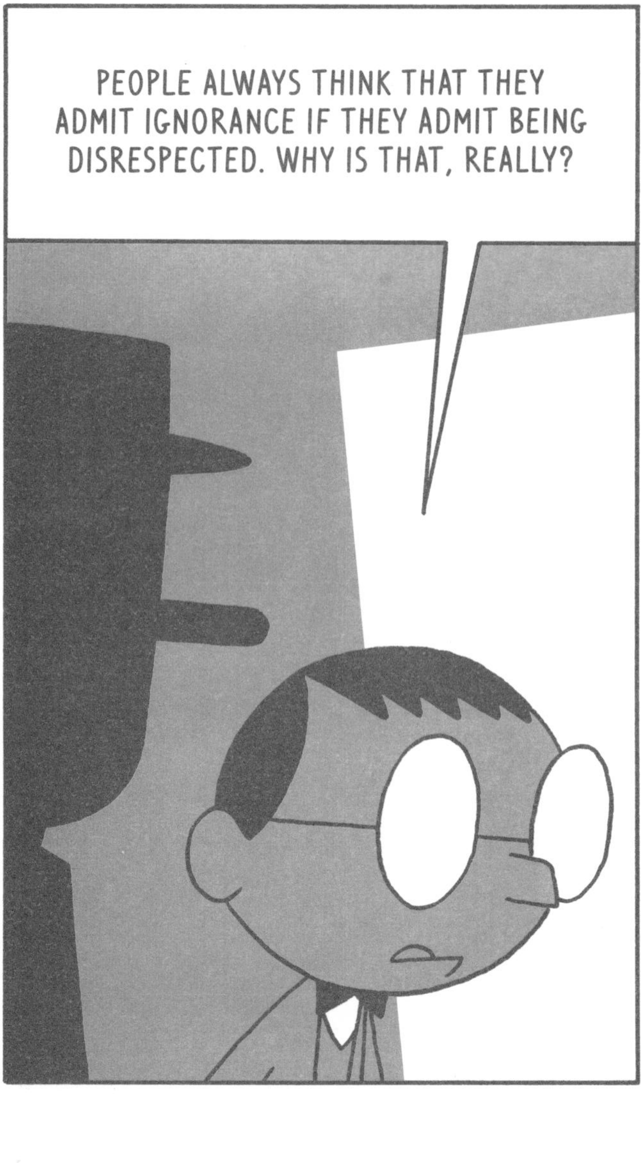
PEOPLE ALWAYS THINK THAT THEY ADMIT IGNORANCE IF THEY ADMIT BEING DISRESPECTED. WHY IS THAT, REALLY?

THE INFERIOR DOESN'T COME CHEAP EITHER

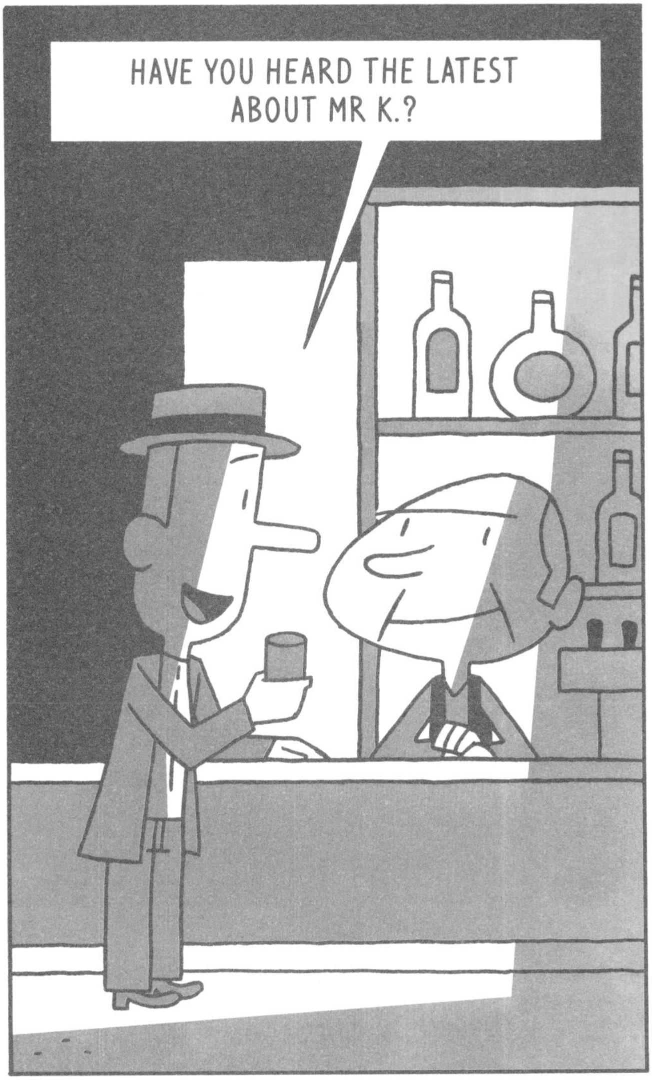
HAVE YOU HEARD THE LATEST ABOUT MR K.?

RECENTLY, AS HE WAS THINKING ABOUT THE HUMAN RACE AGAIN, THE THOUGHT OCCURRED TO HIM ABOUT THE DISTRIBUTION OF POVERTY.

THEN HE WISHED, WHILE SURVEYING HIS APARTMENT, FOR DIFFERENT FURNITURE . . .

. . . SOMETHING MORE INFERIOR, CHEAPER, SECOND-RATE.

SO, IMMEDIATELY, HE WENT TO A CARPENTER AND TOLD HIM TO STRIP THE FINISHES FROM HIS FURNITURE.

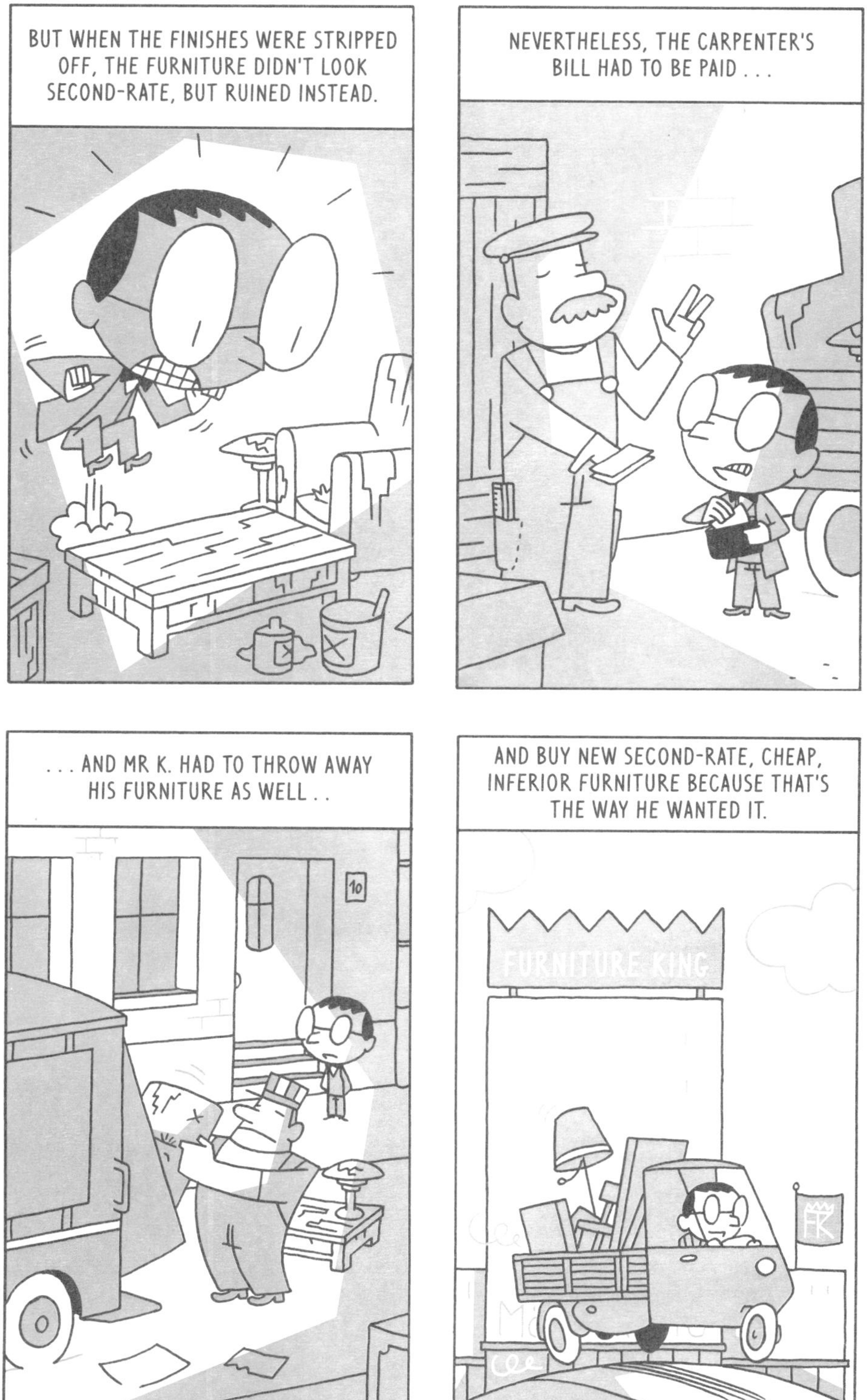
BUT WHEN THE FINISHES WERE STRIPPED OFF, THE FURNITURE DIDN'T LOOK SECOND-RATE, BUT RUINED INSTEAD.
NEVERTHELESS, THE CARPENTER'S BILL HAD TO BE PAID . . .
. . . AND MR K. HAD TO THROW AWAY HIS FURNITURE AS WELL . .
10
AND BUY NEW SECOND-RATE, CHEAP, INFERIOR FURNITURE BECAUSE THAT'S THE WAY HE WANTED IT.
FURNITURE KING
FK

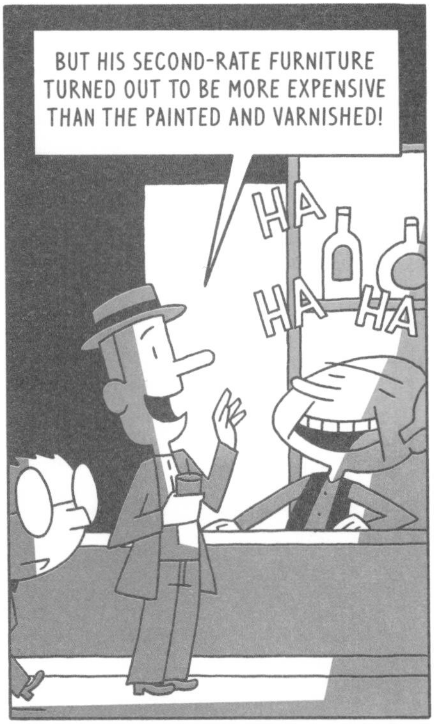
BUT HIS SECOND-RATE FURNITURE TURNED OUT TO BE MORE EXPENSIVE THAN THE PAINTED AND VARNISHED!
HA
HA
HA

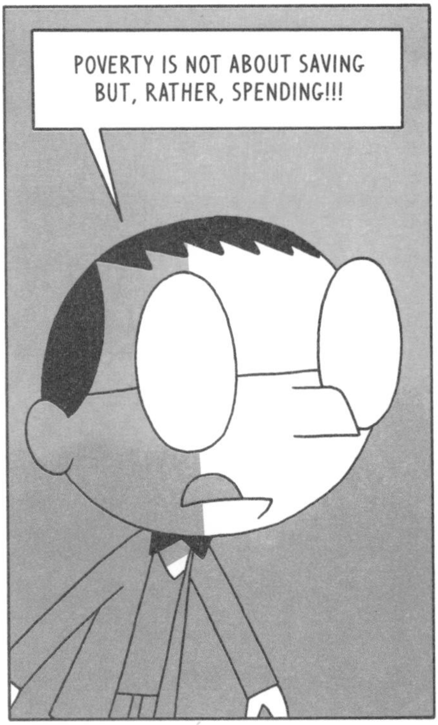
POVERTY IS NOT ABOUT SAVING BUT, RATHER, SPENDING!!!

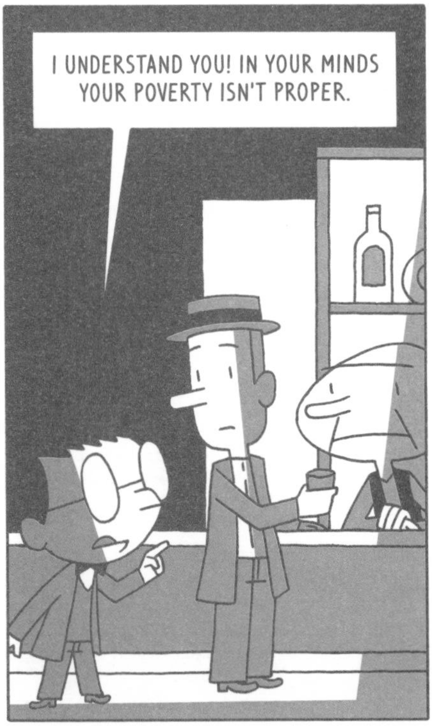
I UNDERSTAND YOU! IN YOUR MINDS YOUR POVERTY ISN'T PROPER.

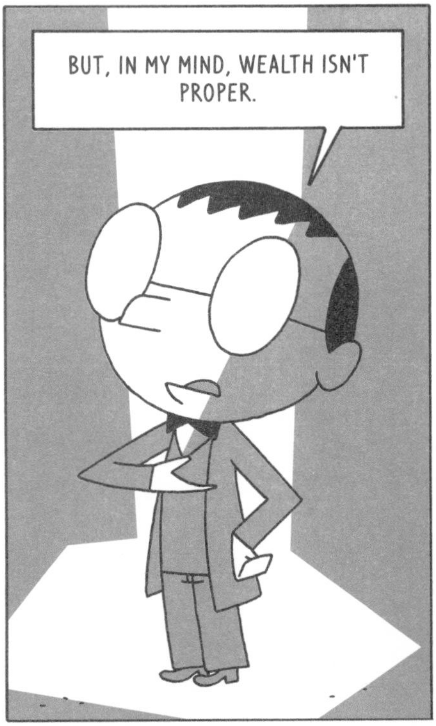
BUT, IN MY MIND, WEALTH ISN'T PROPER.

ON SYSTEMS

MANY MISTAKES OCCUR WHEN ONE DOESN'T INTERRUPT THE SPEAKER OR DOES SO NOT ENOUGH.

THIS WAY A DECEPTIVELY SINGLE ENTITY EASILY EMERGES . . .

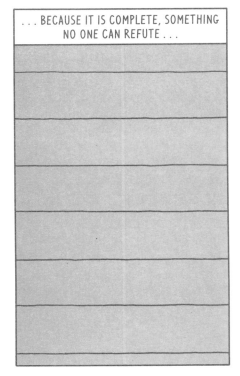

. . . BECAUSE IT IS COMPLETE, SOMETHING NO ONE CAN REFUTE . . .

. . . IT SEEMS TO FIT IN ITS INDIVIDUAL PARTS AS WELL . . .

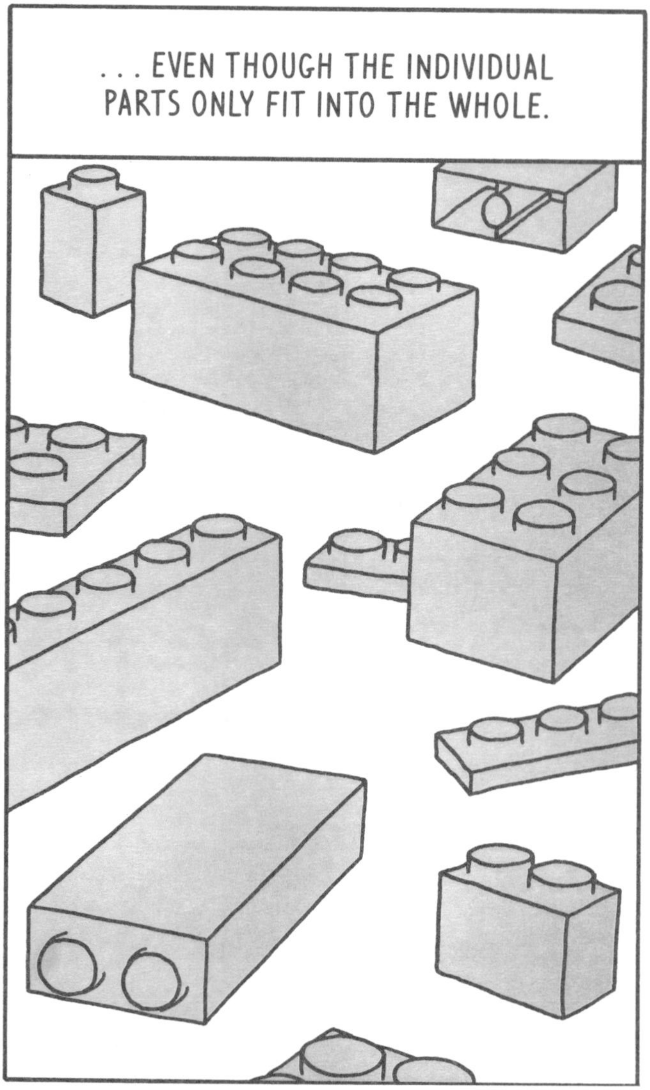
. . . EVEN THOUGH THE INDIVIDUAL PARTS ONLY FIT INTO THE WHOLE.

PATRIOTISM, HATE FOR PATRIOTS

ONE DAY MR K. WALKED . . .
. . . THROUGH A CITY . . .
. . . WHICH WAS OCCUPIED BY THE ENEMY OF THE COUNTRY . . .
. . . IN WHICH HE LIVED.

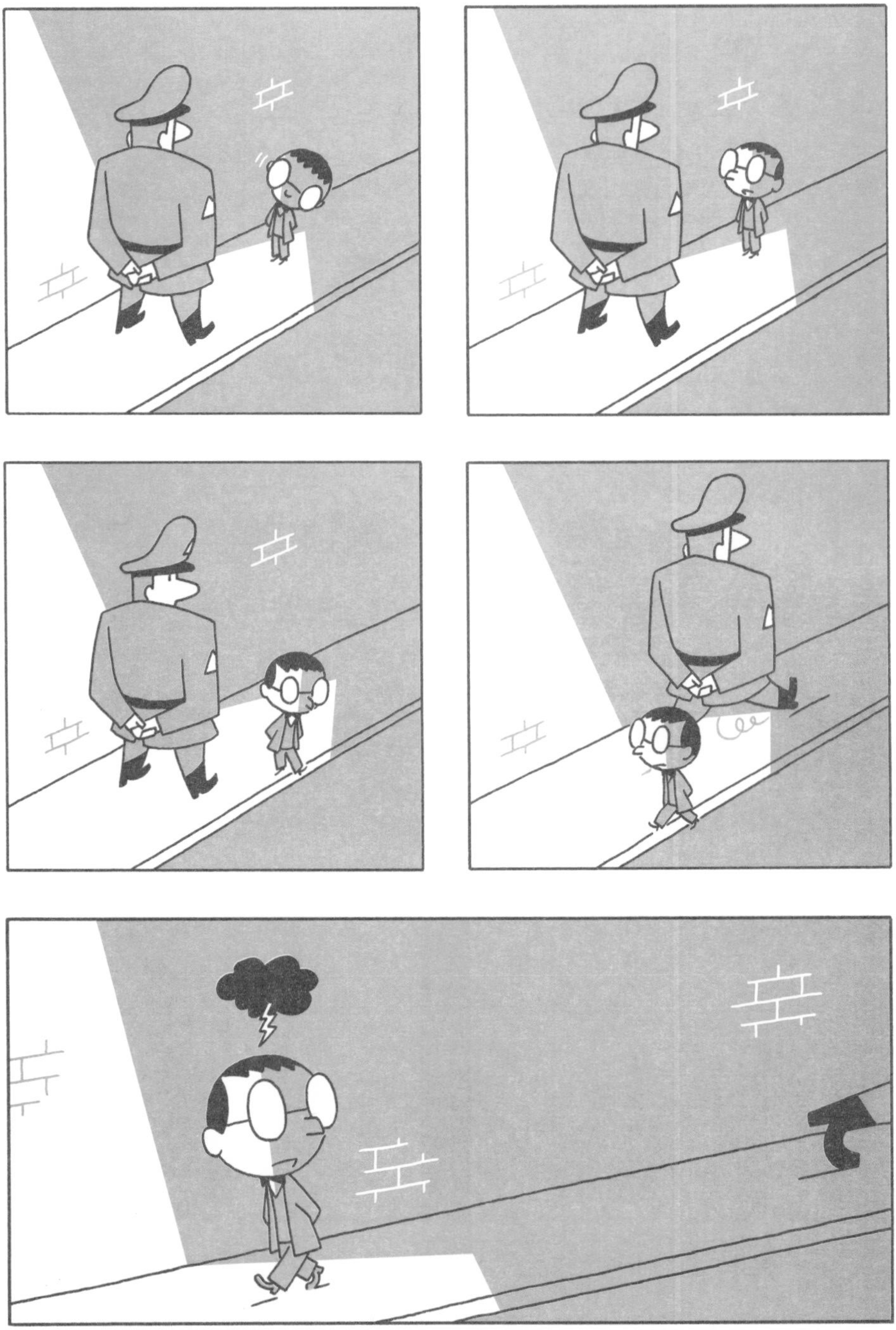

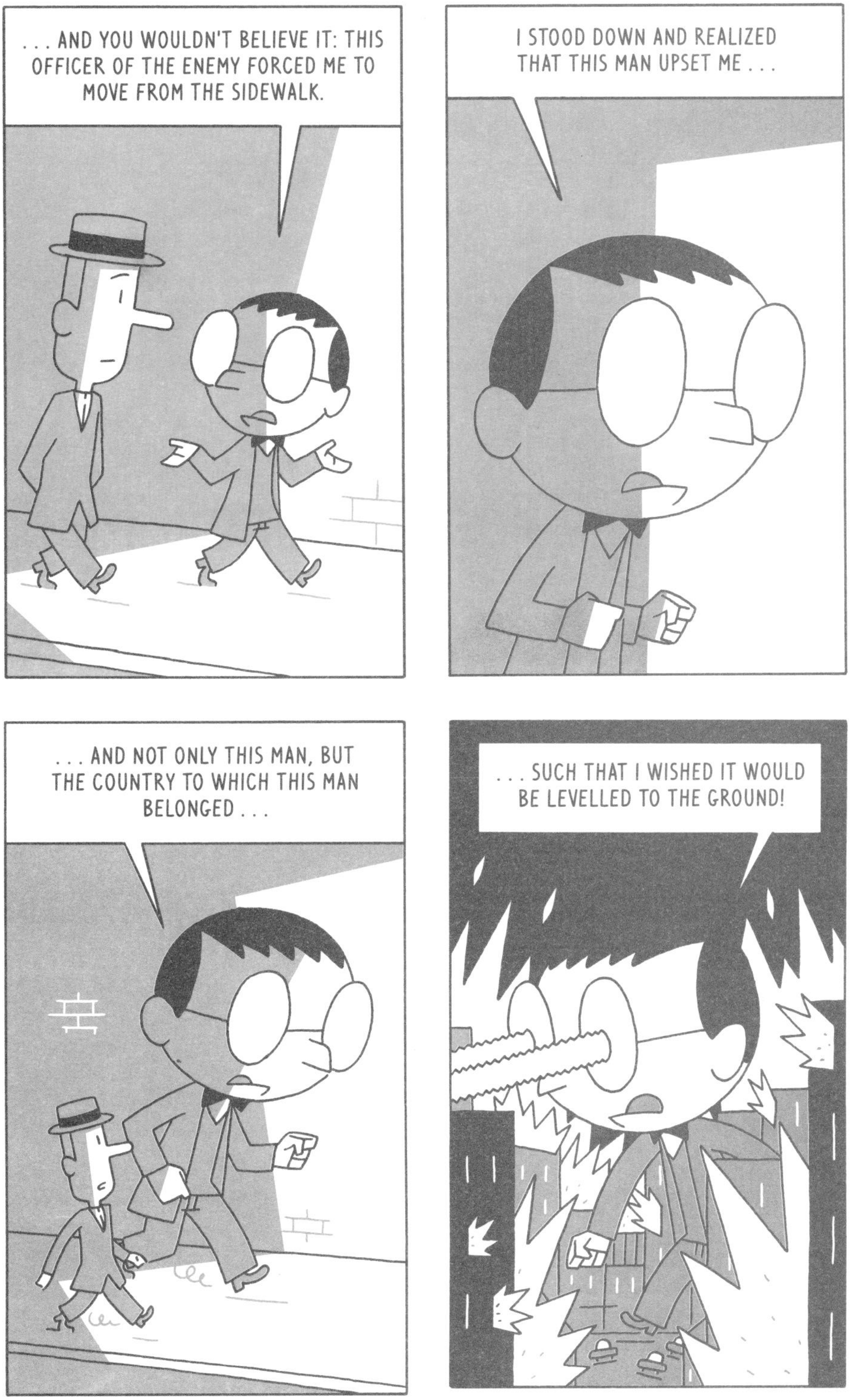
. . . AND YOU WOULDN'T BELIEVE IT: THIS OFFICER OF THE ENEMY FORCED ME TO MOVE FROM THE SIDEWALK.
I STOOD DOWN AND REALIZED THAT THIS MAN UPSET ME . . .
. . . AND NOT ONLY THIS MAN, BUT THE COUNTRY TO WHICH THIS MAN BELONGED . . .
. . . SUCH THAT I WISHED IT WOULD BE LEVELLED TO THE GROUND!

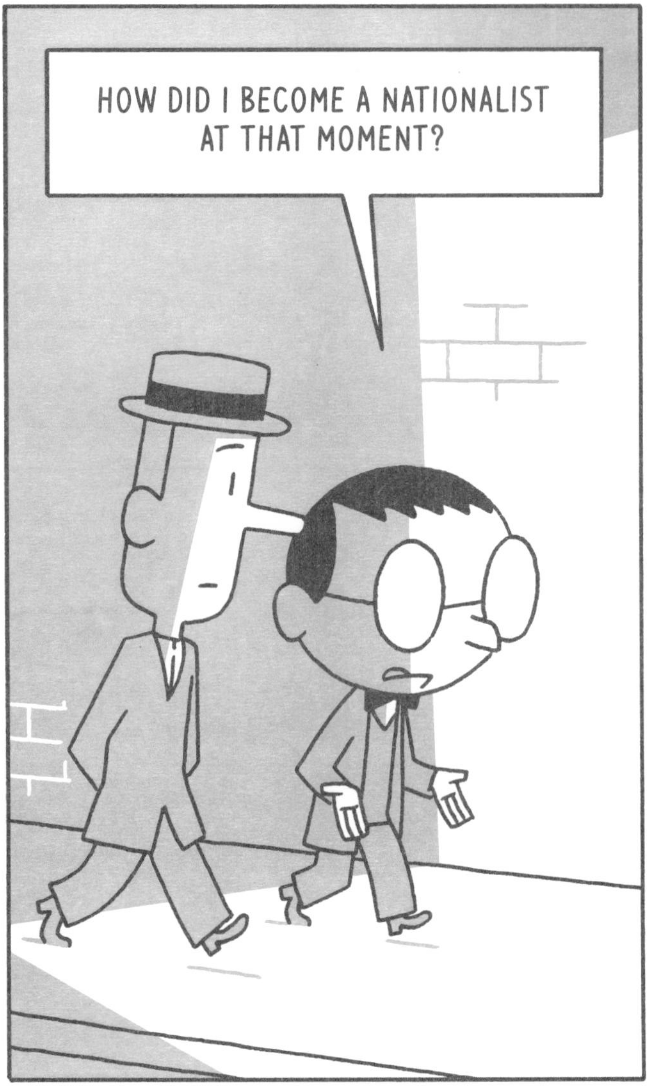
HOW DID I BECOME A NATIONALIST AT THAT MOMENT?

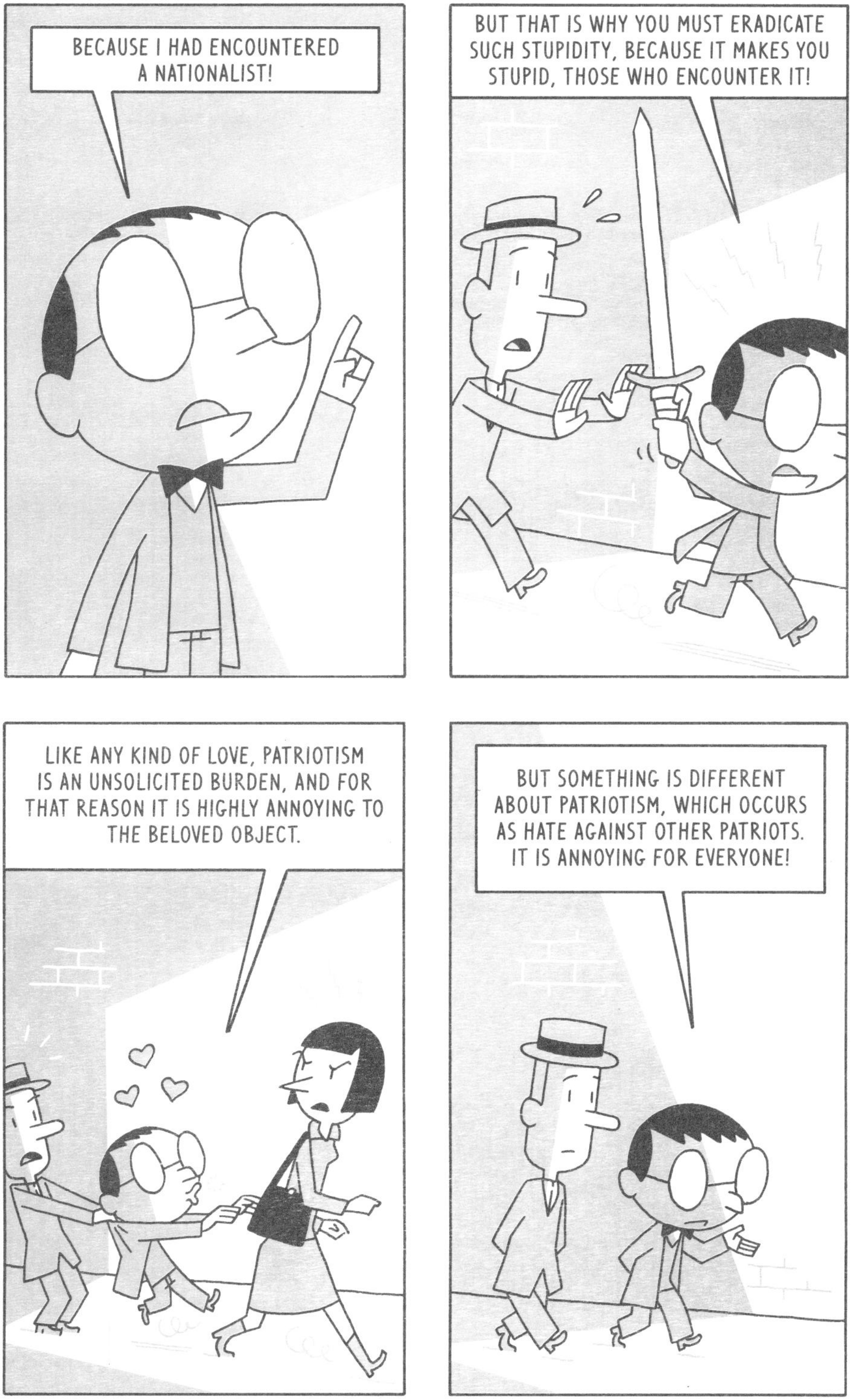
BECAUSE I HAD ENCOUNTERED A NATIONALIST!
BUT THAT IS WHY YOU MUST ERADICATE SUCH STUPIDITY, BECAUSE IT MAKES YOU STUPID, THOSE WHO ENCOUNTER IT!
LIKE ANY KIND OF LOVE, PATRIOTISM IS AN UNSOLICITED BURDEN, AND FOR THAT REASON IT IS HIGHLY ANNOYING TO THE BELOVED OBJECT.
BUT SOMETHING IS DIFFERENT ABOUT PATRIOTISM, WHICH OCCURS AS HATE AGAINST OTHER PATRIOTS. IT IS ANNOYING FOR EVERYONE!

HUNGER

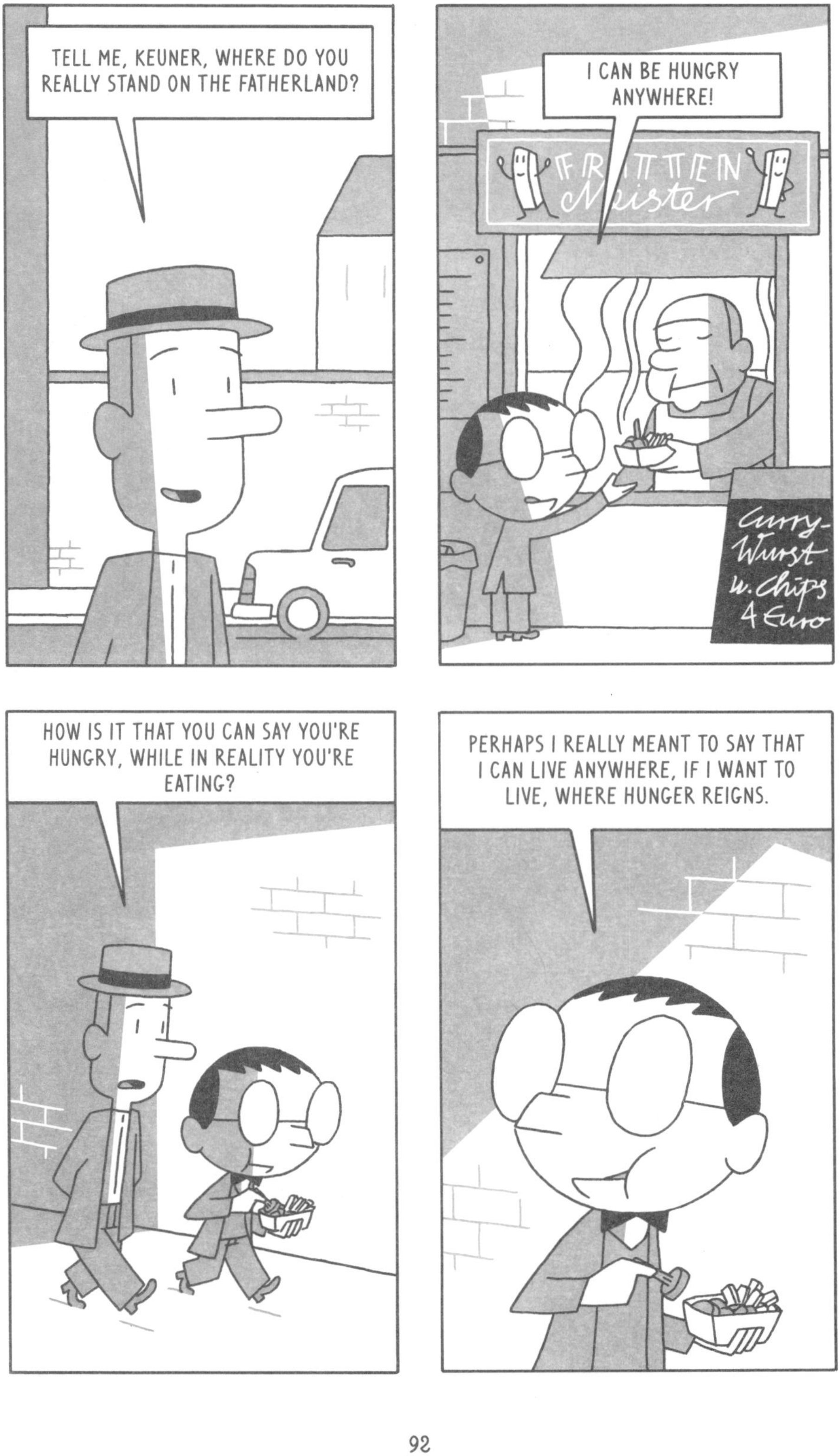
TELL ME, KEUNER, WHERE DO YOU REALLY STAND ON THE FATHERLAND?
I CAN BE HUNGRY ANYWHERE!
FRITTEN Meister
Curry-Wurst w. Chips 4 Euro
HOW IS IT THAT YOU CAN SAY YOU'RE HUNGRY, WHILE IN REALITY YOU'RE EATING?
PERHAPS I REALLY MEANT TO SAY THAT I CAN LIVE ANYWHERE, IF I WANT TO LIVE, WHERE HUNGER REIGNS.

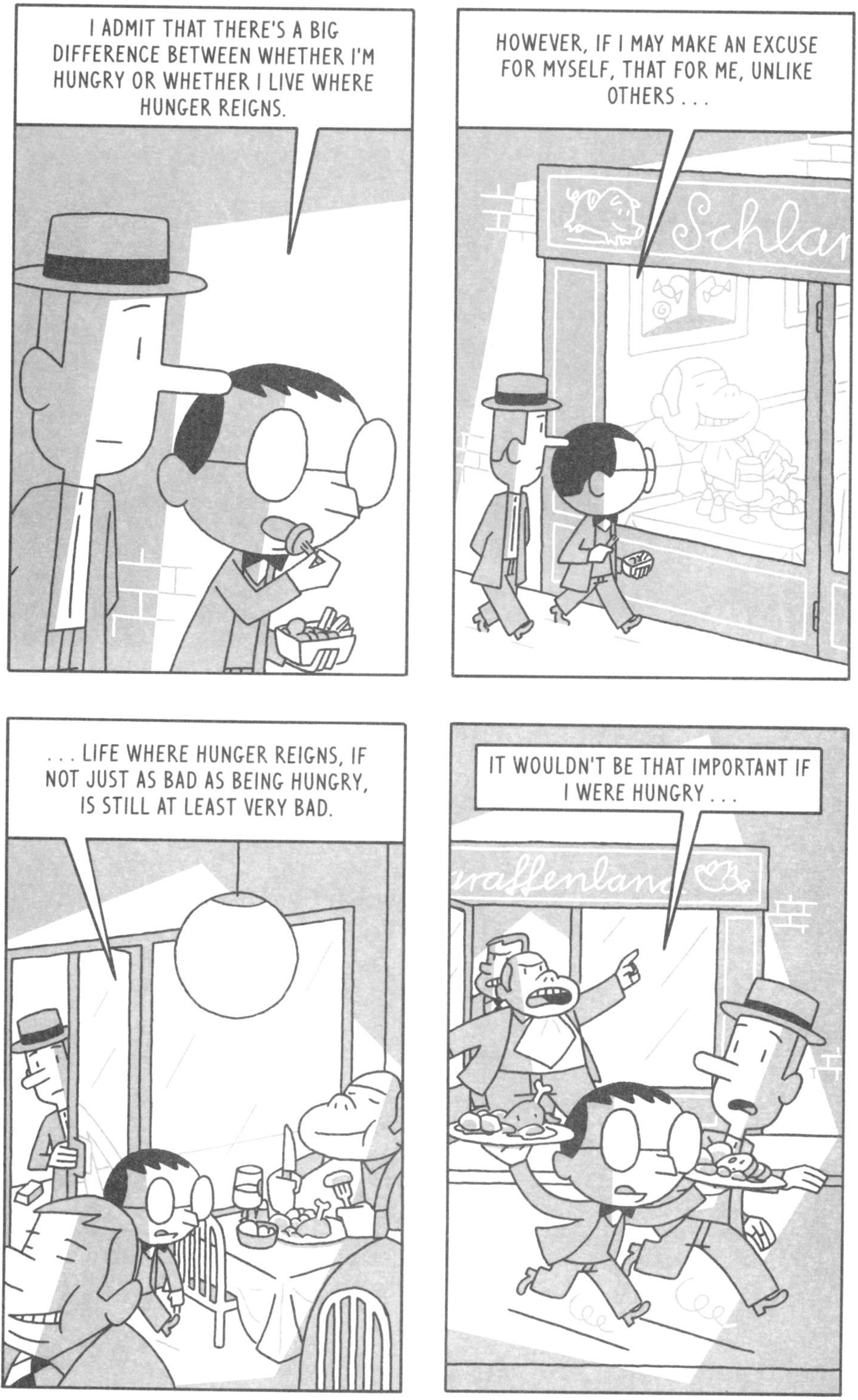
I ADMIT THAT THERE'S A BIG DIFFERENCE BETWEEN WHETHER I'M HUNGRY OR WHETHER I LIVE WHERE HUNGER REIGNS.
HOWEVER, IF I MAY MAKE AN EXCUSE FOR MYSELF, THAT FOR ME, UNLIKE OTHERS . . .
. . . LIFE WHERE HUNGER REIGNS, IF NOT JUST AS BAD AS BEING HUNGRY, IS STILL AT LEAST VERY BAD.
IT WOULDN'T BE THAT IMPORTANT IF I WERE HUNGRY . . .

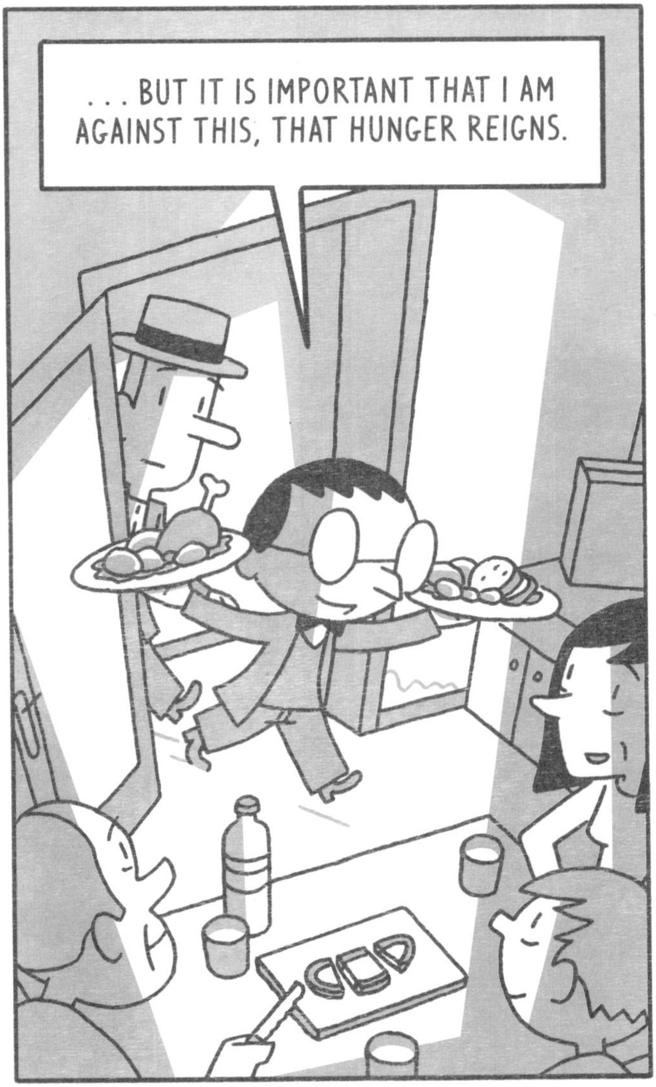
. . . BUT IT IS IMPORTANT THAT I AM AGAINST THIS, THAT HUNGER REIGNS.

MR KEUNER'S FAVOURITE ANIMAL

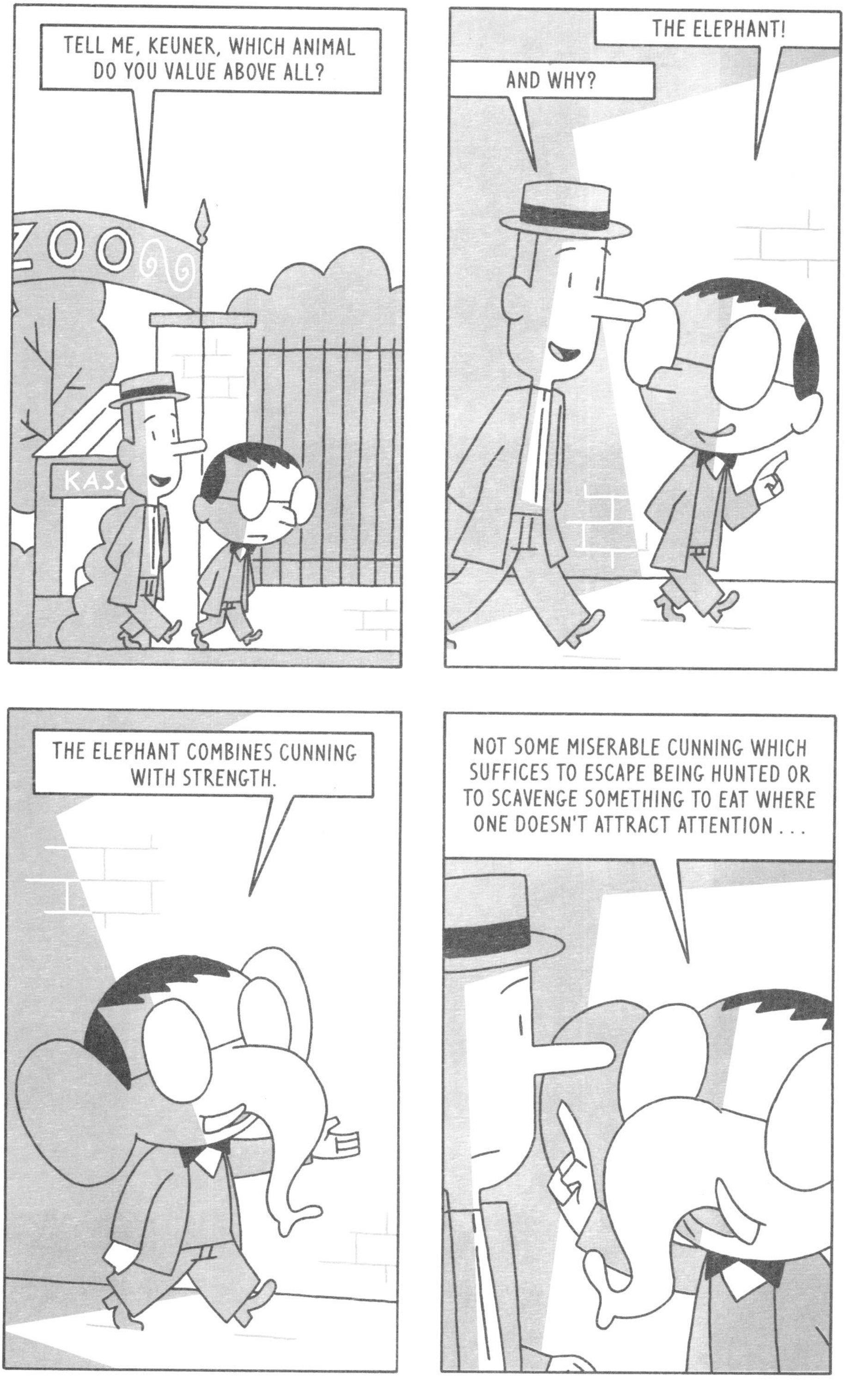
TELL ME, KEUNER, WHICH ANIMAL DO YOU VALUE ABOVE ALL?
ZOO
KASS
THE ELEPHANT!
AND WHY?
THE ELEPHANT COMBINES CUNNING WITH STRENGTH.
NOT SOME MISERABLE CUNNING WHICH SUFFICES TO ESCAPE BEING HUNTED OR TO SCAVENGE SOMETHING TO EAT WHERE ONE DOESN'T ATTRACT ATTENTION . . .

... BUT RATHER THAT CUNNING WHICH IS THE STRENGTH FOR ENORMOUS UNDERTAKINGS OF ORDER.

THE ELEPHANT LEAVES A WIDE SWATHE WHEREVER HE HAS BEEN. NEVERTHELESS, HE IS GOOD TEMPERED AND TAKES A JOKE.

THIS IS NO JOKE!

HE MAKES A GOOD FRIEND...

... LIKE HE MAKES A GOOD ENEMY.

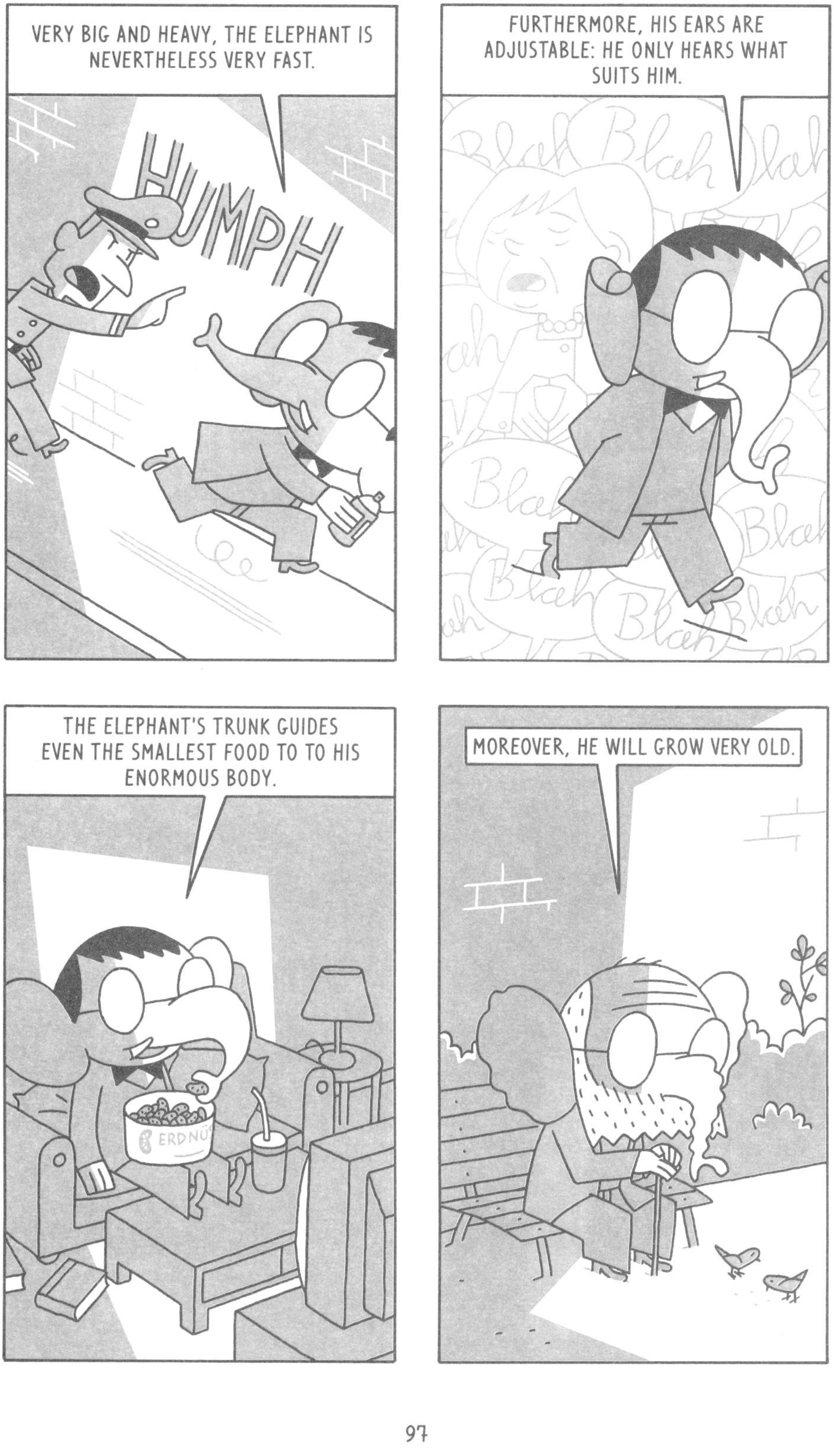
VERY BIG AND HEAVY, THE ELEPHANT IS NEVERTHELESS VERY FAST.
HUMPH
FURTHERMORE, HIS EARS ARE ADJUSTABLE: HE ONLY HEARS WHAT SUITS HIM.
Blah Blah Blah
Blah Blah Blah Blah
THE ELEPHANT'S TRUNK GUIDES EVEN THE SMALLEST FOOD TO TO HIS ENORMOUS BODY.
ERDNÜS
MOREOVER, HE WILL GROW VERY OLD.

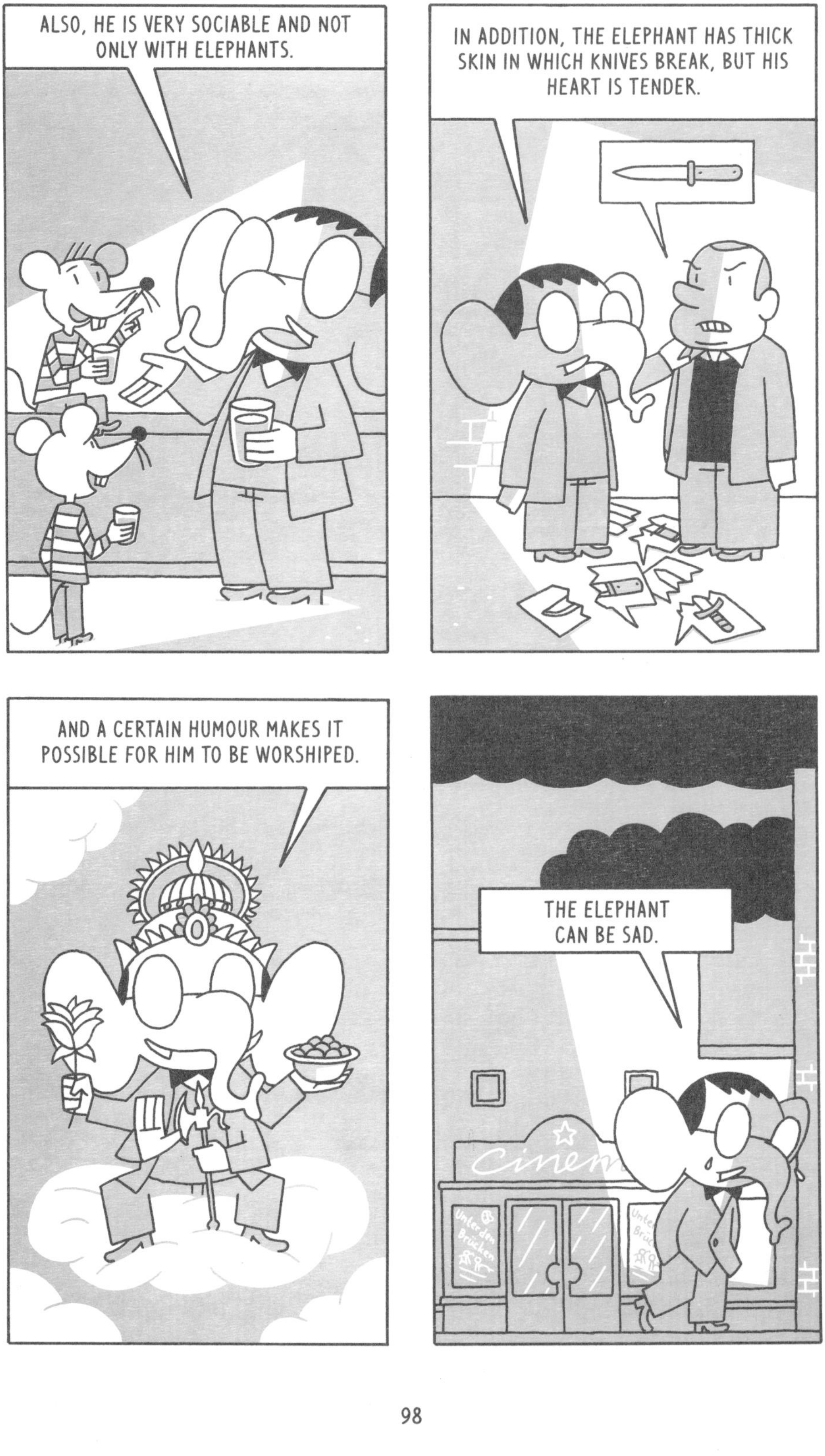
ALSO, HE IS VERY SOCIABLE AND NOT ONLY WITH ELEPHANTS.
IN ADDITION, THE ELEPHANT HAS THICK SKIN IN WHICH KNIVES BREAK, BUT HIS HEART IS TENDER.
AND A CERTAIN HUMOUR MAKES IT POSSIBLE FOR HIM TO BE WORSHIPED.
THE ELEPHANT CAN BE SAD.

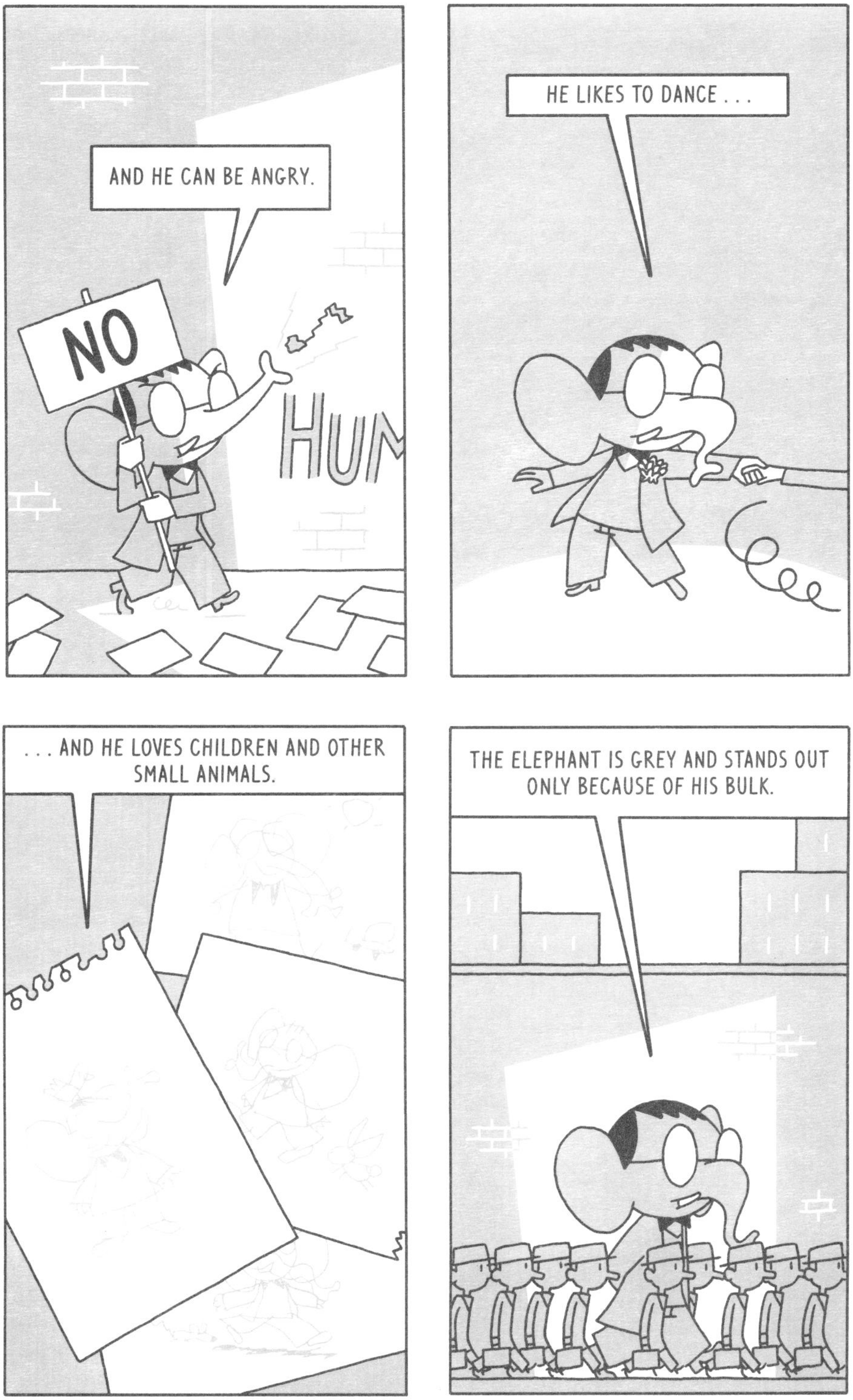
AND HE CAN BE ANGRY.
NO
HUM
HE LIKES TO DANCE . . .
. . . AND HE LOVES CHILDREN AND OTHER SMALL ANIMALS.
THE ELEPHANT IS GREY AND STANDS OUT ONLY BECAUSE OF HIS BULK.

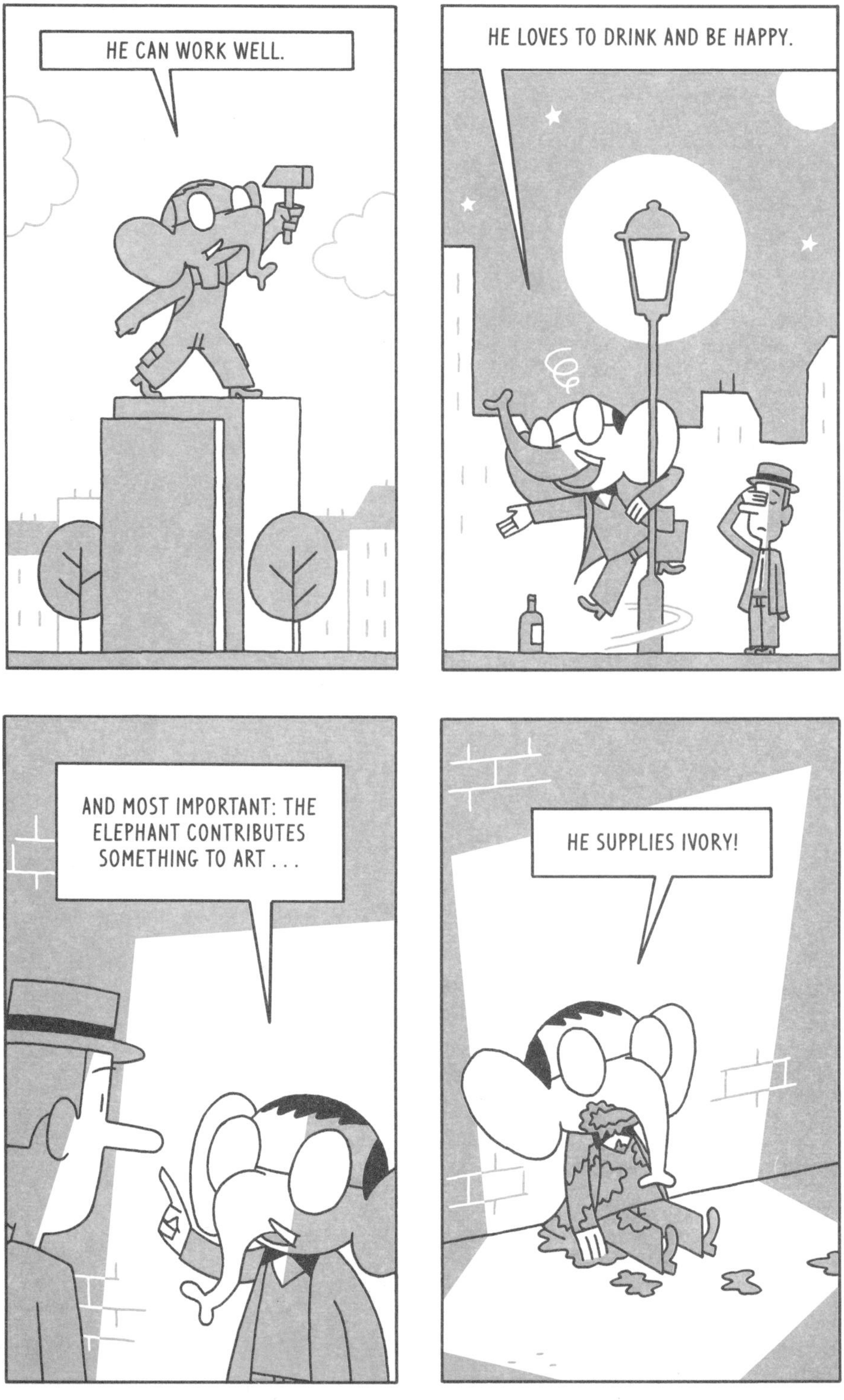
HE CAN WORK WELL.
HE LOVES TO DRINK AND BE HAPPY.
AND MOST IMPORTANT: THE ELEPHANT CONTRIBUTES SOMETHING TO ART . . .
HE SUPPLIES IVORY!

MR KEUNER AND THE TIDE

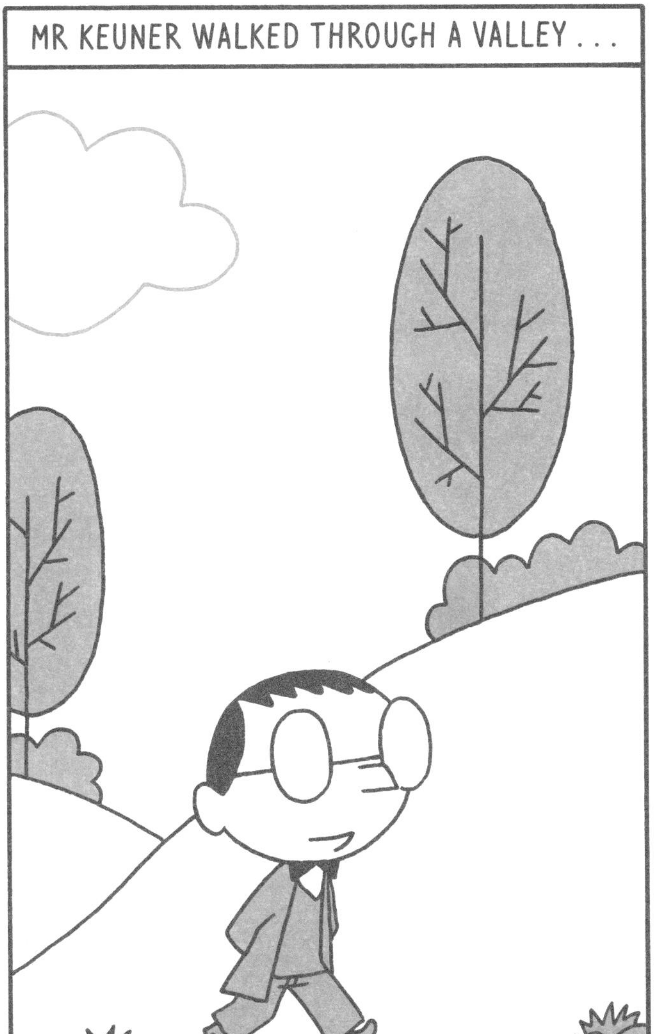
MR KEUNER WALKED THROUGH A VALLEY . . .

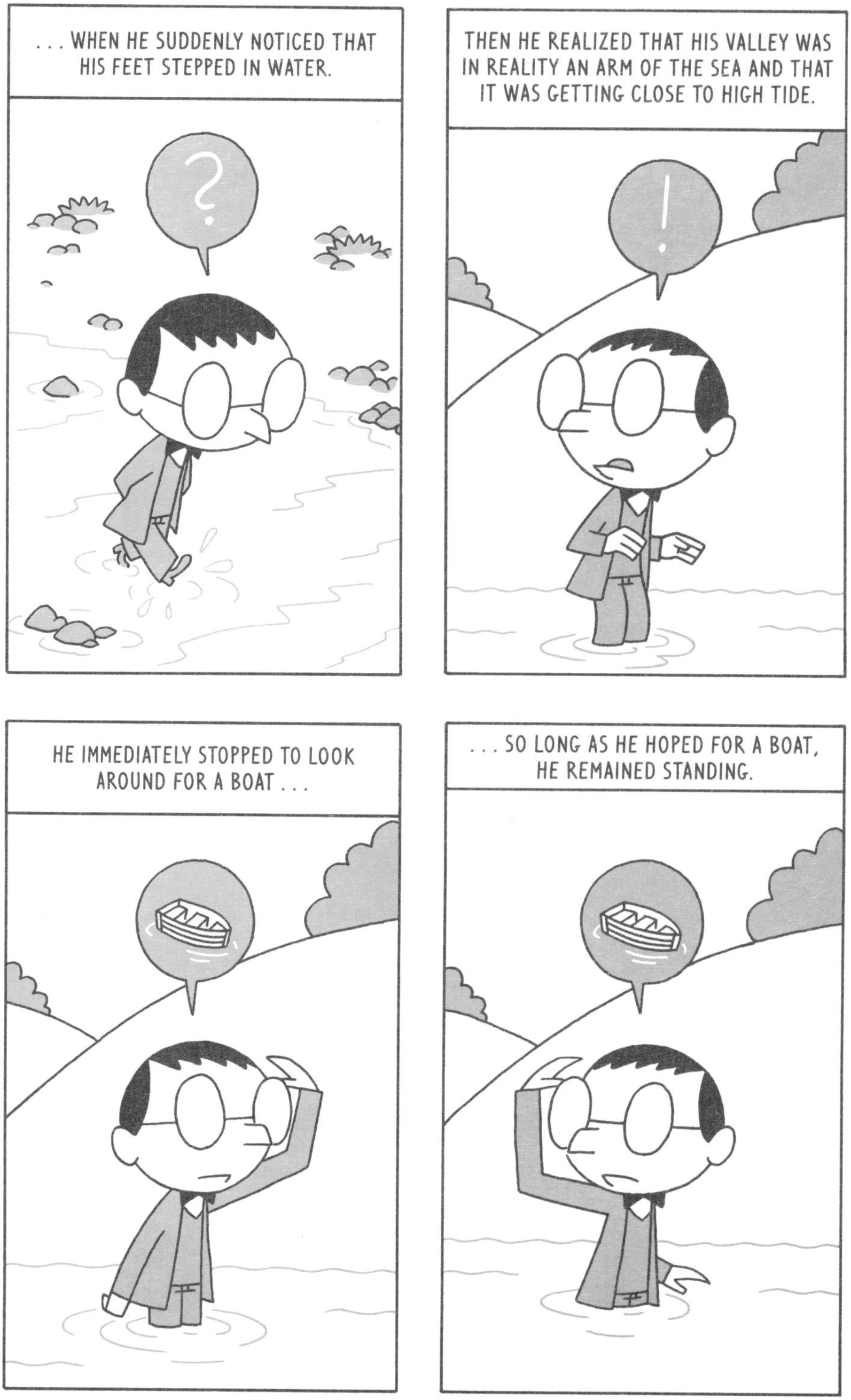
. . . WHEN HE SUDDENLY NOTICED THAT HIS FEET STEPPED IN WATER.
?
THEN HE REALIZED THAT HIS VALLEY WAS IN REALITY AN ARM OF THE SEA AND THAT IT WAS GETTING CLOSE TO HIGH TIDE.
!
HE IMMEDIATELY STOPPED TO LOOK AROUND FOR A BOAT . . .
. . . SO LONG AS HE HOPED FOR A BOAT, HE REMAINED STANDING.

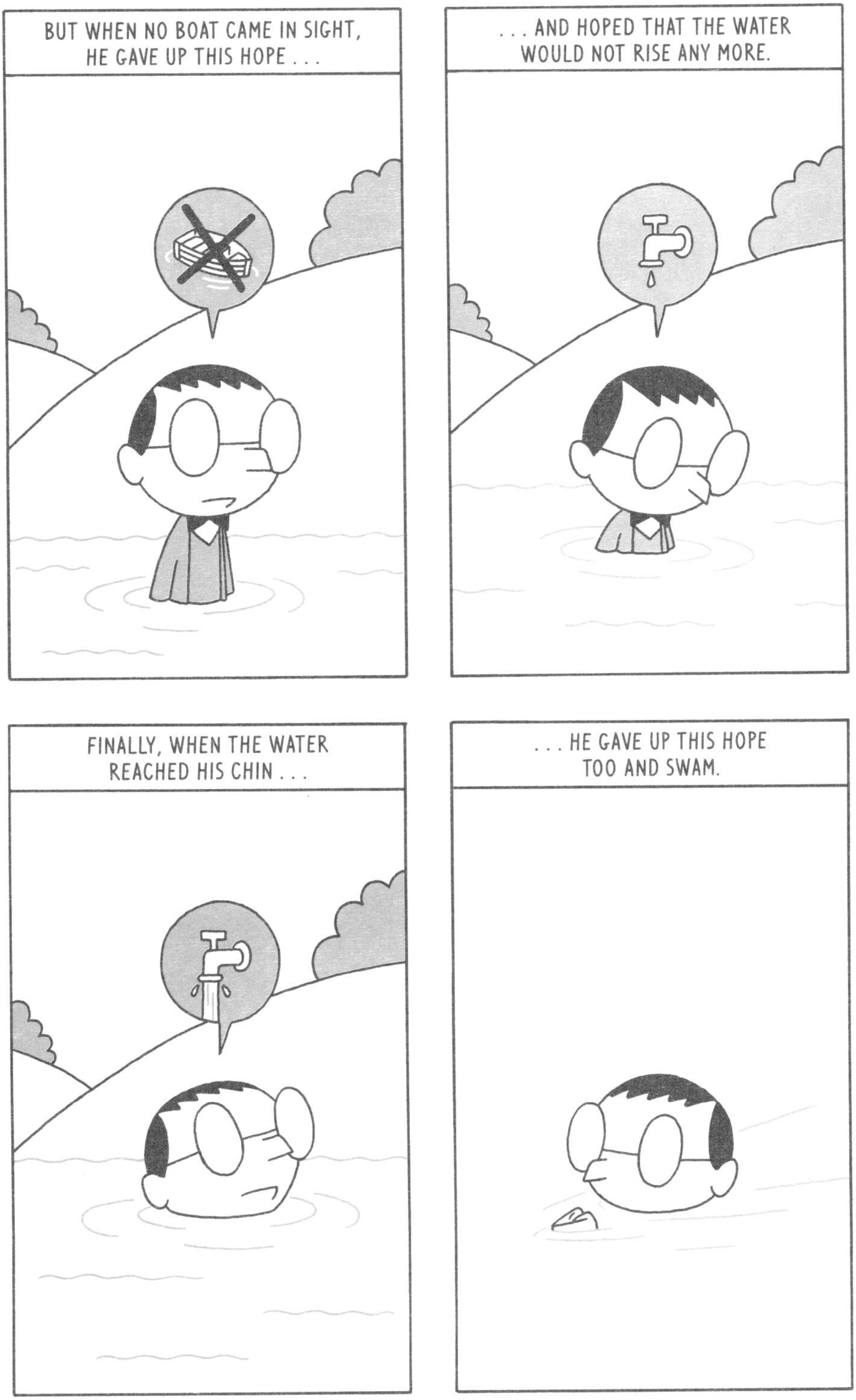

BUT WHEN NO BOAT CAME IN SIGHT, HE GAVE UP THIS HOPE . . .
. . . AND HOPED THAT THE WATER WOULD NOT RISE ANY MORE.
FINALLY, WHEN THE WATER REACHED HIS CHIN . . .
. . . HE GAVE UP THIS HOPE TOO AND SWAM.

MR K. REALIZED THAT EVEN HE WAS A BOAT.

DEPORTMENT

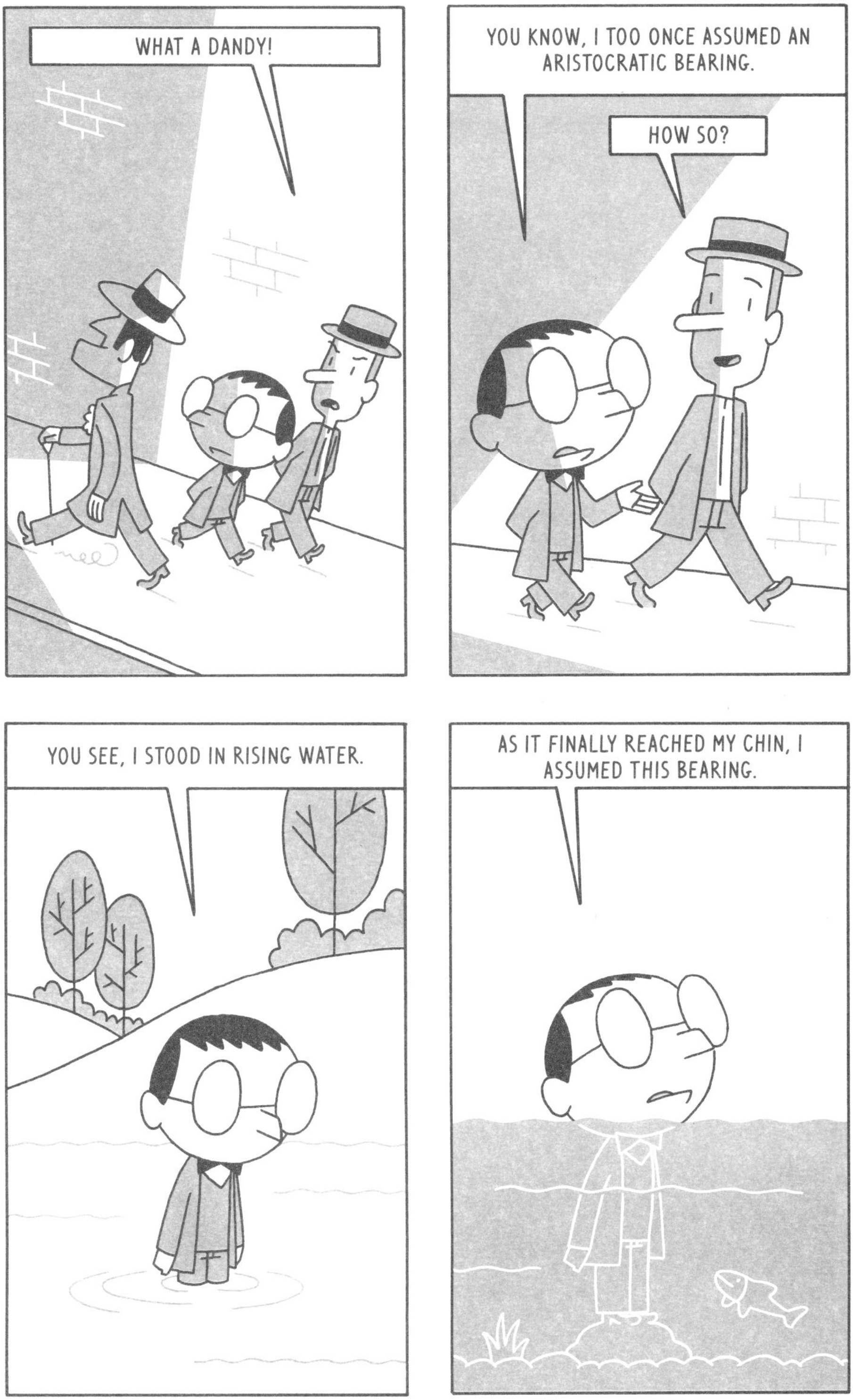

WHAT A DANDY!
YOU KNOW, I TOO ONCE ASSUMED AN ARISTOCRATIC BEARING.
HOW SO?
YOU SEE, I STOOD IN RISING WATER.
AS IT FINALLY REACHED MY CHIN, I ASSUMED THIS BEARING.

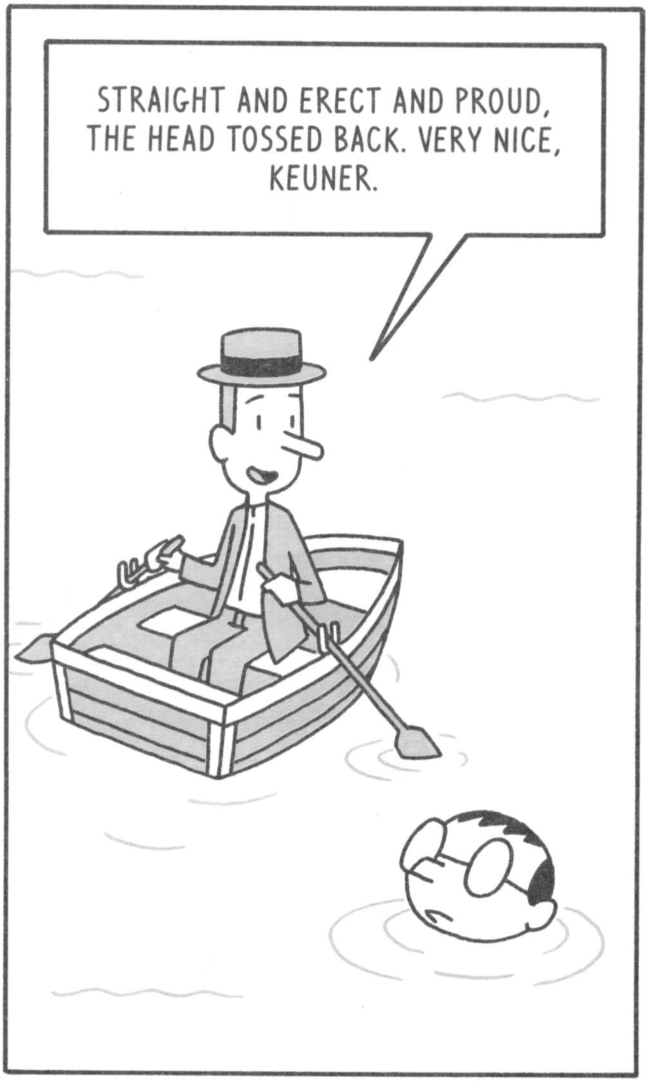
STRAIGHT AND ERECT AND PROUD, THE HEAD TOSSED BACK. VERY NICE, KEUNER.

FAME

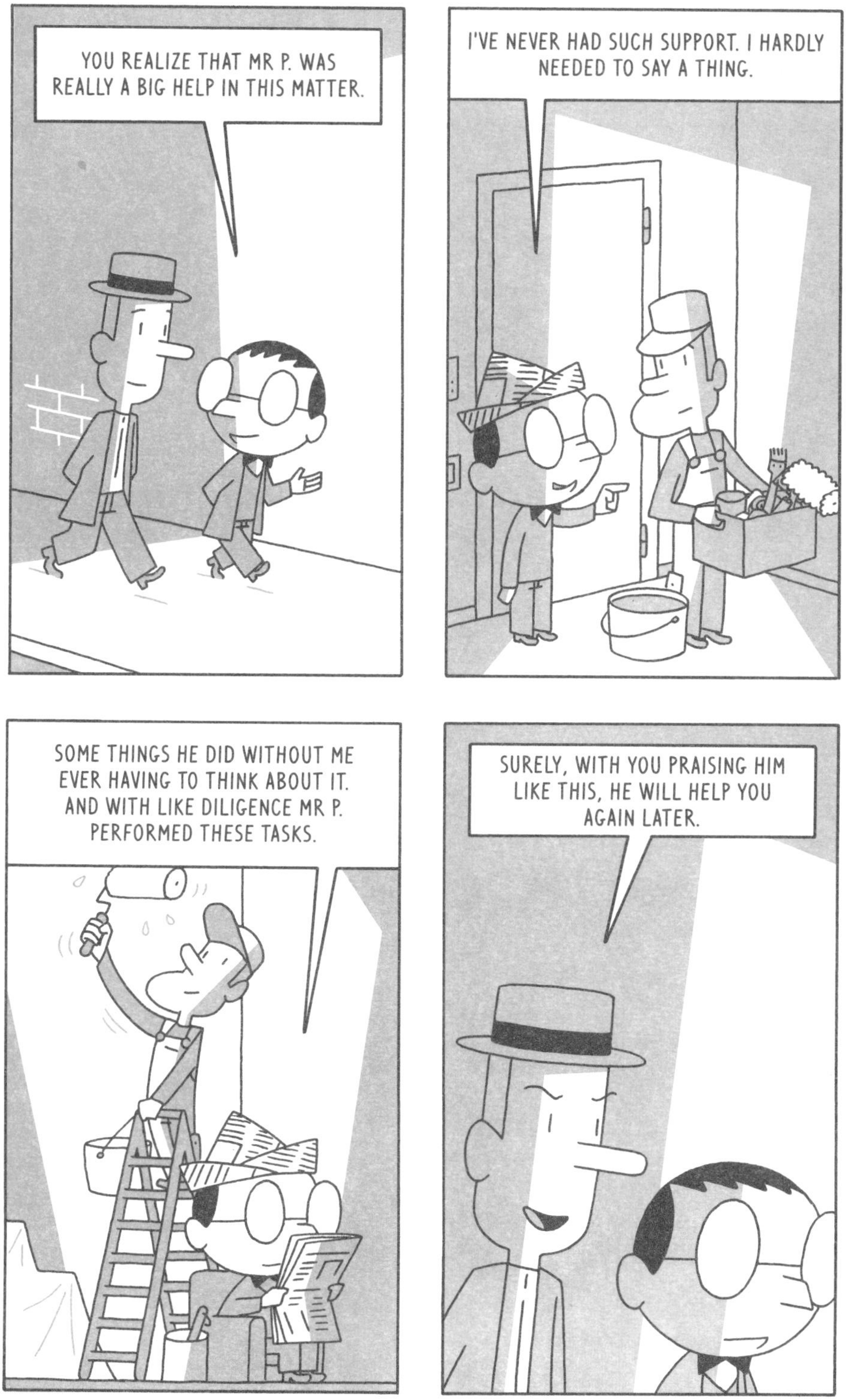
YOU REALIZE THAT MR P. WAS REALLY A BIG HELP IN THIS MATTER.
I'VE NEVER HAD SUCH SUPPORT. I HARDLY NEEDED TO SAY A THING.
SOME THINGS HE DID WITHOUT ME EVER HAVING TO THINK ABOUT IT. AND WITH LIKE DILIGENCE MR P. PERFORMED THESE TASKS.
SURELY, WITH YOU PRAISING HIM LIKE THIS, HE WILL HELP YOU AGAIN LATER.

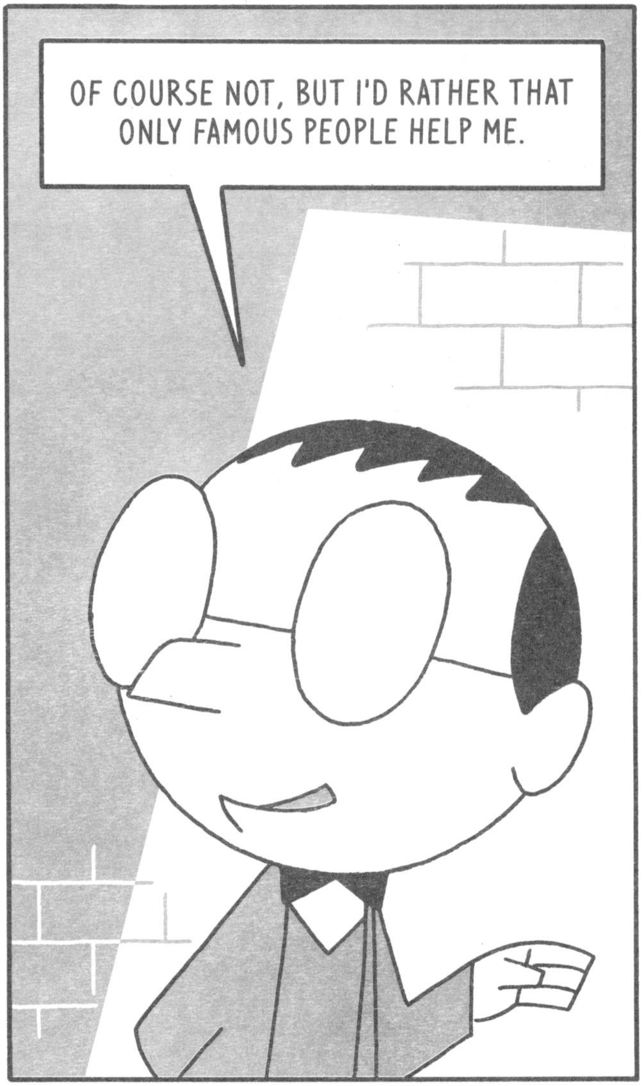
OF COURSE NOT, BUT I'D RATHER THAT ONLY FAMOUS PEOPLE HELP ME.

A BEARABLE INSULT

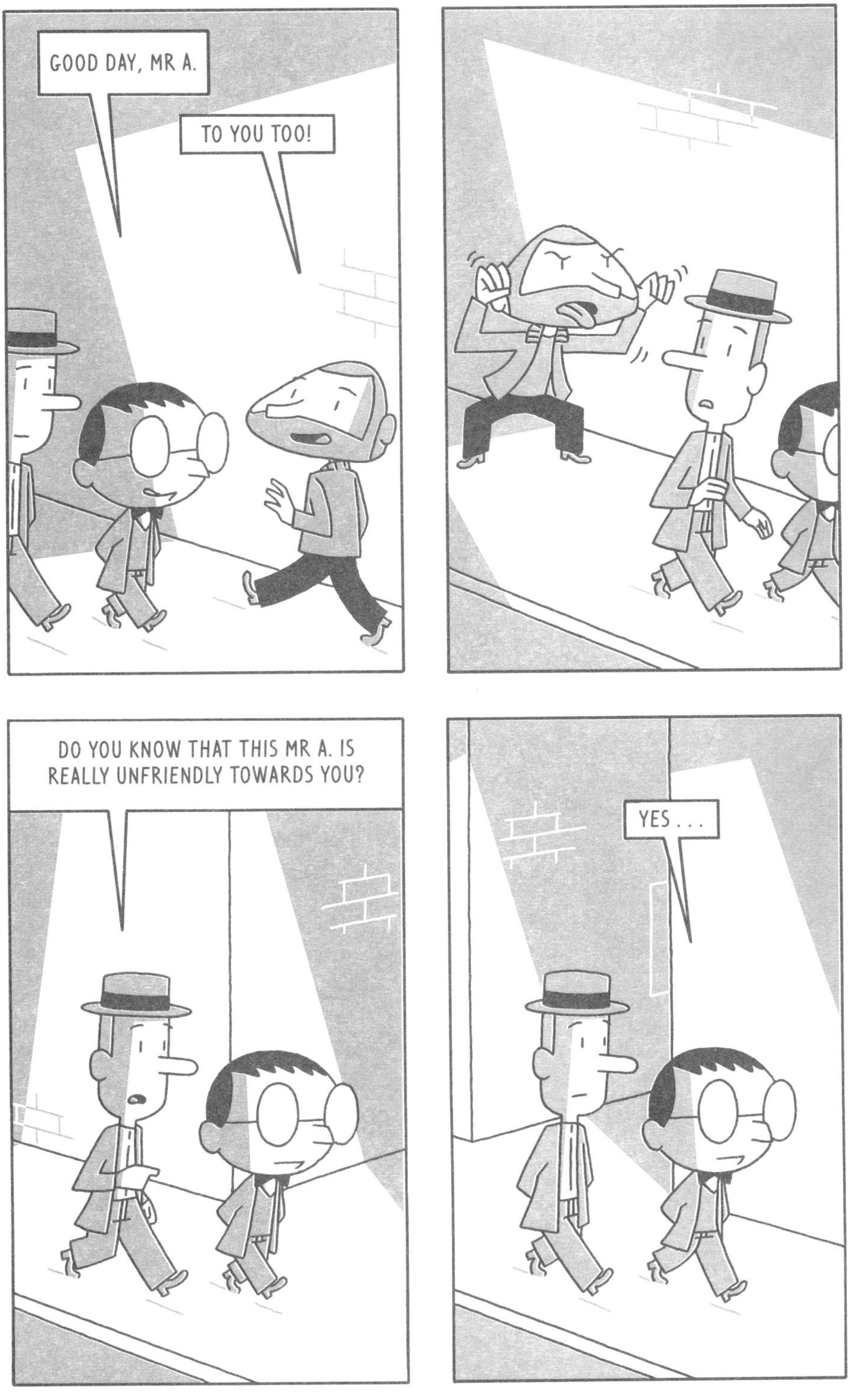
GOOD DAY, MR A.
TO YOU TOO!
DO YOU KNOW THAT THIS MR A. IS REALLY UNFRIENDLY TOWARDS YOU?
YES . . .

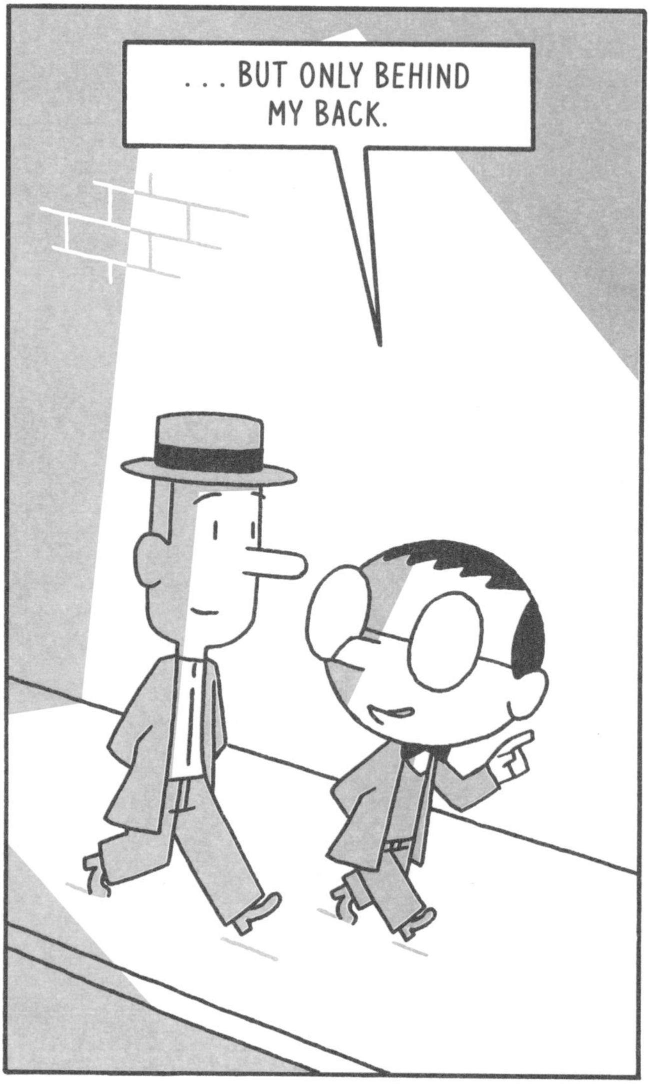
. . . BUT ONLY BEHIND MY BACK.

MR KEUNER AND THE QUESTION OF WHETHER GOD EXISTS

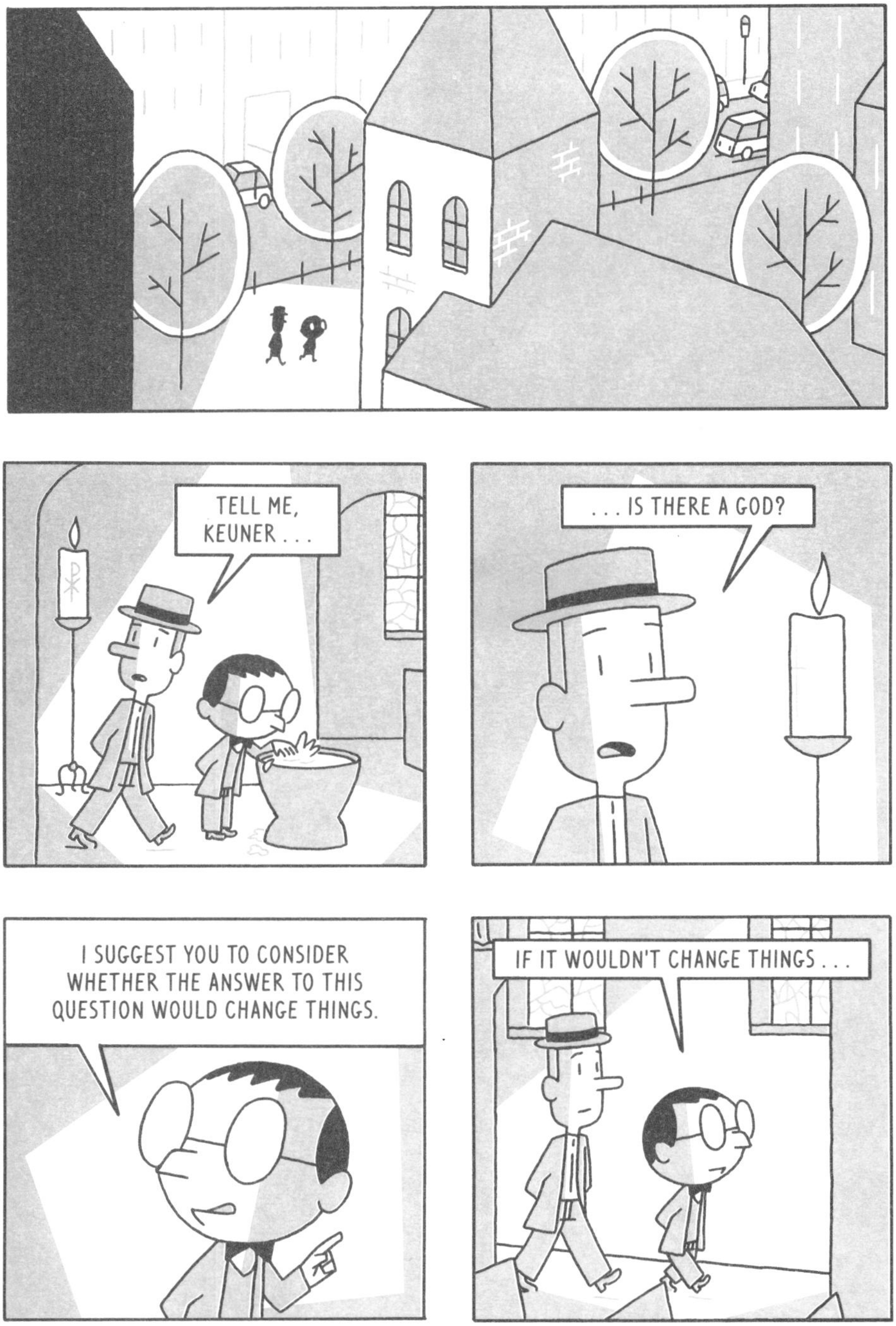

TELL ME, KEUNER . . .
. . . IS THERE A GOD?
I SUGGEST YOU TO CONSIDER WHETHER THE ANSWER TO THIS QUESTION WOULD CHANGE THINGS.
IF IT WOULDN'T CHANGE THINGS . . .

. . . THEN WE COULD DROP THE QUESTION.
IF IT WOULD CHANGE THINGS, THEN I CAN AT LEAST TO SOME EXTENT BE OF HELP TO YOU AND TELL YOU . . .
. . . THAT YOU HAVE ALREADY DECIDED . . .
. . . THAT YOU NEED A GOD!

THE HOROSCOPE

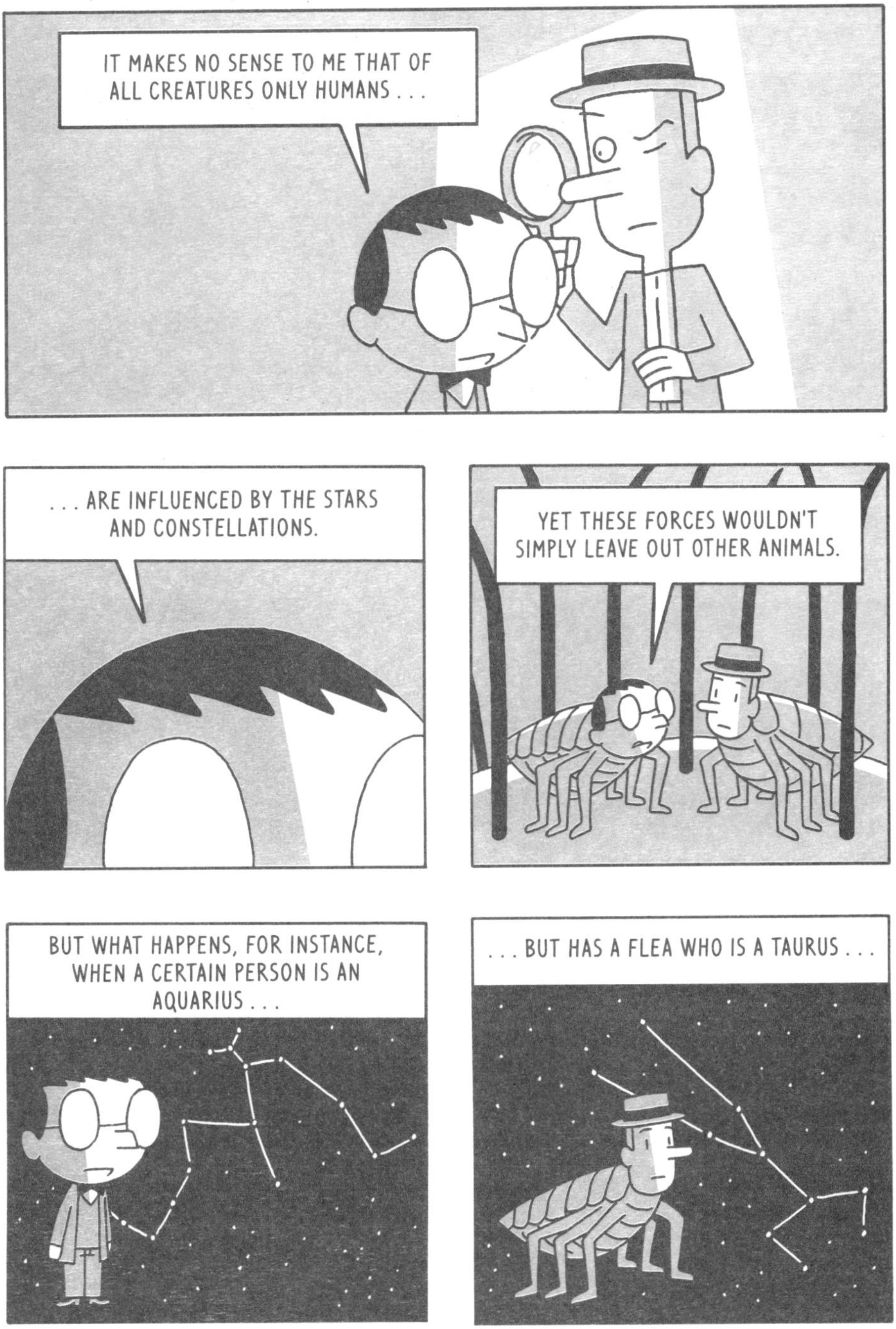
IT MAKES NO SENSE TO ME THAT OF ALL CREATURES ONLY HUMANS . . .
. . . ARE INFLUENCED BY THE STARS AND CONSTELLATIONS.
YET THESE FORCES WOULDN'T SIMPLY LEAVE OUT OTHER ANIMALS.
BUT WHAT HAPPENS, FOR INSTANCE, WHEN A CERTAIN PERSON IS AN AQUARIUS . . .
. . . BUT HAS A FLEA WHO IS A TAURUS . . .

. . . AND DROWNS IN A RIVER?
PERHAPS THE FLEA DROWNS WITH HIM THEN . . .
EVEN THOUGH THE STARS MIGHT FAVOUR HIM.
I DON'T LIKE IT.

MR KEUNER AND THE HELPLESS BOY

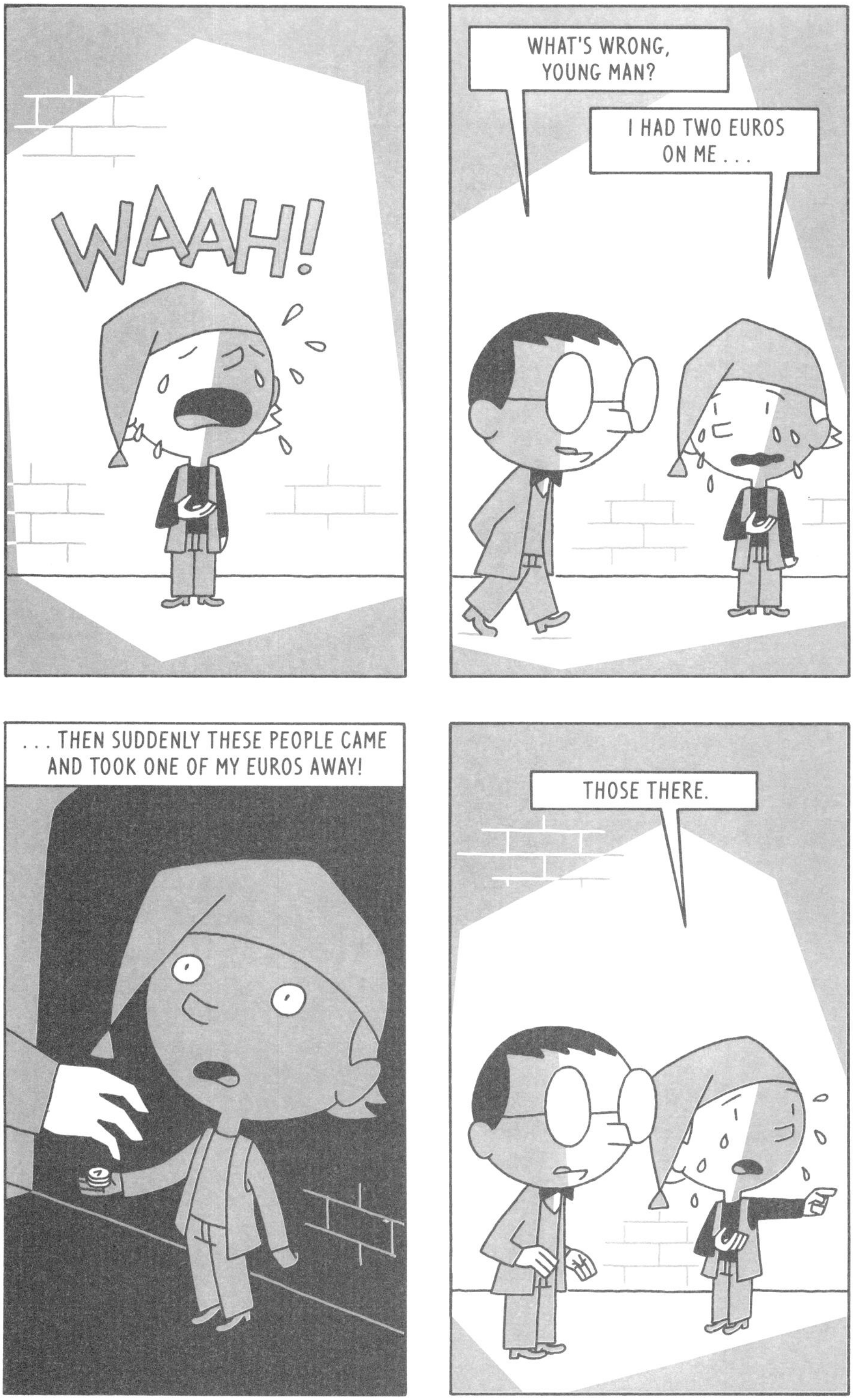
WAAH!
WHAT'S WRONG, YOUNG MAN?
I HAD TWO EUROS ON ME . . .
. . . THEN SUDDENLY THESE PEOPLE CAME AND TOOK ONE OF MY EUROS AWAY!
THOSE THERE.

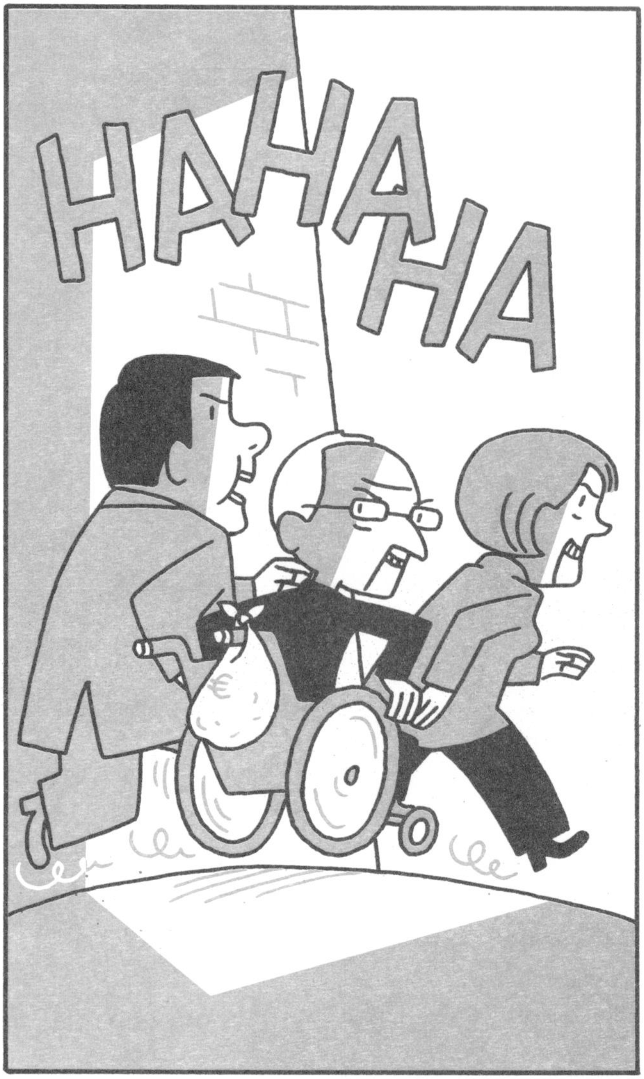
HAHAHAHA

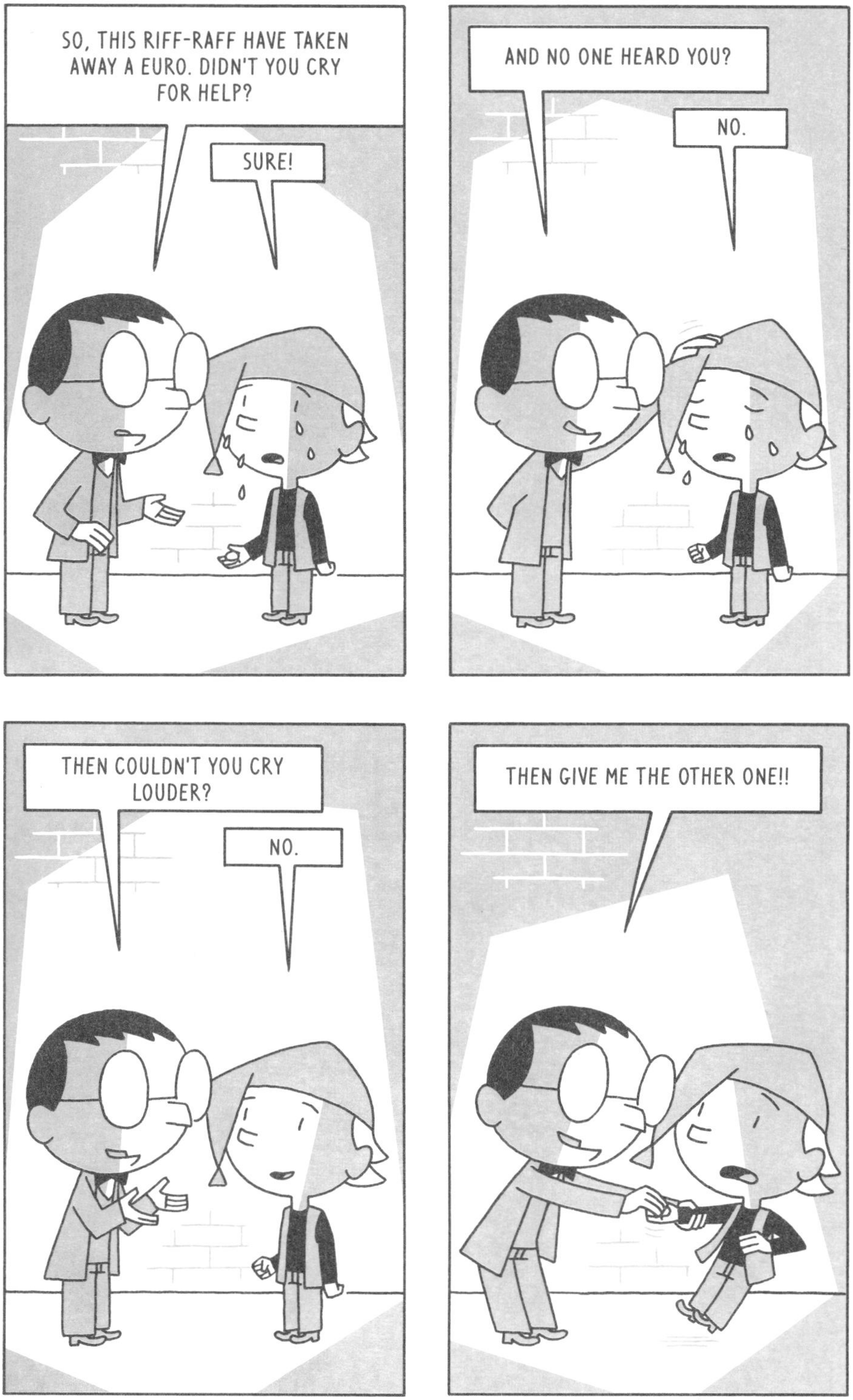
SO, THIS RIFF-RAFF HAVE TAKEN AWAY A EURO. DIDN'T YOU CRY FOR HELP?
SURE!
AND NO ONE HEARD YOU?
NO.
THEN COULDN'T YOU CRY LOUDER?
NO.
THEN GIVE ME THE OTHER ONE!!

WAITING

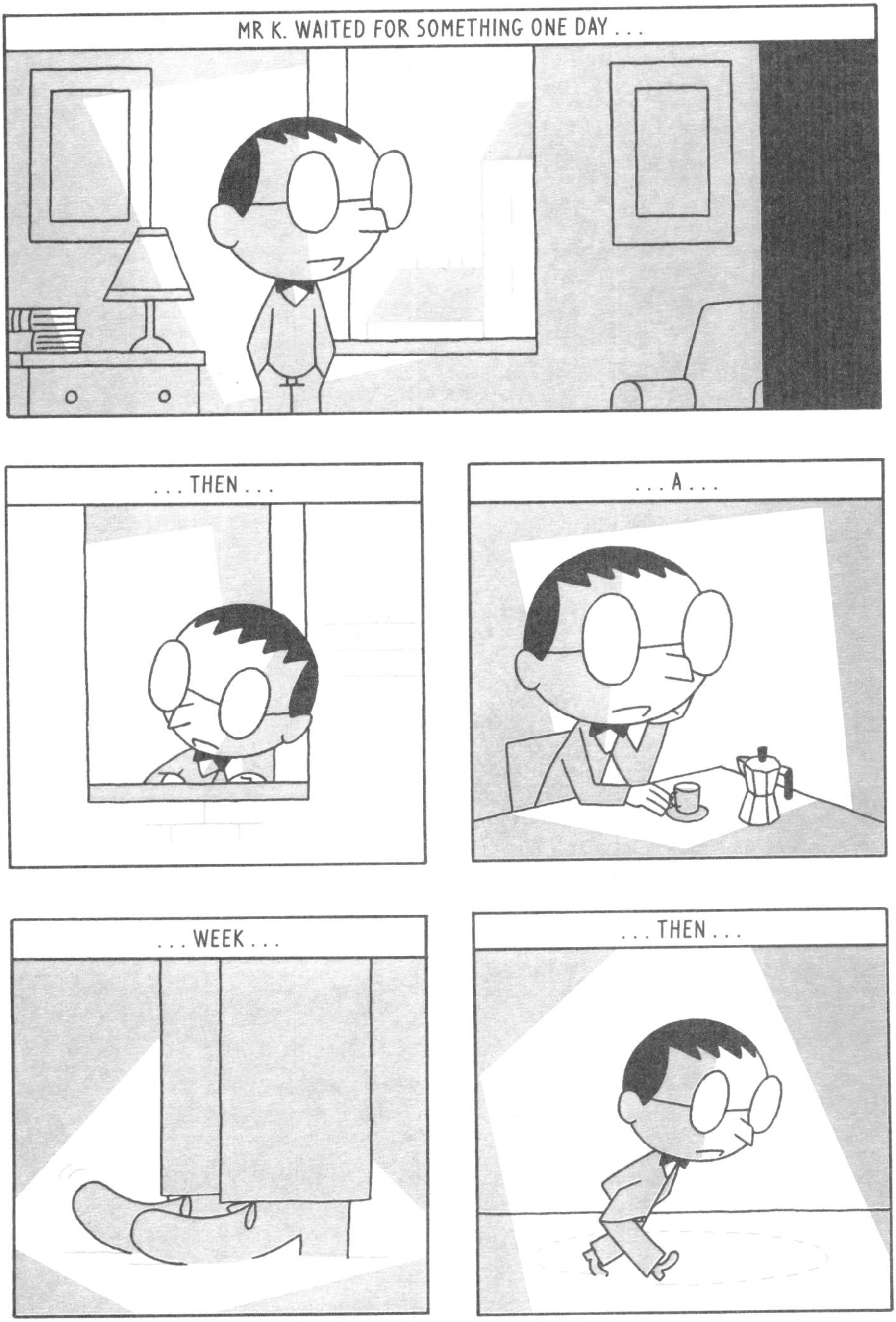
MR K. WAITED FOR SOMETHING ONE DAY . . .
. . . THEN . . .
. . . A . . .
. . . WEEK . . .
. . . THEN . . .

. . . FOR . . .
. . . A . . .
. . . MONTH . . .
I COULD HAVE WAITED A MONTH WITH NO PROBLEM, BUT NOT THAT DAY AND THAT WEEK!!!

MR KEUNER AND MR WOOLY

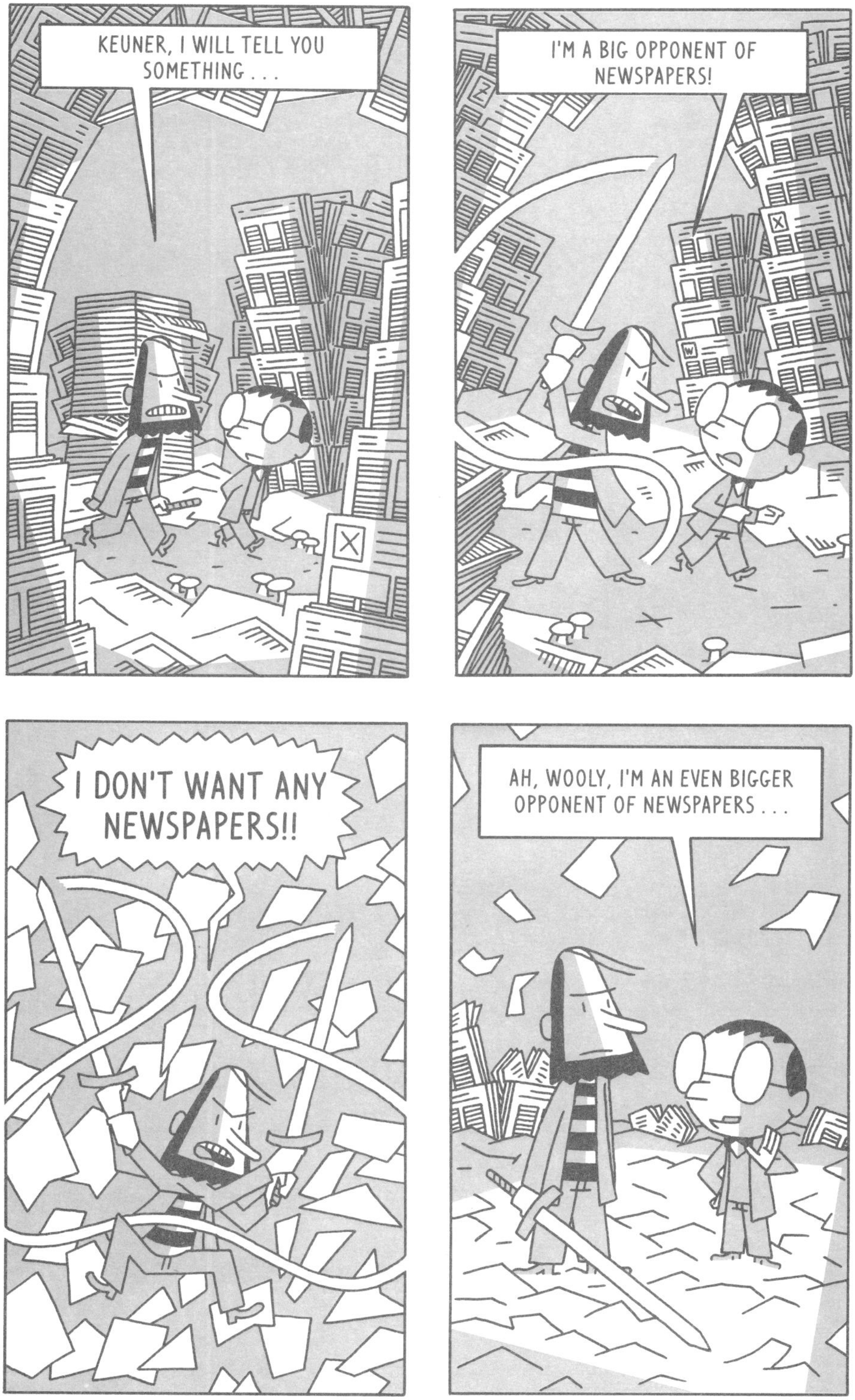
KEUNER, I WILL TELL YOU SOMETHING . . .
I'M A BIG OPPONENT OF NEWSPAPERS!
I DON'T WANT ANY NEWSPAPERS!!
AH, WOOLY, I'M AN EVEN BIGGER OPPONENT OF NEWSPAPERS . . .

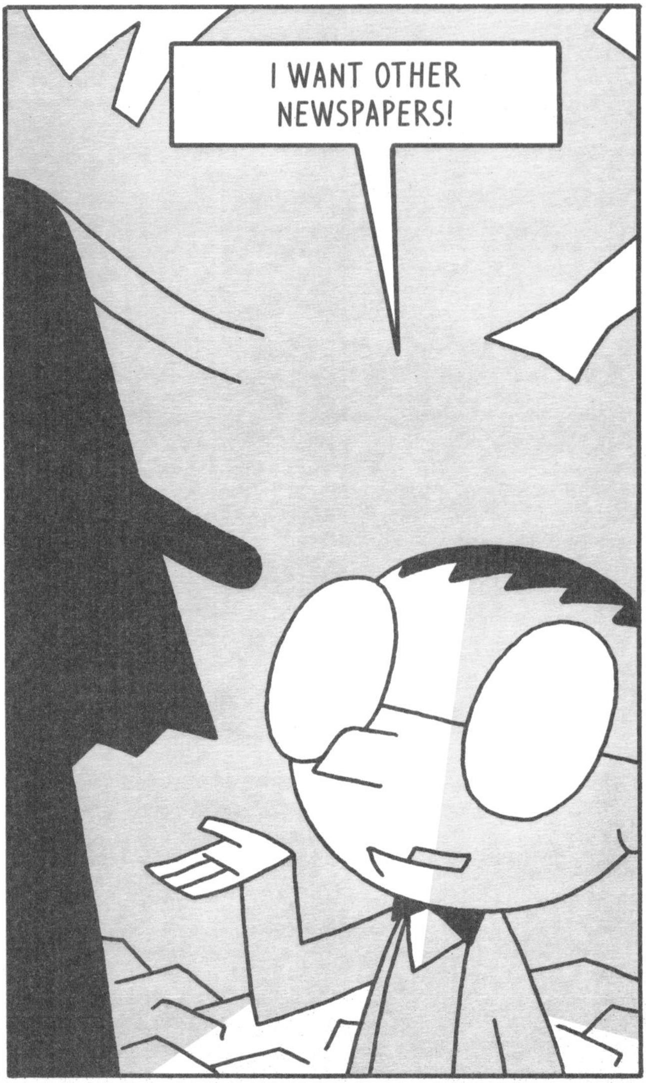
I WANT OTHER NEWSPAPERS!

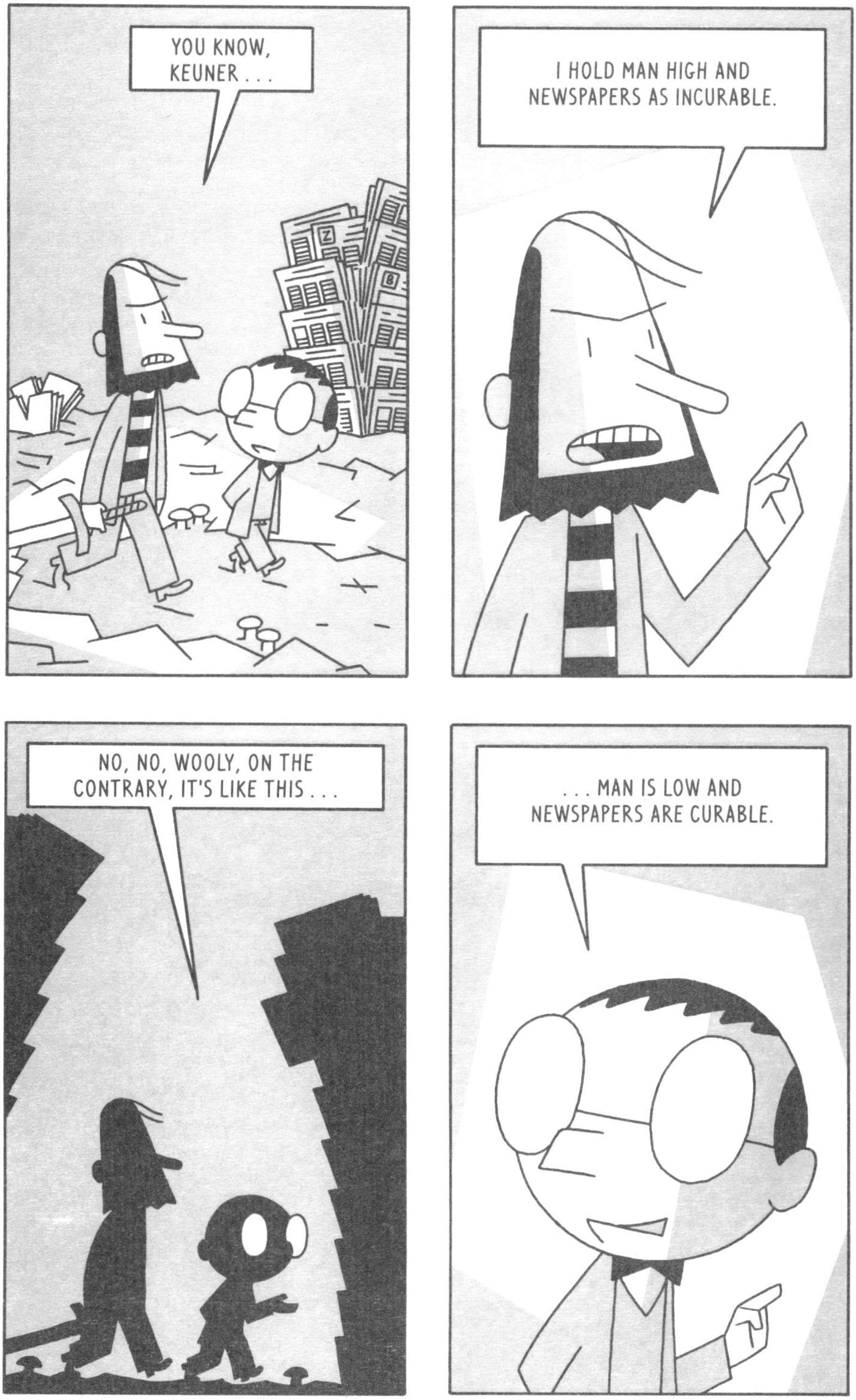
YOU KNOW, KEUNER . . .
I HOLD MAN HIGH AND NEWSPAPERS AS INCURABLE.
NO, NO, WOOLY, ON THE CONTRARY, IT'S LIKE THIS . . .
. . . MAN IS LOW AND NEWSPAPERS ARE CURABLE.

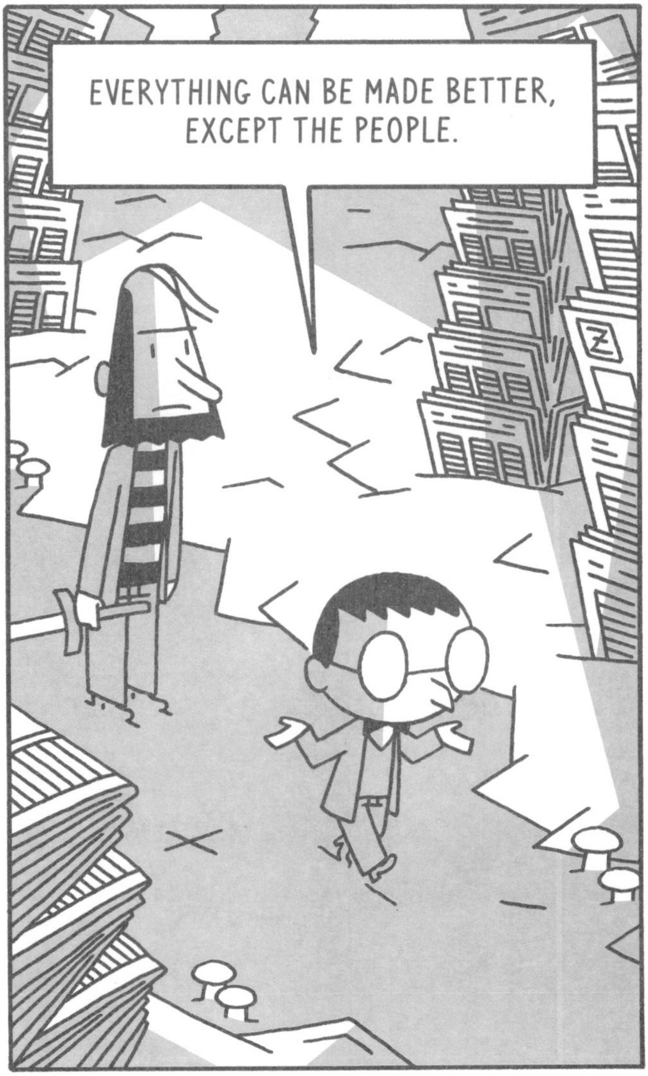
EVERYTHING CAN BE MADE BETTER, EXCEPT THE PEOPLE.

CONVERSATIONS

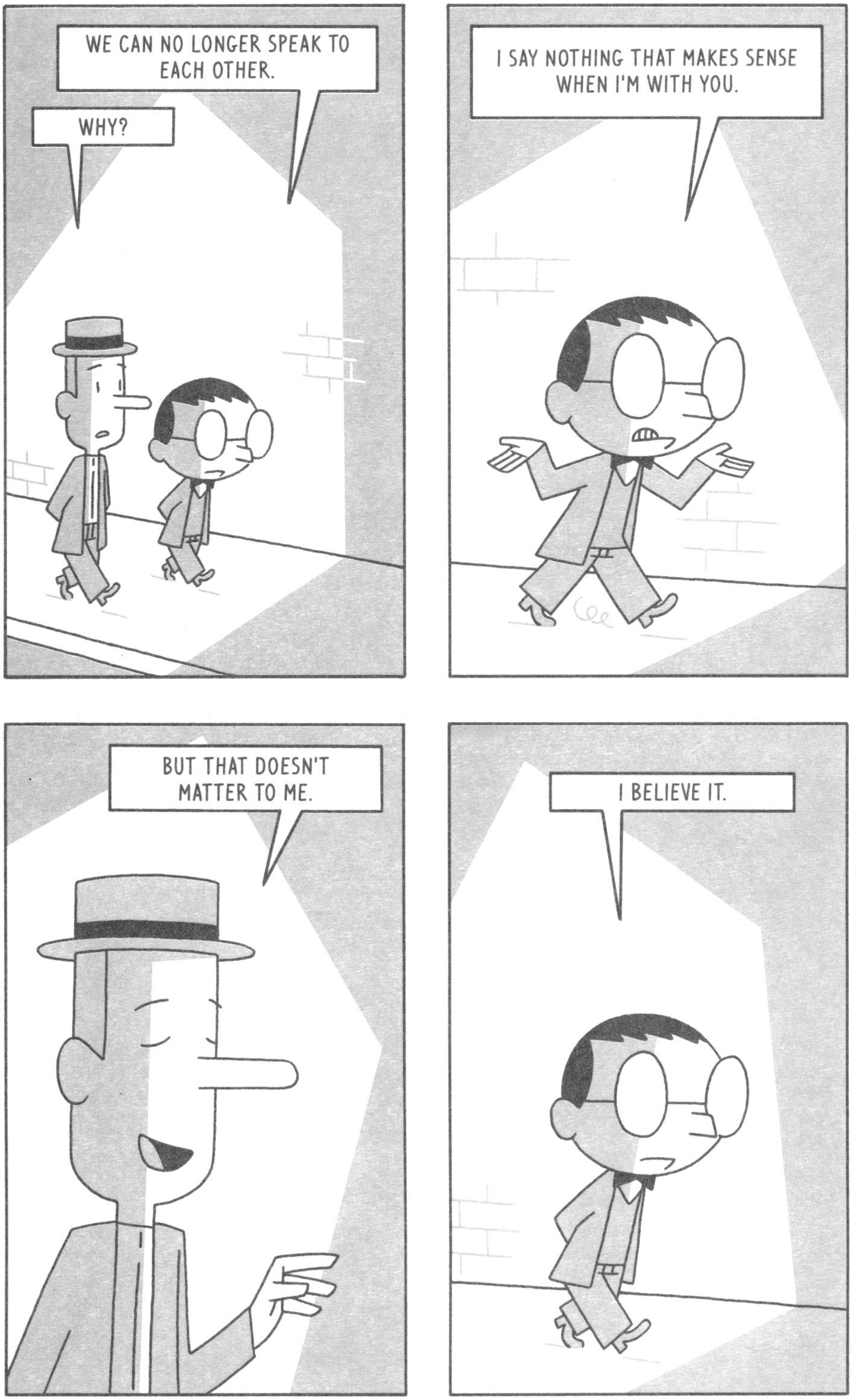
WE CAN NO LONGER SPEAK TO EACH OTHER.
WHY?
I SAY NOTHING THAT MAKES SENSE WHEN I'M WITH YOU.
BUT THAT DOESN'T MATTER TO ME.
I BELIEVE IT.

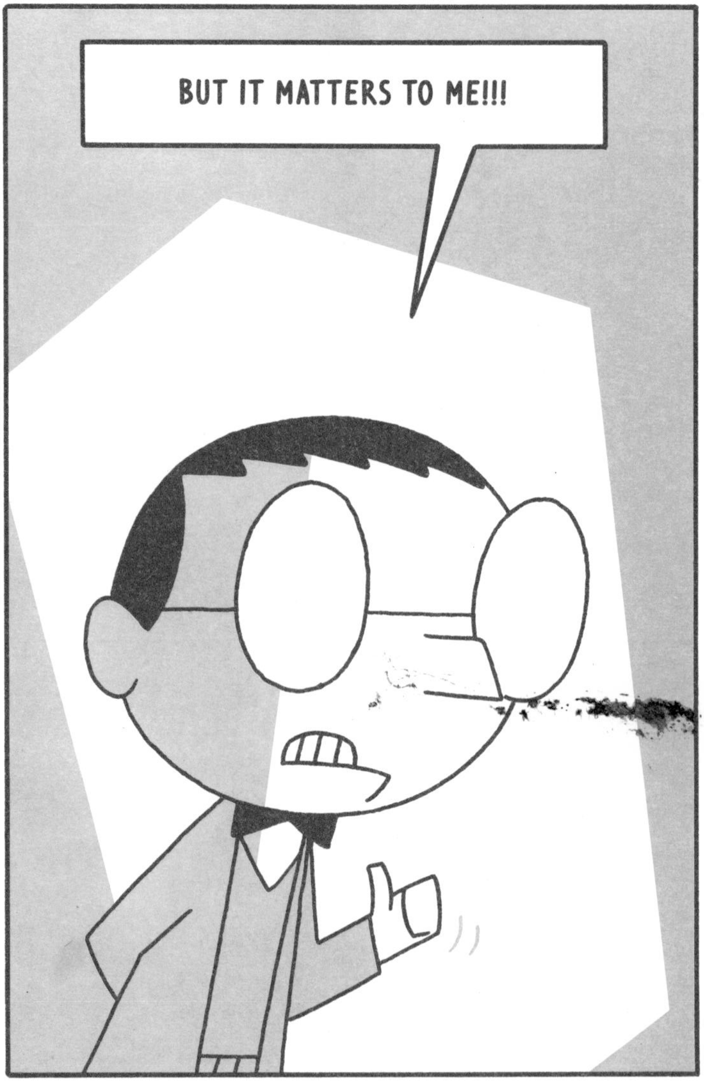
BUT IT MATTERS TO ME!!!